A TEXAS LEGACY CHRISTMAS

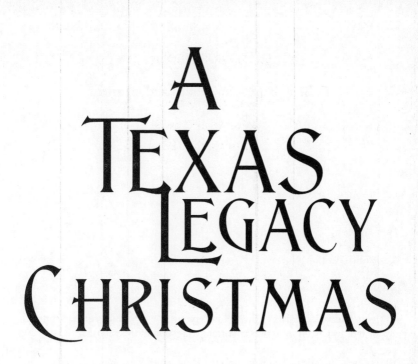

A TEXAS LEGACY CHRISTMAS

DiAnn Mills

BARBOUR
PUBLISHING

DEDICATION

To Betty Barrett, my mother and my friend.

© 2007 by DiAnn Mills

ISBN 978-1-59789-822-5

All scripture quotations are taken from the King James Version of the Bible.

Cover design by Lookout Design, Inc.

For more information about DiAnn Mills, please access the author's Web site at the following Internet address: www.diannmills.com.

Published by Barbour Publishing, Inc., P.O. Box 719, Uhrichsville, Ohio 44683, www.barbourbooks.com.

Our mission is to publish and distribute inspirational products offering exceptional value and biblical encouragement to the masses.

ecpa Member of the
Evangelical Christian
Publishers Association

Printed in the United States of America.

Unto the upright there ariseth
light in the darkness:
he is gracious, and full of compassion,
and righteous.
Psalm 112:4

CHAPTER 1

A blast of wind seized Zack Kahler's breath and threatened to keep it captive. He tightened the scarf around his neck and pulled up the collar of his wool coat. Buttoning it before he left the newspaper office on Times Square had done little good, for the wind still whipped up inside his coat and chilled him to the bone.

Zack lowered his head and held on to his derby hat as he continued to trudge down the street toward his small apartment. He noted the huge snowflakes covering the white ground from earlier in the day. New York's winters were entirely too cold for him. Exhaling an icy vapor, he remembered his first winter here and how the little chilled clouds appeared like magic in the frosty air. That optimistic attitude about freezing temperatures soon ended.

Three more days and he'd head home to Texas, where he'd never complain about the heat again. Although he would miss the Broadway plays and a handful of fine restaurants, he would not miss the woman who expected him to spend his entire pay on her entertainment, frowned on his interest in church, and turned her affections to a wealthier man who carried an impressive name.

Still fuming about the mannerisms of Miss Elizabeth Hanington and how she hadn't really broken his heart, Zack realized the said young woman and the cold blowing around him had much in common. They were probably kin. Zack chuckled. He needed to get home and take over ownership of the *Frontier Press* before he wished dire circumstances upon Elizabeth.

An automobile horn blared a few feet behind him. Zack lost his footing on the ice and snow, sending him backwards onto the sidewalk. He despised those newfangled machines. Give him a horse any day. With his posterior smarting, his pride definitely damaged, and irritation soaring through his veins, Zack attempted to right himself.

"Mister, let me help you," a small voice said. "You took a nasty spill."

Zack stared up into the face of a curly-headed, freckle-faced little boy. The child held out a thin hand. "No thanks." Zack smiled. "I'm not that old yet. But I appreciate the offer." He dug his gloved hand into the snow for leverage and slowly stood.

"Looks like you did all right without me." The boy shivered. No doubt his dirty and torn clothes provided little warmth. A quick glance down revealed bare toes sticking out from the ends of his shoes.

"How about a quarter for your trouble?" Zack reached into his pocket and pulled out the coin.

The boy's eyes widened. "Thanks, mister."

"You're quite welcome." Zack blinked. He must have fallen hard, because he suddenly saw two of them. But he'd fallen on his rear, not his head. "Are there two of you?"

"Yes, sir." Two voices chorused a reply.

Zack winced at the pitiful, ragged pair and dug deep into his pocket for another quarter. He handed the other boy a coin. The two grinned. Never had he seen so much carrot-red hair and matching freckles.

"We'll be on our way," the first one said. "Thank you very much. Be careful and don't slip again."

Zack nodded and watched the two hurry down the street. Perhaps he should have offered to buy them something to eat or asked them where they lived. He patted his back side and adjusted his heavy woolen coat, feeling a bit guilty for its warmth. What kind of parents allowed children to run about the street so scantily clad? Unless they were. . . Reaching inside his coat pocket, he realized his wallet was missing.

"Hey, you two. Come back here."

The twins raced off, leaving a trail of laughter in their wake.

Anger propelled Zack to cast aside his fear of falling again, and he took long strides after the two pint-sized troublemakers.

"You little thieves. Wait till I get my hands on you." All of the frustration of the weather and Elizabeth's discarding him culminated in the pursuit of the two imps scurrying down the street with his wallet.

The boys crossed a busy street into the path of a horse and buggy from one direction and those dreaded automobiles from the other. Horses whinnied and car horns blared like an off-key orchestra. The boys made it across the street, and Zack was gaining ground. His dash into the street triggered the traffic to protest one more time.

His left foot slipped, but he caught himself and realized the distance between him and the pair was narrowing. In the next instant, he had his hands on both of their arms.

Zack whirled the two boys around to face him. They couldn't have been more than six or seven years old. Fright dug deep into their amber-colored eyes.

"My wallet."

The boy on the left reached inside his tattered pants and pulled out the wallet.

"Did you take anything?"

They shook their heads while he dropped his wallet into his coat pocket.

"Are you lying?" He'd throttle the two if they were his. What a conspiracy.

"No, sir," the boy on the left said. "We didn't have time to look through it."

"Sir, is there a problem here?"

Zack studied the face of a square-looking policeman who had obviously seen the wild chase. "I'm not sure." He refused to let go of the boys until he finished lecturing them on the consequences of stealing. Also, he intended to take them to their parents.

The policeman shook his finger at the pair. "Curly, Charlie—are you two pickpocketing again?"

Wide eyes stared back at the policeman and then at Zack.

"I thought as much. This time I'm personally taking you back to the orphanage. You're too young to be living on the street. Gets much colder and I'll be hauling your bodies to the morgue."

Orphans? Twins? Zack's ice-hard heart quickly began to thaw.

"We gave back his wallet," one of the boys said. "We don't like the home. It ain't a good place to live."

"You know better. Those sisters take good care of you with what they have. Doesn't matter. I'm tired of chasing you. You're thieves at the ripe old age of six. Your mother, God rest her soul, must be turning over in her grave." The policeman turned to Zack. "I'm sorry, sir. I'll take over from here."

"Thank you." He glanced down at the woebegone looks on the boys' faces. "You two need to learn what is right and wrong."

The fear on their faces changed to rebellion. "We're tired of being cold and hungry," the spokesman said. "We can take care of ourselves workin' as newsboys."

Zack had seen children as young as these two selling newspapers. What about their schooling? What did they eat?

The policeman cleared his throat. "But you won't freeze to death at the orphanage." He grabbed their thin arms.

Remorse slammed into Zack's heart. "I'm not pressing charges against them."

"You aren't doing them any favors. They're like all street kids— hard and mean. And some of those newsboys are teaching them all the wrong things."

Zack had heard plenty of stories about newsboys and their struggle to survive on the streets of New York. "What orphanage are you taking them to?"

"Saint Vincent de Paul on Forty-second Street."

"And they're treated well?"

The policeman chuckled. "Better than they deserve. But yes, they are fed, clothed, disciplined, schooled, and given religious instruction. These two have had a rough time since their mother died in the Triangle Factory fire last March."

Zack had witnessed that tragic incident. One hundred forty-six immigrants, mostly women, had been trapped inside and killed when the factory caught fire. He was one of the reporters who had covered the inhumane treatment of the workers.

Zack bent to the twins' eye level. "I'm real sorry about your mother."

The spokesman's round face hardened. "She wasn't around much."

Zack peered up at the policeman. The man nodded.

"Come along, you two. Sister Catherine and Sister Agatha are sure to be worried about you."

Zack watched them disappear down the street. He should have done something more, but what?

Chloe Weaver smoothed her worn dress and opened the door of Kahlerville's finest boardinghouse. Taking a deep breath to steady her nerves, she vowed to swallow her shyness. The establishment had a new owner, who had advertised for a front-desk clerk and bookkeeper. She wondered if he needed two positions filled or one. Chloe would take either or both because she desperately needed a job.

The door creaked open. She smelled paint and listened to hammering. A man shouted and another laughed. The sounds nearly deafened her, but she refused to cower to her fears. She'd learned the new owner had also purchased the feed store. No wonder he needed help.

"Mr. Barton?" *Oh, that was not assertive at all.* "Mr. Barton?"

"I'll be there in a minute. I'm up to my elbows in paint. Do you need a room?"

"No, sir. I—I want to apply for the position of desk clerk and bookkeeper."

Silence. Her heart thumped against her chest like a cornered rabbit. "Mr. Barton, I meet your qualifications, and I'll wait until you can talk to me."

She'd done it, made a commitment, and now she must endure the noises, the smells, and perhaps the annoyance of a man who'd been interrupted from his work. But he couldn't have any more of a temper than her father, and she'd tolerated his vicious tongue for eighteen years.

Mr. Barton walked through to the foyer of the boardinghouse, wiping his hands on a soiled cloth as he went. Yellow paint splattered his overalls, and a huge dollop rested on his forehead, reminding her of an egg yolk.

"We're a little busy." He frowned, but she expected that.

"I see, sir. I came in response to the advertisement in the *Frontier Press*."

"I believe I need a man for the job. It involves work here and a combination of bookkeeping for the boardinghouse and the feed store."

"I'm quite good with figures, and I've completed twelve years of schooling."

He lifted a brow. A more pleasant expression crossed his face, and she saw the man was quite pleasing to look at, especially his large blue eyes. "I've seen you a few times around town. What's your name?"

"I apologize for not introducing myself." She stuck out her hand. "Chloe Weaver."

"I need someone who can work long hours." He tossed the paint cloth into a bucket.

"I can work as many hours as you need." A tingling sensation rose from her stomach. "My penmanship is neat, which would be an asset for the duties you've described. Miss Scott at the school will give me a good recommendation."

"You married?"

"No, sir."

"Fixin' to be?"

"No, sir."

"Jacob, we need a hand back here," a male voice in the back shouted above the hammering.

"I'm on my way." He focused on Chloe. "I need someone to start at seven o'clock in the morning. No, make that six. You meet the customers, tend to their needs, show them to their rooms—that means carry their luggage if I'm not around. Also, you'll take care of the money and the books for both businesses."

"I understand. I'll do a good job for you."

"You can take a room in the back if you need a place to live. That can be part of your pay. It'll be ready tomorrow. We're painting the doors, and everything is wet. Just a bed and a small dresser in there."

"I appreciate that. And yes, I can use a place to live."

"You can eat here as long as you're working. I pay a dollar a day."

"Agreed." She hoped she didn't sound too eager.

"I'll see you in the morning at six. And part of the duties means helping out in the dining room or kitchen if needed."

"Whatever you need, I can do."

He peered at her. "If you're late, you're fired. A pretty face might get you a job, but I demand hard work." He whirled around and hurried back to where he'd been working.

Chloe clenched her trembling fists and stepped out into the

street. At last, she'd found a way to support herself. Life and all of its adversity would smooth out beginning tomorrow morning. Tomorrow, she'd eat. Tomorrow night, she'd have someplace to sleep other than the outdoors and be able to bathe somewhere other than the creek. Today was a blessing. *Thank You, Lord.* One more day and she would have been forced to knock on Brother Whitworth's door and beg. Not that she didn't like the preacher and his sweet wife, but she'd starve before accepting charity. Her father had no problem asking for handouts, but Chloe did.

Her stomach growled, reminding her she hadn't eaten since this morning. She'd found an apple tree behind the livery and selected a piece of fruit that wasn't full of worms. After wrestling with her conscience over whether taking the apple was stealing or not, she finally bit into it and quickly devoured all of the tart flesh. Right now, she needed to bathe and prepare herself for the morning. A pecan grove rested on the road to the creek. She could use a rock to break the nuts. Shaking her head, she imagined how desperate her circumstances would be if she fainted on the first day of work from lack of food.

A memory twisted in her mind that took her back many years. She was eight years old and had no lunch for school. She usually sat apart from the other children at noon because so many of them teased her. One of the older boys made his way to her side. He bent down and handed her a sandwich.

"I'm full and wondered if you wanted this."

Chloe stared at the sandwich, thick with meat. She'd not had breakfast, either. "Are you sure?" Her mouth watered.

"Absolutely sure." He spoke softly and smiled. His dark hair and eyes were gentle.

CHAPTER 2

Zack shivered in the early morning air as he dressed. His trousers felt like they were lined with ice, and shaving nearly cost him the skin from his face. The stove in the corner of his room had gone out during the night, and he didn't have time to build another fire from the scant supply of coal and kindling. He'd rented the apartment because of the low rent, not considering the cost of keeping it warm in winter. Two more days, and he'd board a train that would carry him to central Texas.

As he lifted his suspenders over his shoulders and pranced across the cold wooden floor toward his socks, Zack realized that New York had been a good experience. He'd obtained his education and worked three long, hard years for the *New York Times* while he finished college. God had been good to him. Not many young reporters were able to cover big stories, but those opportunities caused him to long for a newspaper of his own—back home.

With a grin, he laced up his shoes, thinking how grand to say he was now the proud owner of the *Frontier Press*—editor, reporter, typesetter, deliverer, and janitor. *My, that felt real good.* He sure was glad the previous owner planned to help him for a while.

And no more women. From here on out, he was married to the paper. Sure would save a lot on the old heart and the wallet.

Wallet. . . What did Curly and Charlie have for breakfast today? Did the sisters find them better shoes and clothing? Were they cold last night?

The Triangle Factory fire had shaken him to the core. Never had he seen such senseless death. He'd labored long hours to report the tragedy accurately and without bias, but he'd discovered the management had ignored basic safety measures for all those people. Low wages and deplorable working conditions still fueled anger in him. That stain in New York's history had killed Curly and Charlie's mother. He couldn't shake the fire, and he couldn't shake the memory of those incorrigible twins. Zack paused a moment. He'd been rebellious and stubborn, too, after his father had died, but he'd been redeemed. He hoped the same for them.

Yawning, Zack shook his head and considered once more why he hadn't slept much the night before. The twins stayed fixed in his mind. He'd seen that mass of curly red hair and those pitiful shoes in every dream. Telling them he was sorry for their mother's death made him feel like one of those Christians who paid homage with their mouths and did nothing to alleviate the problems of the poor. Why hadn't he the foresight to buy them a hot meal and make arrangements for some decent clothes? In short, regret had taken root in his heart.

A memory crept into his mind. . . . A long time ago while he was still attending school in Kahlerville, he'd noticed a little girl who never seemed to have any lunch. He got into the habit of bringing an extra sandwich. The twins reminded him of her.

I can't leave New York without looking into the situation. After making the final rounds at the newspaper, he'd find the orphanage and check on the boys.

Chloe rose long before dawn and bathed in the chilly waters of the creek. She washed her hair and let it drape about her shoulders in hopes it would dry before time to pin it up for work. A satchel held her worldly possessions, but tonight they'd have a better resting place than lying hidden beneath the trunk of a fallen cypress tree. She'd washed her dress last night and wrapped a discarded blanket around her until this morning. The dress was a little more than damp, but it was clean. If only she had something to eat. Maybe she'd be offered some breakfast this morning.

With a sliver missing from a full moon and a sky full of twinkling stars to light her way, Chloe lifted her satchel and started her trek toward Kahlerville. Mr. Barton had indicated she might not be able to handle her new position. She'd show him. Her days had been filled with hard work ever since she could remember. School had been a joy, and she enjoyed the challenge of all her subjects, especially arithmetic. To her, solving number problems was like putting all the pieces of a puzzle together and caused her to temporarily forget her bleak circumstances.

Glancing up at the sky, she figured 80 percent of the right portion of the moon appeared, and that phase was called something. . . . She'd remember it later. Ah, a waxing gibbous moon. Her step picked up.

Life had taken a definite turn for the best.

The boardinghouse windows revealed a hint of light, and that meant signs of someone up and about. From Chloe's estimation, the time was around five o'clock. *The cook must be starting breakfast before the boarders rise.* She could smell the coffee, the bacon sizzling, biscuits baking. . . . Shaking the dizziness from her head, she entered the boardinghouse.

"Good morning. Mr. Barton?"

When no one responded, she made her way back to where the smell of coffee nearly gave her chills.

"Good morning. Mr. Barton?"

"He's not here," came a gravelly voice. "Whatcha need?"

Chloe walked toward the voice. "I'm Chloe Weaver, the new desk clerk and bookkeeper."

A short, chubby fellow with an apron tied around his waist flipped bacon in a huge, cast-iron skillet. "Mornin', Miss Weaver. You're a mite early, aren't you?"

She attempted to ignore the tantalizing smells wafting about. For a moment, she thought she'd faint. "Uh, yes. I'm early. A little eager to get started."

"Well, Mr. Barton ain't here yet. Sit a spell. Coffee's done. He opened the oven door. "And so's the biscuits. I bet you haven't had breakfast."

"No, sir." Her mouth watered, and she glanced away.

"Call me Simeon." He nodded toward the coffeepot on the stove. "Open up that there cabinet and get yourself a mug. Butter and honey are on the table for a biscuit."

Chloe dug her fingers into her palms to stop the shaking.

"Don't be nervous about your first day at work. Barton's fair, but he expects ya to do what he's paying ya for. You can put your bag behind the door."

"Oh, I intend to. I mean do a good job." She set her satchel in the appointed spot and poured the coffee, willing her hand to stop trembling. She licked her thumb and forefinger before reaching for a hot biscuit. In the next instant, thick sweet honey and melted butter oozed from *her* biscuit. "Thank you. This is delicious."

He chuckled. "That's what I like to hear. From the looks of you, I'd say you've missed a few meals. Ol' Simeon will take care of fattenin' you up. You can be my tester."

"Tester?" she asked between bites.

"Yeah. Taste my food and see if it needs anything."

She smiled. "I'd be happy to help you with that little chore." Once she finished the biscuit—in as ladylike a manner as possible—she sipped the coffee. "All right. How can I help you?"

Simeon grinned wide, revealing a mouthful of missing teeth. "You and me's gonna get along just fine." He leaned toward her. "You shore are purdy. Too bad I'm not thirty years younger. We'd be doin' some courtin'. All that shiny black hair. My mama was part Indian, too."

Chloe let him talk. She had no intentions of ever courting or making any excuses about her mama. Today was a fresh start for a new life.

Zack took a bittersweet look around the newspaper office. He loved the sights of people scurrying about, the smell of ink, the sound of typewriters, the hum of reporters and editors relaying the pertinent facts of their latest stories, and the touch of a newspaper. To him, few things compared to the thrill of handing a reader a fresh copy of the *New York Times*. Once he arrived back home in Kahlerville, he'd do the same for those people he'd grown up with and missed during the past few years in the big city.

"Good luck to ye, boy," a typesetter said.

"Tear 'em up with your own newspaper," another man said.

"Enjoyed working with you," still another said.

Zack returned their well wishes with his sights set toward his cold apartment and then home. He gathered up last night's newspaper—a keepsake—and headed out onto Times Square into the wintry morning. But before he trudged the streets to his apartment, he needed to stop at the Saint Vincent de Paul Orphanage on Forty-second Street to see about Curly and Charlie. Once he finished there, he'd have time to pack up his few belongings before noon and do a little sightseeing on his last afternoon in New York City.

Taking the trolley, he arrived at the building housing the motherless and fatherless children of the area. A mixture of wondering why get involved and a deep need to make sure the boys were well taken care of swirled about his mind. How easy it would be simply to forget yesterday and carry on with his own affairs. Unfortunately, that hadn't happened. God had pushed him to make sure the twins hadn't run off again and to contribute a few dollars to their welfare. He could even send a little money regularly to the orphanage. Yes, that was a fine charitable consideration.

Opening the door, he noticed that the inside of the building wasn't much warmer than the outside. Bare toes and ragged coats flashed across his mind.

"May I help you?" a veiled sister asked.

Zack moistened his lips. "Yes, ma'am. My name is Zackary Kahler, and I'm checking on a set of twins who I believe were delivered here by a policeman yesterday."

She smiled. "Welcome. My name is Sister Catherine. You must mean Curly and Charlie."

He nodded. "Have they decided to stay put?"

"At least for the day. The two often work with the newsboys. Are you a relative?"

"No. I met them prior to the policeman escorting them back to you."

"Oh, you must be the man with the wallet."

"I am." He relaxed slightly and smiled. "Are they all right? I mean they sure are young to be wandering the streets. I know the city is full of orphans."

"They are doing well."

"I understand their mother was killed in the Triangle Factory fire." When the sister affirmed this, he braved forward. "And their father?"

"The family immigrated here from Ireland. According to the children, he died when they were babies. They have no family in this country. Would you like to see the twins?" Sister Catherine folded her hands in front of her, making him wonder if she was praying. An uneasiness swept over him, and he couldn't shake it off.

"No need to trouble yourself. Actually, I wanted to take care of the paperwork for setting myself up as a benefactor of sorts."

"I see. If that is the case, they need to thank you properly."

Before Zack could object, she disappeared down a dark hallway. Did he really want to see those two again? With his gloved hands behind his back, he glanced about and noted the draft from the door, the threadbare rug, and the lack of light. But he did hear the faint sounds of children in the distance. From what he'd heard, this orphanage was much better than most.

Just when he was about to give up and get busy with the ever-growing list of preparations to be made before he boarded the train for Chicago tomorrow and from there the Northern Pacific to Texas, Sister Catherine appeared with Curly and Charlie. Her hands firmly grasped a shoulder of each twin. From their reddened faces, the two had been scrubbed clean. Their clothes were ragged but patched, and the shoes were the same ones he had noticed earlier.

"Children, Mr. Kahler has been so kind to visit you."

The two exchanged wide-eyed glances but said nothing. She tapped their shoulders.

"Thank you, sir."

"You're welcome. I trust you have been behaving yourselves." When neither responded, he bent to their level. They reminded him of leprechauns. His mother would call them two peas in a pod. She'd also say how cute they were. *Cute but thieves.* A curious thought twisted through his mind, then planted itself firmly in his heart. He must have taken leave of his good senses. Standing, Zack smiled at the sister.

"I'd like to complete the paperwork necessary to send money for these two until they are adopted."

"Adoption, sir, is highly unlikely, unless you were contemplating the idea."

Zack's heart suddenly felt like freshly churned butter. "I'm not married."

"A father is better than no parent at all. Our Lord would bless you for this act of charity."

What could he say? He sensed the twins staring at him—more like boring a hole through his coat, jacket, and shirt. "I'm leaving the city tomorrow. Returning home to Texas."

"And what will you do there?"

Somehow, the twins had moved closer to him. Their thin bodies touched his, but he refused to look their way. "I recently purchased the town's newspaper."

Sister Catherine pulled the twins closer to her side. "Did you hear that, children? This kind man owns a newspaper in Texas. Oh, Mr. Kahler, what a fine home you could provide for these little angels."

Angels? Obviously, the kind sister had not seen these two in action. "How old are they?"

"Six. They will be seven on June—I'll have to look at their file."

Zack regretted ever considering visiting the orphanage. "I know nothing about raising children."

"Do you have family in Texas? A mother? Sister? Aunt? Any female relatives?"

"I have all of those and an eight-year-old brother." Why did his heart slam against his chest? *No, God. Absolutely not. I have things to do when I get home.*

"Splendid. Large town or small?"

"Rather small."

Sister Catherine stood on her toes and laughed aloud. "You are an answer to prayer, kind sir." She hugged the children into her black skirt. "My precious Curly and Charlie, you are leaving us for a new home and a father." Tears filled her eyes and spilled over her cheeks. "God bless you. God bless you. I'll leave you to get acquainted with the children while I retrieve the necessary papers for you to sign and find Sister Agatha to start the preliminary proceedings."

What had he gotten himself into? "Do you mean adoption papers?"

"Oh yes. Why, you can't simply walk out of here with these children. There are certain legal steps that must be followed."

"And how long will this process take?"

She touched her forefinger to her chin. "I'm not sure. Please excuse me while I find Sister Agatha. You can wait in our parlor." Sister Catherine guided Zack and the twins to the small room, which apparently was rarely used.

The twins had nothing to say, which surprised him, and in turn he could think of nothing clever. Adoption papers? He knew about the orphan trains that headed west with children; some of those children found good homes, and others became nothing more than servants. Those couples didn't meet with judges. Of course, he wasn't married.

An hour later, Sister Agatha and Zack boarded the trolley to pay a call on the judge. Numb best described Zack. In his hand, he carried a copy of New York's laws regarding the legal adoption of minor children by adult persons. Because of his scheduled departure the following afternoon, Sister Agatha wanted the judge to hear the case immediately.

The judge welcomed Sister Agatha and Zack into his chambers. He scrutinized Zack as though he were a criminal.

"Why do you want these children?" The judge removed his spectacles and laid them on his mahogany desk.

Why did he want them? "Well, sir, I'm a newspaper reporter, and I covered the story about the Triangle Factory fire. It was a tragic event, and when I learned about the twins orphaned by it, I wanted to do something to help."

"Adopting them is quite a 'something.' Who is going to care for them while you are working?"

"Actually, I'm leaving New York tomorrow afternoon for my home in Texas. I've purchased a newspaper there."

"He has family in the town," Sister Agatha said. "Women who could care for the children."

The judge nodded. "Were you and the children's mother, uh, involved?"

Zack sensed his face reddening. "No, sir. I know nothing about her."

"It's highly suspicious for you to want the children and immediately leave the city. Especially since you're unattached and do not plan to marry in the near future."

Zack moistened his lips. "I come from a good family and an excellent little town. My stepfather pastors a church there. One of my uncles is a doctor, and another is an attorney. Both sides of my family are good people of the community."

"So they would vouch for you?"

"Yes, sir."

"You're not planning to sell them, are you?"

"Absolutely not. As a Christian man, I don't believe in such practices."

The judge lifted a pen and dipped it into an inkwell. "I want both of your uncles' names and how to contact them. I expect the attorney to write me concerning the welfare of the children." The judge squinted at the paper. "The Sullivan children. This adoption will not be finalized until I hear from him. Is that clearly understood?"

"Yes, sir."

"That will be all." The judge studied him again. "I hope you have a good head on your shoulders, young man, because this undertaking will not be easy. You can't return children like they were puppies who chewed up your shoes." He dismissed him and Sister Agatha with a nod.

Zack glanced at a smiling Sister Agatha. Her wrinkled face and apparent joy did not relieve his apprehension.

Lord, help me. I think my impulsive nature just got the best of me.

CHAPTER 3

Chloe stirred up eggs, peeled potatoes, and set out dishes for the boarders' breakfast before Mr. Barton arrived on this first morning of her employ. He strode through the kitchen door like a noble king ready to issue a proclamation. She took note of his banded hat and fitted suit. Obviously, he wasn't picking up a paintbrush this morning. She hadn't noticed before, but his right hand was shriveled.

"I've had some good help this mornin', Mr. Barton." Simeon poured him a cup of coffee and added a generous spoonful of honey and lots of thick cream. "Would you like yer breakfast now?"

Chloe's stomach still growled, but she'd not complain.

Mr. Barton pulled out his pocket watch. "We've got a good twenty minutes before getting started. Miss Weaver, you may not get a chance to eat until evenin'. Let's get us a plate of breakfast and talk about all of your duties."

She had no idea what she'd done right to deserve a whole plate of food, but she'd not refuse it. "Thank you, sir."

They sat in the corner of the dining room. Mr. Barton said nothing while he hurried through his breakfast. He reached for his coffee. "I did some askin' around and learned you're a smart young woman."

She thanked him with a nod since her mouth contained a tender piece of crusty fried potato.

"Miss Scott says you were one of her prize students. She had a hard time keeping you busy in school. Had to send to Austin for harder arithmetic and more books for you to read."

Chloe swallowed. "I enjoyed learning."

He leaned in closer across the table. "Brother Whitworth says you never miss a Sunday or a Wednesday night prayer meeting. That's real good, 'cause most folks with mixed blood tend to stay away from church."

She wasn't about to tell him her regular church attendance was due to her father's abuse and not the mixture of Comanche and white blood flowing through her veins. God knew her heart.

"He also said your father died in a house fire a few weeks ago on a Wednesday night while you were at church."

Chloe gazed into Mr. Barton's deep blue eyes. What hadn't he found out about her? Yet the newspaper had reported the fire and her father's death. "Yes, sir."

"I don't believe in hiring someone just because they need a job or been subject to hard times. I need people who can perform a task and do it well. If you can't, you're gone." His voice raised a tad. "See this?" He held up his withered right hand. "I've made it in this town because I work hard. Not because I expected someone to give me a handout."

"Yes, sir. I understand."

"The only reason I'm not doing the bookkeeping is that my penmanship is deplorable." He took another swallow of coffee, then pulled out his pocket watch again. "Three minutes to six o'clock. Time to get started."

In the next hour, Chloe learned how to register a new boarder, including what information to gather and how much money to collect in advance. Mr. Barton gave her a key to the small cash box and instructed her to guard it with her life. She pulled her only ribbon from her hair and threaded the key through it. Turning her back on Mr. Barton, she slipped the ribbon and key inside the bodice of her dress.

Mr. Barton's instructions included showing her an empty boarder's room, as well as the spare room behind the registration desk.

"Now, when a customer asks what the rooms look like, you can describe them in detail. Also, when a customer checks out, you remove the sheets and pillowcases and bring them downstairs to the kitchen. On Saturday mornings, all the beds are changed. Simeon has someone who picks up the linens and returns them clean. You make the bed and dust and sweep the room, too. The chamber pots are to be emptied in the outhouse every morning and evening. Make sure you use the back staircase at all times. Treat this boardinghouse like your own home. Keep it clean and perform whatever duties need to be done. The customers are to be treated with the utmost respect and courtesy. No matter what they say, they are always right. No matter what they need, you fetch it for them. If Simeon needs help and you aren't busy, you make sure those customers are happy. I'll tell you more as you go along." He snapped his fingers. "Newspapers are delivered on Saturday morning. Keep them on the front counter for the customers to purchase. It's an honor system, but keep a watchful eye for those who take one and don't leave a nickel."

Mr. Barton took a deep breath as though he'd just delivered a regal declaration and pointed to the parlor. "On Thanksgiving, Christmas, and Easter, you're free to go after breakfast. And with Christmas coming, we'll want to decorate everything."

How could she do all those things and keep an ear out for the bell above the door? "When the work is caught up after supper, then I'm free to go to my room?"

"That and all the entries made for the day. Once a week, I'll bring you the books and receipts from the feed store to post figures. And you are free to do as you please on Sundays. I'll help Simeon with meals before and after church. It gives me a chance to visit with the boarders."

Chloe hoped she remembered everything Mr. Barton had told her. He wanted the numbers written in the ledger a particular way and the book stacked beneath the counter with the spines out so he could grab them at any time. She saw strength and perfectionism in him, no doubt instilled at an early age from his crippled arm. A new respect for him surfaced. She'd been crippled, too. Her spirit limped from the years of abuse, but things were changing. Soon she'd be able to walk the streets of Kahlerville with her head held high and ignore the jeers.

<hr />

"Now that you two have eaten, a bath is in order. Once we get to my apartment and build a fire in the stove, you are going to scrub long and hard." Zack stood from the small table at a restaurant where he and the twins had eaten their fill of vegetable soup and bread.

"A bath?" the spokesman said. "Why? We had one not too long ago."

"You're Curly?"

The child nodded. Zack studied him and Charlie. How would he ever tell them apart? First thing in the morning, the boys would get new clothes for the trip home. That way he could assign them a particular color.

"It's like this, Curly. You're dirty, and tomorrow we're heading to Texas on the afternoon train."

"How far is this Texas?"

"It'll take us a few days to get there."

Curly ran his finger around the soup bowl and then popped it into his mouth. Those two definitely needed to learn some manners.

"Mr. Kahler, why did you take us?" Curly crossed his arms over his chest.

"Not sure myself. It just happened. Looked to me like you needed a good home, so I'm going to try to provide one." Zack nodded at Charlie. "How's come your brother never talks?"

Curly frowned. "Guess Charlie doesn't have much to say."

"Charlie, anything you want to ask me?"

The little boy shook his head.

"How much work are you going to give us?" Curly glanced over at Charlie's bowl, which still held part of a spoonful of soup.

Without a word, Zack handed him his own piece of bread. "The only kind of work I can think of is schoolwork and a few chores."

"Where are we gonna live?"

Zack rubbed his chin. He'd been thinking about that very thing. What *was* he going to do with twin boys? "I haven't decided yet. I bought a newspaper office, so we need to live close to town."

"What's this Texas like?"

"It's mostly country. Lots of farms and ranches in the community." Zack waved his hands around the room. "There's only one restaurant in town, and it's at the boardinghouse. But I heard another restaurant is opening soon. It's quieter there. Slower pace of life. I can tell you more about it on the train."

Curly rested his hands under his chin. "Are you sure this isn't a trick to make us work for you?"

Zack understood the suspicions. The twins probably didn't trust anyone. New York had its share of mistreated children. "I give you my word. I don't have any intentions of seeing you boys come to any harm."

Curly fidgeted, glanced over at Charlie, then back to Zack. "There's somethin' I have to tell you."

"Go ahead." Zack had long sensed the boys were wasting time to prolong the bath.

"Charlie's not a boy."

Long after sundown, Chloe labored over the cash box holding the day's money. A number of guests had taken rooms, and she had counted the money twice before unlocking the cash box and placing it inside. She'd placed it behind the ledger book just like Mr. Barton had instructed. But when she'd added a new boarder's money, Chloe discovered the cash box was short two dollars.

Her stomach churned. She could only imagine the accusations. Mr. Barton would have her arrested, and the town's gossip would rise like chimney smoke on a cold morning. What had happened to the money? She'd been sure of the correct amount before helping

Simeon with dinner. If only she had the two dollars to put into the cash box. This position had been her opportunity to better herself, and now her mistake would give her free room and board at the jail.

The boardinghouse hushed as the residents retired to their rooms. Chloe removed every item she could find from behind the registration counter in an effort to find the lost money. Tears threatened to surface, but she bit them back. The grandfather clock in the foyer chimed eleven. Thoughts of running crossed her mind, except where would she go without any money?

The bell above the door tinkled, and she held her breath. Mr. Barton made long strides toward her.

"You're working late." His gaze fixed on her as if he knew her blunder.

"Yes, sir. I am."

"Why?"

She thought her heart would burst from her chest. Surely he must have heard it. "I seem to have misplaced something."

"What's the problem?"

Chloe stood. Her knees trembled, and a lump settled in the back of her throat. "The cash box is short two dollars. I don't know how it happened, but when I opened it to add a new boarder's money, I discovered the cash was missing."

Mr. Barton nodded. "I see." He reached inside his trouser pocket and pulled out a wad of bills. "You've passed the test." He peeled off two one-dollar bills. "I wanted to see if you were honest, so I took the money while you were helping Simeon tonight. I have a key to the cash box with me at all times."

Chloe didn't know whether to leap for joy or unleash a bit of her temper. "Mr. Barton, you nearly caused my heart to fail me."

"Good."

Anger dripped through her veins. She opened her mouth to tell him what she thought of his prank but thought better of it.

"You want to say something?"

"No, sir."

He touched the brim of his hat. "Good evening, Miss Weaver. Sleep well. I think this arrangement will work out just fine."

Shortly thereafter, Chloe crawled beneath the sheets of her very own bed. She'd slept so many nights on the hard floor or under the stars that the comforts of a mattress, even though it was threadbare, had to be just short of heaven. Praise God. Come Sunday, she'd be singing the loudest in church—and praying Mr. Barton was finished with his tests. Surely Mama would be looking down from her mansion with Jesus, happy that her daughter was going to be fine. Those boys who'd found her living by the river wouldn't be teasing her anymore, either. Someday she'd leave this town and never look back. Maybe save enough money to buy a business or teach school or even own a little house. She'd grow old taking care of herself with only books as friends.

Exhausted, she hoped the days to come were filled with more hours for sleep.

CHAPTER 4

Zack settled onto a seat on the train across from Curly and Charlie, or rather Carlin and Caitlain. *His children.* They did look cute in their new clothes, especially Charlie in a bright blue dress with a matching hair ribbon in her curls. She looked very much a little girl. He'd splurged a little and bought shoes, socks, and undergarments for both of them. Then he remembered they would need day clothes once they arrived in Kahlerville. More purchases. More money.

He leaned back against the seat and closed his eyes. If he took the time to sort out the past few days, he might become ill. All of this happened because two little thieves had picked his pocket. Now he was...

Zack startled. He was a father? What did he know about children? Where would they live until he found a house? And did he continue to call them Curly and Charlie or their given names?

He glanced at the twins. Both of them had their fingers up their noses. Definitely Curly and Charlie. "Hey, stop that."

They knew exactly what he meant, for their hands now lay in their laps. Zack reached inside his coat for a clean handkerchief and handed it first to Charlie. The twins fought, used language that only a bar of soap would cure, and ate like little animals. Where would he begin?

His mother would be appalled. Zack's original thought of living with his parents until he found a place of his own he now deemed impossible. Never would he subject his family to these two until he worked on civilizing them.

"You don't like us. I can tell," Curly said. "I know you're mad 'cause the sisters made you take us from the orphanage."

How did he reassure them that he did care? "I do like you, and no one made me do anything. I'm just tired and thinking about the future."

"What do you mean?"

"Where we're going to live, your schooling, my newspaper. Those kind of things."

"We used to have only a mama. Then we had nobody. But now we have you." Those were the first words Charlie had spoken without being prompted. "But you hate us."

Curly put his arm around Charlie's shoulder. Big tears rolled over her too-thin cheeks.

What had he done wrong? Zack slipped from his seat and leaned over his little charges. Mischievous as they were, they were now his. "I don't hate you at all. If I didn't care about you, I wouldn't have started the adoption process."

"What does that mean?" Curly asked.

Zack proceeded to wipe the tears from Charlie's cheek with his finger.

"It means we are going to be a family."

The twins quickly exchanged glances. "We thought you'd lied to us and we were going to work at your newspaper," Curly said.

Zack shook his head. "Not at all. Oh, you might help me if I need something special, or you might ride along with me to deliver newspapers. But your job is to be a child and go to school."

Charlie sniffed. "Do I have to give back my clothes?"

"Of course not. And I'll get you more when I start making money."

"I heard you tell Sister Catherine that you had family in Texas."

"I do. And you will have a grandma and grandpa, aunts, uncles, and cousins."

Their smiles were the sweetest this side of heaven. Maybe the two wouldn't be so much trouble after all. He bent and kissed each one on the forehead. Perhaps now was the time to start thinking about these two as blessings instead of a burden.

Chloe carried a load of dirty linens down the back stairs. Today had gone well, and she had expected Saturday to be quite busy. That morning Simeon had whipped up the lightest pancakes she'd ever tasted, while she fried the bacon and set the table. The boarders were friendly, which made her work easier and almost enjoyable. Lugging the chamber pots up and down the stairs and then cleaning them, however, was at the bottom of the list of her favorite duties. Nasty. Smelly. She heard Mr. Barton say that in the next six months he intended to add a couple of water closets. He hadn't stopped by yet this morning, and that was fine with her. Last night's test had pushed her patience nearly to its limits.

She heard the bell above the front door and made her way to the registration desk to see if she was needed. Mr. Barton had a bag of flour and a fragrant bag of coffee beans in his hand. This time he wore overalls. That man sure had a lot of clothes. He made his way toward her.

"Morning, Miss Weaver. I trust you slept well." He grinned broadly.

She clenched her fists. "Very well, thank you. Once I got to bed."

He threw back his head and laughed. "I guess I deserved that." He reached into his pocket and drew out a peppermint stick. "Will this sweeten your day?"

She couldn't help but laugh and reached for the peppermint. "I think it's a grand start."

"Wonderful. Do we have a two-bedroom room available?"

"Yes, we do."

"I just received a telegram from Zack Kahler. Not sure if you ever knew him. He's due in on tomorrow afternoon's train. Says he will have two children with him."

Had Zack married? She remembered him as the handsome boy who was one of the few who hadn't teased her about her Indian heritage.

"From what I hear, he purchased the newspaper. Must have married someone from New York. Odd, the town hasn't heard about it." He tipped his hat and headed for the kitchen.

Zack with a wife and children. She heard he'd gotten into some trouble when he was younger, when his mother was a widow. Then

Brother Whitworth came to town and married Zack's mother. Oh, he had his moments like all boys, but they were playful—not cruel like some of the other boys. When she was a girl, she fancied herself one day wed to him. Ridiculous when she considered he had viewed her as a charity case. Chloe shrugged and decided to check on the empty rooms for Mr. and Mrs. Zack Kahler and children.

Zack carried a sleeping Charlie off the train in Kahlerville. Curly trailed beside him in a similar state of exhaustion. With an air of apprehension whipping about him, Zack glanced about for his parents. The town had grown. New buildings had sprung up, and there were changes in the old. Later he'd study the town and learn about the new businesses. Where were his parents?

When he had made arrangements at the boardinghouse, he should have also wired his parents about the twins, but he didn't quite know how to word the news about them. Odd, he could write a newspaper column, but he could not convey to his parents that they now had two grandchildren.

His gaze swept across the depot. His family made their way toward him. There they were: his petite blond mother who looked more beautiful as the years passed, his far-too-lovely sixteen-year-old sister, his eight-year-old brother, and his stepfather, whom Zack loved as fiercely as his own deceased father. He wished his brother, Michael Paul, was there too, but he was in seminary. Surprise registered on all of their faces. He chuckled and leaned over to Curly.

"Your grandparents, Aunt Lydia Anne, and your uncle Stuart, who is only two years older than you, are straight ahead."

"I'm scared." Curly latched on to Zack's coattail.

41

"No need to be." But Zack sensed his own stomach doing a few flips. Should he wake Charlie? How was he supposed to make introductions?

His stepfather reached him first and leaned over the sleeping Charlie to hug him. "Good to see you, and we're all so glad you're home." He swung a glance first at Charlie, then at Curly. "Are you helping someone with their children?"

"Not exactly." He gulped. "The twins are mine. Well, they will be. I'm in the process of adopting them."

Mama offered a shaky smile. She stepped closer, and Zack bent to let her kiss his cheek. "Welcome home, son. My, you are more handsome every day." She took in a deep breath. "The children are quite a surprise, but a good one. I'm—I'm anxious to hear the story."

Lydia Anne covered her mouth, but a giggle managed to escape. "You look funny carrying a little girl."

Stuart laughed aloud, his dark hair spilling over his forehead. "Big brother, I never thought I'd see you comin' off the train with children."

Concern swept over Mama's face, and she stroked the sleeping Charlie's cheek. "Oh, my dear boy. Are you ready for this responsibility?" Without waiting for a reply, she stooped down to Curly. "I'm your grandma. What is your name?"

Curly appeared to be speechless. Definitely a first.

"You're shy," Mama continued. "I understand meeting all of us must be a shock."

"Their names are Curly and Charlie, and they are six." Suddenly Charlie had gotten very heavy. "Actually, their names are Carlin and Caitlain."

His dad chuckled. "Perfect names. A bit of Irish stew. I like

42

nicknames myself. Let's get your trunk into the wagon and head home."

Zack cleared his throat. He could count on Dad to make the most awkward of situations a little easier. "I've made arrangements for us to stay at the boardinghouse. The twins and I have adjustments to make."

"I won't hear of it." Mama frowned. Her severe look used to work when he was a kid, but not at the age of twenty-four.

"Mama, these two have lived on the s–t–r–e–e–t. They can be an h–a–n–d–f–u–l."

She continued to frown. "But the boardinghouse is no place for children to play."

"I'll find us something suitable soon."

Curly sneezed, and the contents dripped to his chin. Zack scrambled for his handkerchief while balancing Charlie. The hand-kerchief was not exactly clean, but he attempted to wipe the boy's face anyway.

Dad laughed until his eyes filled with tears. Lydia Anne and Stuart joined him, but Mama pulled her own dainty handkerchief from her reticule and proceeded to help.

"Less than a month before Thanksgiving and Christmas to follow. What grand holidays we will have." Dad lifted Charlie from Zack's arms. "We do want you to live with us, but we respect your decision."

"Thanks, Dad. This is best, and it shouldn't take too long for me to find a proper house. How about dinner at the boardinghouse after we've checked in?"

Mama's small shoulders lifted and fell. "I planned to have your favorite chicken and dumplings and apple-cinnamon pie."

"That's tempting, but then you'd have to bring us back into town, and the twins are really tired."

"Will you come tomorrow and spend lots of time? We can have your favorite dinner then."

"Sounds good. The twins have never seen a ranch, and I think they'll love it. But I want to visit the newspaper first."

"I'll show you all the animals," Stuart said to Curly. He puffed up, striking a pose that mirrored his dad at the pulpit.

"It's a shame they weren't here for church on Sunday. I'd love to have shown them off." Mama tilted her head.

Zack didn't want to think about the twins' behavior in church. "There will be other Sundays."

After he retrieved his trunk and made arrangements for it to be taken to the boardinghouse, the small band made their way down the street. By this time Charlie had awakened and begged Zack to hold her.

"I'm sure you will be a fine father," Mama said. "You'll have matters in hand in no time at all."

Zack had his doubts.

His dad opened the door of the boardinghouse. The tantalizing aroma of roast beef and potatoes met Zack's nose. Until this moment, he hadn't realized how hungry he was, and the twins undoubtedly felt the same.

"This sure smells better than food at the orphanage," Curly said.

"You poor baby." Mama sniffed. "I will make sure you have plenty of good meals."

Zack chuckled, then took a fleeting glance at the young woman behind the registration desk. He started. *Chloe Weaver?* He hadn't seen her in years, but he recognized those huge brown eyes and long thick lashes. Here she was all grown up and quite a beauty.

"Good evening." Her voice rang sweet, reminding him of candy.

"Chloe Weaver, right?" Zack's voice cracked like a twelve-year-old.

She nodded. "How good of you to remember me after all this time. We received your wire, and I have your room ready." She smiled. "Your children are beautiful."

"Thank you."

"How long have you been married?"

Here came the questions. "I'm not married."

A glint of something that resembled curiosity and disapproval rested in her eyes. And because he didn't understand her reaction, frustration settled in him. Zack had no intention of explaining why he was now responsible for a set of six-year-old twins. Had he set himself up to be judged and hung because he'd chosen a family without a wife?

"Would you like to see your room? Dinner is awaiting you, too."

"Thanks. We're pretty hungry." His glance moved from one child to the other. "How about we see our room and then eat?"

"Yes, sir," the two chorused.

Ah, the lessons on manners were working.

The room was slightly larger than his New York apartment and definitely warmer. A raised window let in a soft breeze that gently blew back the curtains. Instantly, the twins were pointing out the sights of Kahlerville from the open window.

"How many newspapers in this town?" Curly asked.

"Only one." Zack had a good idea of what he was thinking. "Neither of you will be working as newsboys here."

"How are we going to live?" Charlie asked.

"Let me worry about that." Zack saw his mother exchange a

confused look with Dad. "The twins lived a hard life in New York."

"I can see that." Dad made his way to the window and placed a hand on each of the twins' shoulders. "Do you two like to fish?"

"Don't know," Curly said. "Never done it."

"Well, I'll have to introduce you two to the art of fishing. Zack, Stuart, and I spent some fine days on the creek bank."

"I can show you how, too." Stuart stepped over beside them, and Lydia Anne joined them.

Zack realized Mama would have many questions. She probably thought he should have a wife before children. Most of the time since his trip to Saint Vincent de Paul Orphanage, he would agree. But a wife would only add another burden, as his relationship with Miss Elizabeth Hanington had already proven. "It will be all right, Mama." He wrapped his arm around her waist.

She touched her gloved finger to the tip of her nose and leaned onto his shoulder. "I know, but this road won't be easy."

He didn't need his mama to tell him that.

CHAPTER 5

Chloe turned from one side of the bed to the other, then onto her back in a frustrating effort to sleep, but Zack Kahler's appearance consumed her mind. She still thought of him as the boy who supplied her with food every day. Why was she allowing him to dwell in her thoughts? Could it be her heart had never healed from the childhood infatuation with him? She'd been twelve when he finished school, and she'd seen him at church every Wednesday night and Sunday after that until he left for school in New York. His absence had caused her to cry for weeks.

Zack had been gone four years. And now he'd come home with children who were definitely older than four.

He said he wasn't married. Had his wife died, or had they separated? Where was the twins' mother? The children had immediately attached themselves to her heart, and those cute accents further endeared them to her. So what had Zack been doing in New York? A few immoral thoughts trekked across her mind. "Father, forgive me," she whispered into the darkness. Suddenly she gasped. *What is wrong with me?* The truth ushered in an answer. Chloe touched her heart. A long time ago she'd placed Zack on a pedestal for his kindness toward her, and now with his appearance and questionable past, she'd knocked him clear to the ground.

His morals and the reason he now had two children were none of her business. Chloe thought a moment longer. She'd become just like those gossips who had hurt her all of her life—condemning and criticizing without taking the time to learn the truth. With that realization, she shoved aside everything that had to do with Zack Kahler and vowed to sleep.

Four thirty in the morning came all too soon. Yawning and craving a few more precious moments of rest, Chloe crawled from bed and readied herself for work. She lit a lantern and watched the amber shadows dance across the faded wallpaper. Had Zack grown accustomed to the new electric lights? What did he think of all the people in that huge city? And what of those newfangled automobiles?

Shaking her head, Chloe scolded herself for allowing Zack to creep back into her thoughts. She smelled coffee and hurried to help Simeon. The time spent with the old man gave her a lift for the day. His wisdom and views about living a good life were often amusing, and she stored his sayings in her head to contemplate during mindless chores.

"Morning, Simeon. What's for breakfast today?"

He tossed his familiar toothless grin her way. "Scrambled eggs with bits of onion and jalapeños, corn bread, sausage, and grits."

"Are the eggs real spicy?" She didn't want the children to burn their mouths.

"Not any more than usual. Opens up the head, I always say. Takes care of what ails a body. Coffee's done and waitin' on ya." He wagged the knife her way. "Has anybody complained about my eggs?" He frowned.

Chloe planted a kiss on his whiskered face, then proceeded to tie an apron around her waist. "Now, Simeon, the only reason I asked was because we have a couple of children staying with us. They're from New York, and I doubt if they have ever tasted jalapeños."

He attempted to scowl but laughed instead. "Do you want to keep a couple of eggs separate for 'em? Far be it from me to tamper with a young'un's sensitive nature."

"Oh, you will be blessed for sure."

"I already have been. Seein' you each morning since you started working here is like having my own private angel. God knew this old man had seen his share of strife and needed a glimpse of heaven."

She shook her head. "You sure have a way with words."

"I'm speakin' the truth. And I'm not the only one who's noticed ya." She threw him a puzzled look.

"Mr. Barton. Yep, he sure is smilin' the last couple of days, and I saw him watchin' yer every move."

"He only wants to make sure I'm doing a good job." His little test still caused her stomach to churn and her temper to surface.

Simeon turned back to cutting up pieces of onion and pepper while whistling "The Yellow Rose of Texas."

Mr. Barton? Heaven forbid. Simeon needed to concentrate on cooking and not matchmaking. First a sleepless night because she couldn't get Zack out of her mind and now the prospect of Mr.

Barton's interest. She whipped her attention to measuring grits and water into a huge pan. The twins might like butter in their grits or sugar or maybe both.

"The Yellow Rose of Texas" continued to waft about the kitchen while Chloe fumed about two men who didn't interest her in the least. Eighteen years with her father had shown her what men were really like. She'd be better off sticking with Simeon in the kitchen.

Zack gathered up the wet sheets from the twins' bed and descended the back stairs that he thought led to the kitchen. His nose detected what had awakened him this morning. Curly had been humiliated and defensive at the same time. How had those two managed at the orphanage or on the street?

A woman used to pick up the laundry from the boardinghouse and return it later. He hoped that was still the procedure, considering they would be staying there until he found a home for them. God must have known what He was doing when He urged Zack to save his earnings. He also could have warned Zack about a few things regarding a pair of six-year-olds.

At the foot of the stairs, he opened a door and inhaled tantalizing smells that tugged at his empty stomach. Another door opened to the kitchen. An old man with an apron stirred something in a bowl, and Chloe pulled plates from a cabinet. He gulped. The little girl he remembered sure had changed.

Clearing his throat, he forged ahead. "Ah, morning." Awkwardness for what he carried in his arms hit him like a blast of New York wind.

Chloe swung her attention his way and smiled. "Why, good

morning, Zack." She walked his way and took the sheets from his arms, then deposited them in a heap outside the door behind him as though the problem was common place. "We'll have these taken care of today. And I'll remake the bed after breakfast."

"I'm sorry. One of the twins had an accident." He ventured to study her face. For a moment, he thought he'd drown. An image of the little girl who always thanked him with her wide eyes and sweet smile flashed across his mind.

"Don't think a moment about it. What else do you need?"

"A pitcher of water. . .for the wash basin." What had come over him? Words had fled from his brain.

"Certainly." She reached into the cabinet again and pulled out a pitcher. "I'll make sure it's warm."

While she busied herself with the water, he observed an old man who poured eggs into a huge skillet. "I'm Zack Kahler."

The whiskered old man nodded. "Pleased to meet you. I'm Simeon, the cook. I'd shake your hand, but they're soaked in onion and jalapeños."

"Sure smells good." All this time, Zack watched Chloe from the corner of his eye. Hadn't he decided that no woman would ever capture his attention again after Elizabeth had pierced his heart? Yet in all of her finery, Miss Elizabeth had never possessed the same beauty as his eyes feasted on this moment.

"Here you are." Chloe held out the pitcher and draped a cloth over it.

"Thanks." He took the pitcher and lingered a moment longer on her face. If not for the high cheekbones, she could have passed for the Italian women he'd seen in New York. Not that her Indian heritage bothered him. He'd seen a mix in America's melting pot. The people of this country weren't known for color or race but for their courage and purpose. He had no use for prejudice. No time for it. Besides, it went against God's character.

"Please remember I'll take care of your room after breakfast."

Zack swallowed hard. "The twin refused to go to sleep last night for fear of this. . .problem. So I took a few precautions for the mattress."

She smiled again. "I appreciate that. What are the children's names?"

"Curly and Charlie. Curly is the boy, and Charlie's the girl." Now he sounded stupid. "Their names are Carlin and Caitlain, but they like the nicknames."

"I do, too. They are adorable children. All those curls and freckles."

"Yeah, they are special. I hope to find a house for us soon."

"Little ones need room to run and play."

"And they can be a bundle of energy. I never dreamed adoption would be so difficult."

Simeon cleared his throat. "Miss Chloe, your grits are going to boil over if you don't watch 'em."

She blushed and hurried to the stove. Her waist-length black hair clung to her back, tied with a narrow strip of leather.

"Thanks for the water and cloth."

"You're welcome." She pulled the pan of grits from the stove and glanced up at him. "Let me know if there is anything else you need."

As Zack carried the water pitcher carefully up the back stairs, he heard Simeon whistling "The Yellow Rose of Texas." Chloe laughed. A very delicious sound.

Once back in the room, he helped Curly wash and change into

dry clothes. The little boy sniffed and avoided Zack.

"Hey, little man, it's all right."

"It's what babies do."

"You are not a baby, and I remember my little brother had the same problem after our dad died."

"When did it stop?"

Zack thought back through the tragedy of his father's illness and death. "I don't remember, but it couldn't have been very long. I'll help you with it. How about I wake you up in the middle of the night to use the chamber pot?"

Curly nodded but still avoided Zack's gaze. Poor little fellow.

Charlie touched Zack's arm. "You're alone like us, except your mama and papa are close by."

Zack reached out to touch her soft curls. "I'll do my best with you two, but you have to do your part and behave."

She tilted her head and nodded. "Me and Curly do get into trouble."

"Try real hard, all right?" He smiled at the two with the full understanding they could break into a punching match in the next five minutes. "Are you ready for breakfast? When I fetched the water, the food sure smelled good."

Their eyes widened. "We never ate so much before you got us," Curly said.

The simplicity of his statement touched Zack in the pit of his stomach—he'd never known true hunger. "Here on out, you two will eat regularly. And I'm going to see if I can get each of you another set of clothes."

"And a warm coat and scarf?" Charlie rubbed her hands together as if anticipating wintry temperatures.

"Honey, it doesn't get that cold here." He'd told them before about Kahlerville's mild temperatures, but they must not have believed him.

The twins exchanged a puzzled look.

"You may need a jacket, but most of the time the weather's pleasant."

Curly giggled and covered his mouth. "This must be the heaven Sister Catherine talked about. Plenty of food and no cold weather."

Zack swiped a tear from his eye and vowed to remember this moment the next time they tried his patience to the hilt.

They made their way down the front steps to the dining room. No sooner had they sat down than Chloe stood before them and described breakfast.

"I have a couple of scrambled eggs put aside without the onions and jalapeños for the children."

What a good idea. "Thank you, Chloe. Me, I love the onions and hot peppers in mine."

"I want mine like yours." Curly lifted his chin.

"Tell you what." He leaned toward the little boy. "I'll let you taste my eggs, and if you like them, we'll get you some."

When he focused his attention on Chloe, a faint smile played on her lips. Did he see admiration in her eyes?

"Mr. Zack, when you told us to be good, does that mean you're sending us back to the orphanage if we're bad?" Curly asked.

"I want to know that, too, Mr. Zack." Charlie folded her little hands under her chin. "I don't want to go back there. I'll do anything you want."

"We can sell newspapers and give you all the money." Curly sat straight in his chair.

Chloe's smile immediately whipped into a frown, and she whirled around toward the kitchen. Did she think he'd been mistreating the twins? Threatening them? What had he done wrong?

CHAPTER 6

Chloe poured the twins each a glass of milk. She didn't understand their relationship to Zack, and she wasn't sure she wanted to. Their welfare had nothing to do with her, and she had enough duties at the boardinghouse to keep her mind and body occupied. But the sad, fearful look on those children's faces tugged at the memories of herself as a child. She understood loneliness, fear of what tomorrow might bring, and intense hunger. After her mother died, her father had resented Chloe and found fault with nearly everything she did. He used the strap at his every whim and threatened to leave her on the preacher's doorstep where she'd be put to work.

All because she looked like her mother.

He began to drink until he drank himself into a grave. She'd surmised he was drunk the night the house caught on fire.

She rubbed her temples. Indeed, someone needed to protect those children. Why did the twins call Zack by his first name? What had happened to their mother? If he had adopted them, why didn't they call him Dad or Papa? For that matter, was Zack Kahler a saint, or did the children need to be rescued?

Chloe shook her head and loaded the children's plates with the scrambled eggs seasoned only with salt and pepper. There must be a reasonable explanation for all of this. For the children's sake, she had to find the answers. None of this had anything to do with her past feelings for Zack. It had everything to do with how she'd grown up without the basic needs of life. Children needed love and care, plenty of good food, and clothing. Anything less wasn't fair.

Zack didn't have time to contemplate Chloe's sudden coldness to him, but he'd come to realize that was the way of women—especially single ones. Now, if he could find a woman who was more settled in her ways like his mama, then he might have found a jewel. Shaking his head, he cast aside his thoughts. Mama had her moments, too. Right now, he had a list a mile long for the day, and his first chore was to stop by the schoolhouse. Hopefully, Miss Scott had forgotten all the trouble he used to get into before Brother Whitworth became his dad.

With his hand firmly clasped around each twin's hand, Zack made his way through town toward the schoolhouse. Folks stopped to admire his little imps with oohs and aahs. One woman who had taught him in Sunday school asked if they were his children.

"Yes, ma'am. I'm in the process of adopting them."

Her eyes sparkled beneath a layer of wrinkled years of wisdom.

"Oh, my dear boy, you are in for an adventure."

He had been down a few of those paths already.

Zack and the twins continued to make their way through town. Storefronts had taken on a fresh coat of paint, and the new businesses pleased him. He saw two general stores—the larger one had been in the Kahler family for years—a dentist office, a post office, and a millinery. At dinner last night, Mama had said the town's dressmaker had plans to build her own shop and that the cotton gin outside of town had expanded. Progress.

"Got a Methodist and a Lutheran church here now, too," Dad had said. "The German folk don't have to ride so far for services now."

Zack imagined the town dressed up for Christmas. That was one part of New York that he'd miss. The magnificence of the decorated tree in Central Park, the greenery woven around streetlights, and the dressed windows of the businesses put everyone in a festive mood. But as he caught sight of the town's square, he realized decorating the tree there would have more meaning with his children.

"What are they doing?" Curly pointed to a building project on the town square.

Zack stopped to observe men laying brick. "Why, that must be the new courthouse. Kahlerville has been named the county seat." More progress. More people. And more people reading newspapers.

"What's that mean?" Charlie asked.

"It means that the people who are in charge of running the government around here will work in that building."

He could tell she didn't understand, but he hadn't much practice in explaining things to children.

Walking toward the school, Zack pointed out a few of the familiar sights. "Across from the school is the church where I grew up."

"You mean you lived inside the church with the sisters and the priest?" Curly asked. "I thought you had a mama and papa."

Zack laughed at the serious look on the little boy's face. "I meant that is where I attended church while I was growing up. A lot of memories there. Good ones." Someday when the twins were older, he'd tell them about his difficulty handling life after his father died. Some of which they'd understand now. "When my father died, I was sad and got into trouble."

Charlie's eyes widened. "Like us?"

Zack nodded. "Your grandpa decided to help me and then married your grandma."

"Like you took us?"

"I guess so." Zack chuckled.

"Did the priest and the sisters at your church tell him to do that?" Curly asked.

"We don't have a priest and sisters at our church."

Charlie tugged on his hand. "How can you have a church without 'em?"

"Different people have different ways to worship God. Your grandpa is the preacher at this church." He smiled into her confused face. "You'll see for yourself next Sunday."

The church sat back off the road directly ahead. Beside it was the old parsonage where his grandparents had lived and served the community for years. They'd been laid to rest in the Piney Woods Cemetery behind the church a long time ago. He looked forward to next Sunday when he could walk through the memories that helped form him into a man.

Zack drew in a deep breath. Perhaps he should have arranged a meeting with Miss Scott before the other students arrived. He glanced up at a huge oak tree where he'd once stolen the clothes from Miss Scott's line and hung them on the branches. Unfortunately, his dad—actually this was before the man had proposed to Mama—had figured it out and made him retrieve the clothes and apologize to his teacher. Zack laughed just thinking about it. He'd never forget Miss Scott's bloomers waving in the breeze. Now, here he was bringing his own double-trouble to the town's teacher.

He stopped in the middle of the road. "I went to school here. Miss Scott's a fine teacher."

The twins said nothing.

"Are you scared?"

"A little," Charlie said. "Can't we just stay with you?"

Zack bent down and pulled the two children to the front of him. "No one is going to hurt you. You'll make good friends that will last until you are very old. Miss Scott will make you behave, but she'll also love you and teach you the things you should know. Aunt Lydia Anne and Uncle Stuart attend here, too."

"But we can't read or do numbers," Charlie said. "We didn't go to school much in New York."

"That's what Miss Scott is for. But you won't stay here today. Tomorrow we'll start school. Remember, today we're going out to the ranch after lunch."

The two nodded. Charlie blinked back a tear, but Curly looked just plain defiant. That sent a whirling sensation to the pit of Zack's stomach. He started to make a comment about what he expected from them at school, but that lecture could wait until tomorrow.

"Let's get going. We have much to do today."

Opening up the schoolhouse door brought a flood of more memories—good and bad. He thought about little Chloe Weaver. She wasn't so little anymore. She used to sit in the back of the room away from the other children. He'd sat in the back, too, on the other side of the room, partly out of orneriness and partly as a self-made guardian for Chloe. He hoped someone took that role for his twins. From the looks of her all grown up, she still needed someone protecting her.

Miss Scott started at the sight of him. "Why, Zack Kahler. I heard you were coming back to town. What a fine way to start a morning. I'll be right with you."

She issued a few instructions to the students and joined him in the back of the room, her skirts bustling as she went. He well remembered that sound, especially if she was after him. Good thing he had mended his ways when he acknowledged Jesus as Lord.

A fire had been built in the stove near the front, no doubt to take the chill out of the air. The scent of wood warmed him more than the heat the fire provided. Miss Scott had a large class. Looked like she could use a little help, but then, he well recalled how she kept a classroom in order.

"And who are these beautiful children?" she asked. "I heard you returned from New York with a delightful set of twins."

"News travels fast. They are mine. I'm in the process of adopting them. Charlie, Curly, this is Miss Scott. She will be your new teacher."

Charlie turned her little face bathed in freckles up toward him. "Where is her long black dress?"

"Miss Scott is not a sister. We don't have those ladies in this school." He offered Miss Scott a smile. "They were previously taught by Catholic sisters."

"How much schooling have they had?"

Zack dragged his tongue over his lips. He stared down at the two. "How long have you been going to school?"

Curly shook his head. "Usually we just sneaked off to sell newspapers."

Zack thought he'd sink right through the floor. "Miss Scott, these children lived in an orphanage in New York. Life was hard, and—"

"Never you mind, Zack. We'll do just fine." She smiled wide, her round face a picture of caring and concern.

He wanted to hug her. "Thank you. I'd like to start them tomorrow. This is their first day in Kahlerville, and I'd like to get them a little more settled."

"Excellent idea. I'll be looking for them in the morning. Don't forget to bring lunches. And I'll need for you to provide me with their full names and birthdays." Miss Scott placed her hands on her ample hips. "I suggest you have your Uncle Grant take a look at them to make sure they're healthy."

He hadn't thought of that. "I will." He grasped Charlie and Curly's hands. "Have a good morning." He gazed down at the twins. "What are you supposed to say?"

"Have a good morning," they chorused.

Once outside, Zack complimented the twins on their good behavior. He focused his attention on the newspaper office—feeling like a boy again heading for penny candy. The town's paper had gone through a few owners, but he had visions of a daily paper that incorporated news from the neighboring communities and essentially brought the folks together.

They stepped inside, and he cautioned the children not to bother anything until he was finished, especially if they were looking forward to fun at the ranch. Maybe his bribery approach wasn't the best, but how else could he manage them? The familiar smells of paper and ink were better than a quilt on a cold night.

"Mornin', Zack," Hank called out. "I heard you got back to town."

"Yes, sir. Last evening's train. I sure am glad you decided to stay on and help me with the paper. I appreciate your talking Gilbert into staying, too. I really need a master printer and journeyman, and you two are the best. Thanks for convincing the fellas to stay in the back to set type. Without everyone here, the paper will not fulfill the vision we've talked about." He took in the familiar sights of the press and the typesetter. The *Frontier Press* was peanuts next to the size of the *New York Times*, but this paper was his. And the ownership made him feel powerfully good.

"Helpin' you will be a whole lot easier than trying to run it all myself. Gil is a smart man, and he's learning real fast. When there are edits to do, he has a good eye for catching mistakes. We need a couple of reporters, but that will come."

A small desk cluttered with papers sat at an angle in the corner of the room. A typewriter rose from the middle of the disarray like a chimney soaring above a roaring fire—a fire of news. Life. Truth. Homespun and worldwide. Yes, he was home. The smells, the sound of the typesetter, and the taste of excitement in the air were in his blood. He wanted so much for this paper to bless and inform the people of Kahlerville, and he hoped his ideas would soon take form. Not today, but tomorrow he'd tell Hank that the *Frontier Press* would soon become a daily paper, an evening edition. Before the twins, he'd wanted to print a morning paper, but he couldn't leave his children until eleven at night. Press time at noon made more sense.

Electricity was now a luxury. He'd gotten spoiled with it at the *Times*, but new advances would come to Kahlerville in due time—as well as a printing press that ran the pages instead of requiring the lengthy process of doing it by hand.

"Zack, you're grinning like the mouse that ate the cat." Hank laughed.

"I feel like Christmas came early." He felt a tug on his coattail.

"Mr. Zack, where's the newsboys?" Curly said. "I ain't seen anyone sellin' papers."

"The proper word is 'I *haven't* seen anyone.' We don't sell papers here like in New York. Some folks come into the office to buy them. We also have a stack at the general store and the boardinghouse. Hank and I will deliver newspapers to folks who live on farms and ranches, and a young man here in town takes them to the people of Kahlerville. We mail some of them, too."

The little boy shook his head. "Sure is strange. No sisters or priests and no newsboys. Makes me wonder what a body is supposed to do to earn a livin'."

Hank laughed until tears rolled down his cheeks. He lifted his hat from his bald head and laughed some more. "The city has just met the country."

Zack worked with Hank and discussed the paper until the twins could not handle another moment of behaving themselves.

"You hit me one more time, and I'm going to black your eyes and break your arm."

Zack whirled around to see Charlie with her little arm drawn back. Curly lay sprawled on the wooden floor, and she sat atop him.

"Is that any way for you to treat your brother?"

She lifted her chin. "He said girls can't fight as good as boys."

"You've already proven him wrong. Get off of him, and we'll leave here in just a minute."

Hank muffled another laugh. Zack turned and grinned. "I know

I tried my mother's patience, but these two will make an old man out of me."

"You need a woman."

Zack blew out an exasperated sigh. "My luck with the female gender has had its share of problems."

"You need a Texas girl to treat you right. Me and my missus have been married for forty years, ever since she was sixteen and I was eighteen. Love will come courtin' you, son. I can feel it in my bones."

Chloe had chores well under control. One boarder had checked out and another had arrived. All the rooms were in order, and the scent of pork roast and creamed corn swirled through the air. Never had she eaten so well. As the boarders drifted into the dining room along with other townspeople who enjoyed Simeon's good cooking, she found herself watching for Zack and the twins.

While balancing three plates of food from the kitchen to a table, she saw Zack and the children enter the dining room and take a small table in the corner. Her heart betrayed her, for it raced at the sight of him. No, it must be impossible. Her concern was for the welfare of Curly and Charlie. A few moments later, she made her way to the trio.

"Did you have a good morning?" she asked.

Zack leaned back in his chair. His city-bought suit gave him a dashing look. "We've been to school and visited with Miss Scott," he said. "And we've been to the newspaper office."

She hastily tore her gaze from him to the children. "Busy morning for you little ones."

"We're going to a ranch after we eat," Curly said.

"That sounds like tremendous fun to me."

The little boy nodded. "We're going to see horses, cows, chickens—and animals."

"And family," Charlie said with a nod.

Chloe swung a quick glance at Zack. The compassion on his face moved her to rethink her earlier opinion of him.

"Every person who is my family is now yours," he said.

Chloe swallowed the emotion rising in her throat. "I'll hurry with your lunches so you won't miss a moment at the ranch."

"Perfect." Zack stared up into her face. "We won't be here for dinner. I imagine my mother will have more food than we know what to do with. Could I ask you for a favor?"

She nodded. Did he really need to ask?

"In the course of folks coming and going, if you hear of anyone having a house to rent or buy, would you let me know?"

"I'd be glad to." She excused herself to fetch their lunch and nearly ran into Mr. Barton.

"You're a busy lady." He stood with his hands behind his back.

"Yes, sir. Simeon is such a good cook, and everyone in town wants to eat here."

"You're doing an excellent job. In fact"—he held out a bouquet of fresh mums in vibrant fall shades of gold and orange—"I thought you might like these."

How sweet of him. She took the flowers tied with a purple ribbon. No one had ever given her flowers before. "Thank you." She inhaled the bouquet, and all the frustration she'd felt about his test vanished. "This was very kind of you."

"It's sort of a peace offering for keeping you up late the other night.

Somehow the peppermint stick didn't quite convey my apologies."

She laughed lightly. "I accept." Glancing about at the busy room, she thought better of lingering. "I'll set these in the kitchen until things settle down. They are lovely."

His face reddened. Simeon's words of his interest leaped across her mind. She took quick steps to the kitchen but swung a look at Zack. He was watching her, as though he'd seen the flower presentation.

Strange. How very strange, for she couldn't read the blank look on his face. Did he think Mr. Barton giving her flowers wasn't proper? A delightful notion filled her brain. *Wouldn't it be wonderful if Zack were just a little jealous?*

CHAPTER 7

"Until Stuart returns from school, I want you to play close to the house." Zack pasted on his best stern look. "I'm sitting inside by the window where I can watch you." Since he'd never tried conducting himself like a father before, he didn't know if the twins took him seriously.

"Yes, sir." Curly grinned. In the sunlight, his freckles popped out like little peach dots.

"And you, Miss Charlie?"

"Yes, sir." She had discovered a mama cat with kittens and appeared to be totally enamored.

Zack stepped inside the two-story white home with its many chimneys, angled roofs, and winding porches. This was still home no matter where he lived. Mama had always made sure the house looked as though a dozen servants crept about at night. The wooden floors caught the glimmer from the afternoon sun, and the drapes were spread wide to let in every bit of the outside. She loved the kitchen and helping Juanita with the huge meals for all the ranch hands. Sometimes a couple of the hands rode their horses right up to the kitchen window, where Mama would hand them leftover biscuits with sausage patties tucked inside. Dad had helped her run the ranch since the day they were married, and she had helped him edit his sermons. They were a good match. Maybe someday Zack might find the perfect woman.

He smelled chicken and realized the promised chicken and dumplings were simmering on the stove. The tantalizing aroma of apples and cinnamon confirmed an apple pie. Lydia Anne and Stuart would be home from school, and he wanted to spend time with them, too.

"I'm sure the twins will be fine." Mama glanced out the parlor window where they played.

"They could handle themselves on the street, but a farm is another matter."

"I hope you will let them spend lots of time here. I want to get to know my grandchildren. They remind me of little angels." She made her way back to the sofa beside Dad. "I love their curly red hair and freckles."

"You haven't seen them in action."

"I wish you'd tell us what happened in New York and how you came to adopt them. Juanita has dinner in order, so time is not a problem."

"Are you sure you want to know the whole story?"

"Yes, we do. Isn't that so, Travis?"

Dad muffled a laugh behind his hand, as though he knew the secret about the double-trouble grandchildren. Mama shot him one of her this-is-no-laughing-matter looks.

Zack took a deep breath. Curly and Charlie were not to blame for their impoverished life in New York. "They lived on the streets. Their father died when they were babies, and I don't know who raised them while their mother worked. She died in a tragic factory fire last March, apparently leaving no one to care for them. I'm not sure how long they fended for themselves before being placed in an orphanage."

"Those poor children," Mama said. "How did you find out about their horrible circumstances?"

Zack knew this question would come, and he had yet to form a response—except he may as well tell the truth.

"I think this is going to be a tremendous story." Dad placed his hands behind his head and tossed a teasing grin Zack's way. "How *did* you meet Curly and Charlie? I might want to use this in a sermon. How you and I met has worn out through the years."

Zack clearly recalled the day Brother Whitworth arrived in town. While on the way to the parsonage, he broke up a fight between Zack and another boy. That story had spiced many a sermon.

"Now, Travis, give him time." Mama paused. "But I want to know, too."

This time Zack laughed. "They picked my pocket."

Once he finished the story and confirmed the twins were still playing where he'd placed them, he relaxed slightly.

"We're right here to help." Dad stood and made his way to the window and observed the twins. "You've bitten off a God-sized project. But I believe you're the man for the job."

"Thanks. I'm not so self-assured. Glad you two are here for me. When I consider the fate of those two being picked up on the street and sold to work until they were adults or put onboard an orphan train, well, I'm glad they're in my care. The twins have no living relatives."

"But how were you able to take them from the orphanage without a wife?" Mama asked.

Zack chuckled. "Oh, I have to send the judge recommendation letters from key people in town."

"First off, I'm going through Stuart's outgrown clothes for Curly," Mama said. "And I know I have a box of things for Charlie that Lydia Anne used to wear."

"I appreciate that, Mama. Life will be easier once the newspaper is running smoothly and we're out of the boardinghouse." He hesitated. "How long has Chloe Weaver been working there?"

"I have no idea."

"She sure has grown up."

"We noticed you noticed." Dad chuckled.

"Now, Travis. He was only admiring a pretty girl."

"He nearly dropped little Charlie."

Zack didn't respond. Had he made a fool of himself in front of Chloe? Why, he was supposed to be the sophisticated man from the city. The memory of Mr. Barton presenting her with flowers crept into his thoughts.

Search your mind, man. Say something!

"I was merely surprised at how quickly she'd grown."

"I see." Dad coughed.

Mama shook her finger at him.

Zack peered behind him and didn't see Curly or Charlie. He

stood and stared out the window toward the red-painted barn and pasture just in time to see the two climb over the fence—that held the bull.

"Oh no!" He hurried past Mama and Dad and on through the kitchen and out the door. "The twins are in with the bull." He raced down the back porch steps and toward the fence. "Curly, Charlie, get out of there now."

Neither twin looked his way. They'd skipped toward the animal with no thought or fear. Didn't they question its massive horns? Then he saw why. Two of the kittens scampered at the children's feet.

Dear Lord, please. Don't take them away before I have a chance to take care of them.

"I got the gate," Dad called from close behind.

Zack couldn't waste his strength in responding. The fence loomed a few feet ahead of him. Suddenly the twins realized the mammoth black bull stood in front of them. "Get out of there," he repeated.

As though paralyzed, the children stared at the bull. Zack grabbed the top of the wooden rail fence and vaulted over. The bull snorted and pawed at the ground. In the next breath, Zack grabbed the children at their waist, one in each arm, and whirled around toward the gate. Dad held the gate open wide enough for Zack to squeeze by with the children. Mama ran from the barn with a pitchfork. Dad snatched it up and stepped inside the gate.

Zack could hear the bull behind him, almost smell its breath. The distance to the gate narrowed. Fifteen feet. Ten feet. Dad moved back outside the gate and lifted Curly from Zack's arms as he raced by. The gate slammed shut. Gasping, Zack set Charlie on her feet and held his knees. Every muscle, every nerve in his body protested. His lungs ached.

"Son, you all right?" Dad's hand gripped his shoulders.

Zack nodded, still too out of breath to speak. He inhaled a painful breath. "Are. . .are the twins all right?" He glanced and saw Mama had a firm hand on each twin's hand. Her pale face clearly displayed her fright. Tears streamed down Curly and Charlie's cheeks.

"Don't. . .don't you ever disobey me again." He slowly stood. "You scared the wits out of me."

"What was that?" Curly's voice was barely above a whisper.

Zack saw how frightened they were. He took another breath and reached out for them, drawing their trembling bodies to his. "It was a bull, and it could have killed you with its horns. I asked you to play by the house for a reason. When I tell you something, you must obey."

"Yes, sir."

"Charlie?"

"Yes, sir. I'm sorry."

"I'm sorry, too. Right now, we're going inside the house. You'll stay there until I decide to show you around the ranch."

Long after sundown, Chloe sat at the registration desk and watched the front door for Zack and the children. She really didn't have to wait for them, but making sure that the boarders were happy was part of her job. At least she kept telling herself that. How had one man and two children captured her attention in so short a time?

But Zack had been on her heart and mind for many a year, and try as she might, he held a special spot. The door jingled, and Zack walked in carrying a sleeping Charlie.

"Can you help me?" he whispered. "I've got the key in my pocket, but would you mind opening our door?"

"Of course." She stepped from behind the registration desk and tried not to show her eagerness to help.

Zack balanced the sleeping little girl on his knee and retrieved the key. "Thanks so much."

"Where's Curly?"

"He's asleep in the wagon." He frowned. "I need to return the wagon."

She laughed lightly. "Zack Kahler, I believe you have yourself in a pickle. Bring Curly in, and I'll stay with the twins until you return."

His brown eyes widened, and with his hair dipped onto his forehead, he looked quite the boy she remembered. "I really appreciate this. They wore themselves out at my folks' ranch." Once she unlocked the door, he laid Charlie on a bed. "They had a little problem with a bull this afternoon, but hopefully it taught them a lesson. It did me, anyway."

"You'll have to tell me about it."

"I will." He started to pull off Charlie's shoes.

"Go on ahead. I'll get her tucked in."

"You are a gift from God." Although his words were spoken in a whisper, she wanted to shout them from the rooftops.

Chloe, you are a grown woman. Didn't you insist that you had no use for men? She had made that declaration, but she hadn't considered the possibility of Zack ever being part of her life again.

A moment later, she heard him mount the stairs and met him at the door. "Charlie hasn't moved." She reached out her arms. "I'll take him. Go ahead and return the wagon."

"Thanks." Zack disappeared, but she waited to hear the bell above the door before turning her attention to Curly.

What a sweet face. Both of them. She sat on the side of the

bed and watched their peaceful slumber. She hoped Zack understood these treasures. Once, a long time ago, when she was thirteen, she'd wakened and discovered Pa standing over her. At first she was afraid, but he touched her cheek and told her to go on back to sleep. It was the only time after her mother's death that he ever showed any affection. Chloe treasured that memory.

Within the half hour, Zack returned. "Thank you again," he said between breaths.

"You didn't have to rush. I enjoyed watching the twins sleep."

"I didn't want to take advantage of your kindness. And I didn't want them to wake up and wonder what happened to me."

He *was* a loving father. "Do you want to tell me about the bull?"

"Sure." He motioned to the hallway. "We could talk out there."

Chloe joined him on the wooden floor outside the room. With the door cracked open, Zack leaned against the wall.

"What a day." He shook his head. "What a whirlwind these past few days have been."

"I'm sure the trip from New York was exhausting."

He chuckled. "The trip was only part of it."

"How long have you had the twins? I mean by yourself."

"Always by myself. I've had them about six days."

"Six days?" Surely she'd heard wrong.

"Do you want to hear the whole story?"

A parade filled with automobiles couldn't have stopped her from listening to his every word.

"It started last Thursday. That was the first time I laid eyes on Curly and Charlie. Two days before I left New York, I was walking home from the newspaper office and slipped on the ice. Suddenly one freckled-faced little boy offered to help me up. I politely refused but offered him a quarter for his trouble. He looked terribly thin, and his clothes were threadbare. I looked again, and there were two of them. I gave that one, who I thought was a boy, a quarter, too. They thanked me and took off down the street."

How generous.

"It took only a moment to discover my wallet was missing. I forgot about slipping on any more ice and took out after the two."

A giggle escaped Chloe's mouth. "I'm sorry. It's not funny—"

"Go ahead and laugh. They are a clever pair. Anyway, I caught them and retrieved my wallet. About that time, a police officer approached us. He knew the twins. I learned they had run away from a Catholic Charities orphanage. This wasn't the first time. Their mother had died in a factory fire some months before. Well, I couldn't get those two out of my mind. I kept seeing their thin arms and toeless shoes. The next morning, as soon as I said my good-byes to my friends at the newspaper office, I walked to the orphanage with the idea of making arrangements to send them money on a regular basis." He shook his head. "Now, you will laugh."

"Go ahead. So far, it all sounds very heartwarming." She blinked to disguise a stray tear.

"The sister there thought I'd come to adopt them. I learned that sometimes the twins ran off and sold newspapers for a little money. Unfortunately, New York City is filled with children trying to earn a living that way. And before I knew it, I was convinced that this is what God wanted me to do. I appeared before a judge that afternoon, and here we are." He took a breath. "During the evening, Curly told me Charlie was a girl."

Another giggle surfaced. "Any regrets, Mr. Kahler?"

"No. There are times, however, when I think I must have lost my mind. Like this afternoon when the twins chased some kittens into the bull's pen."

By the time he finished the latest story, Chloe was ready to build a monument in his honor. "I'm not the least surprised at your adopting them. Have you forgotten the hungry little girl you used to bring a sandwich to every day?" Instantly, she wished she hadn't brought up those humiliating days.

"I remember. I used to worry about what you ate on Saturday and Sundays."

"Sometimes I saved part of the sandwich for those days. You're a good man, Zack Kahler. Curly and Charlie are very lucky children."

"I think I'm a lucky man. But I have so much to learn. They scared me today, and I didn't know whether to warm their behinds or hold them tight."

"You'll figure it all out."

"I hope so. They're six, but their lives up to this point haven't been good. And there's so much to do at the newspaper. At least the two are in school during working hours, and my sister and brother volunteered to bring them to the office in the afternoons. Excuse me, I'm complaining like an old man."

"I'll help in any way I can."

"I believe Mr. Barton has you pretty busy."

"My Sundays are free." Should she have been so bold?

He glanced down at his hands, then up at her face. "Would you like to help me with the twins this Sunday? I need to take them to church. I might need to lasso them into a pew."

She started to say that people would talk if she joined them. But if God had decided to answer her dreams by blessing her with Zack and the twins for a Sunday morning, well—"I'd be glad to."

CHAPTER 8

Sunday morning, Zack held the hand of a twin on each side of him, and Chloe walked alongside Curly on the road toward Piney Woods Church. Chloe reminded him of a freshly picked rose—perfect. He could get lost in those enormous dark brown eyes. And her hair. . .it reminded him of black silk draping down her back. It would be hard to keep his attention on the service today. He recalled how Elizabeth always wore stylish clothes and had her hair fixed all over her head in curls, but she paled in comparison to Chloe. Hadn't he convinced himself that he had no time for a woman? Mercy. His resolve must be sitting on the sidewalk in New York—right where he'd fallen.

Chloe gathered Curly's other hand into hers. *Good.* At least he couldn't pick his nose. Heaven forbid what might come from the twins' mouths this morning. But they did look very civilized with cheeks like polished apples and dressed like preacher's kids—or rather, grandkids.

"This church will be strange without sisters and a priest," Curly said.

"Oh, I think you'll get used to it. Remember, Grandpa is the preacher. And Grandma will be your Sunday school teacher."

The twins were silent—a rarity unless they were nervous about new surroundings. A little over a week with them had taught him that much.

"You will have fun and learn about Jesus." Zack glanced over at Chloe in hopes she could add a word or two to ease the twins' uneasiness.

"We don't like school," Curly said. "Do we, Charlie?"

The little girl shook her red curls. "We want to go to the newspaper office with you."

"Why?" This was the first Zack had heard about their discontent with school.

"The kids say we talk funny," Curly said. "And they laugh."

Zack swallowed his amusement. "You and Charlie come from a different part of the country."

"But I want to sound like them. Say *y'all* and *fixin'*."

This time he laughed aloud. "Oh, you will once you've lived here awhile."

"Hope so. I'm tired of them sayin' we talk too fast. And I don't like it when they call us Irish stew. I like it when Grandpa calls us that, but not the kids at school."

"Pretend it doesn't bother you," Chloe said. "When I was a little girl, the children used to tease me, too."

Charlie peeked around Zack to see the lovely young woman

beside him. "Why, Miss Chloe?"

"Because I didn't look like them."

Zack smiled at her. She knew exactly what to say.

He studied Piney Woods Church. A lot of memories lived within those walls. As always, it glistened with the newest coat of paint. The stained-glass windows were intact, a gift to the church from his uncle Morgan and uncle Grant some years before. The church members never found out who had financed them, but Zack had overheard the conversation with his dad. Dad said the hymnals had recently been replaced, and he was proud of them. To the left of the church stood the old parsonage. It too sparkled with a new coat of paint. The church had sold it to one of the deacons under the condition that it would always be kept up. This was the church where his parents had been married and his father had been buried. This was also where Mama and Dad had married and where his grandparents' funerals had been held. Life and death. All a part of each person's journey to eternity. To Zack, this church represented all those things that had molded him into a man and set him on the right road.

Once inside, folks nodded and welcomed him and the twins. Zack held his breath each time someone spoke to them, but the children remembered their manners. He introduced Curly and Charlie to so many people that he began to wonder if he'd remember everyone who had met his children.

"Mornin', Miss Chloe," many said. "Good to see you helping Zack."

She responded to each one of them graciously. As soon as Mama spied them, she snatched up the twins for her class. Poor Mama. Hopefully she could keep the two in their seats. Zack and Chloe sat together for Sunday school, but he was so worried about the twins' behavior that he only half listened. Next week he'd do better. He suddenly remembered family devotions and memorizing scripture. Another thing to add to his list of fatherhood responsibilities.

When his cousin Rebecca started playing the piano as a sign that church was ready to begin, he gathered up his charges, who still looked fairly presentable. For a moment he counted the family members who had not met Curly and Charlie. The upcoming holidays would take care of that. He glanced down the aisle to where his dad stood ready to start the service. The front pew was full with Mama, Lydia Anne, Stuart, and friends, so he took the pew behind them.

"Did you like your lesson?" Zack asked Charlie.

"Grandma told us a story about a giant, a bad man."

He kissed her forehead. "Wonderful. What happened to him?"

"A boy killed him with a slingshot 'cause God said so."

Zack smiled. "Wonderful. We'll talk later."

Chloe had pulled Curly onto her lap, so he did the same with Charlie. Now didn't they look like the perfect family? His thoughts collided inside his mind. What in the world was he thinking? Women were bad news—like a story that didn't make the front page. And he wasn't the least bit interested in Chloe.

Midway through the sermon, Charlie whispered that she needed to go to the outhouse. Great. He'd have to take her outside in front of all these people. He lifted her up into his arms and excused himself as he stepped by Chloe.

"Where are you going?" Curly's words were much too loud.

"Hush, Curly," Charlie said. "You're in church, even if there aren't any sisters or a priest."

"But why are you leaving?"

"We're going to the outhouse."

A snicker rose in the crowd. Zack wanted to sink through the floor. His face grew warm. Not knowing what to say to either twin, he looked to Chloe for help.

"It's all right," she whispered. "They're just children."

He didn't feel any better as he hurried down the aisle to the back door and attempted to ignore the amused congregation. Once church ended, Mama cornered him.

"Zack, why don't you, Chloe, and my precious grandchildren come on out to the ranch? Juanita and I will have fried chicken ready in no time at all."

It did sound good, and the twins had talked about all the fun they'd had at the ranch—except for the bull pen. He swung his attention to Chloe. "Would you join us?"

She hesitated. "Of course. I'd love to."

"Ride with us home." Mama teetered on her heels as though she couldn't contain her excitement. But over what?

He glanced at the twins and then to Chloe. His normal mode of things was to exclude women. Seemed like a man had to have his senses intact and hide his wallet when it came to the female gender. He and Chloe were simply old friends. Right? Had he been taken in by a pretty face and forgotten his wariness because of the twins?

I'm in serious trouble.

❧

"I think Zack will be set nicely with plenty of clothes for the twins." Chloe held up a yellow and green dress with a huge green bow. "Won't Charlie look precious in this?"

"I'm simply glad Lydia Anne and Stuart's clothes can go to someone who can use them." Mrs. Whitworth stacked another shirt for Curly on the bed. She walked to the window and covered her mouth, but a laugh burst through. "Oh, Chloe, come look at what the twins are doing."

Chloe stood beside the petite woman and watched the scene unfold. Stuart held the reins of a pretty nut-colored pony for the twins, who happened to be perched atop it. Brother Whitworth stood on one side of the pony, and Zack stood on the other. Each man balanced a twin.

"Oh my." Mrs. Whitworth planted her hands on her hips. "Do you suppose the twins have ever ridden a pony before?"

"Possibly not in the city."

Mrs. Whitworth studied her, and Chloe's heart sped to a gallop. "Have you and Zack been writing to each other?"

"No, ma'am." She continued to focus on the pony ride. Neither twin looked to be excited about the new adventure.

"So the night he arrived at the boardinghouse was the first time you'd seen him since last Christmas?"

"Before that."

"He certainly appears comfortable with you."

How was she supposed to respond? "I think he's comfortable with me helping him with the twins."

Mrs. Whitworth smiled sweetly. "We'll see."

The remainder of the afternoon floated by Chloe like a dream. She'd never been to the Whitworth ranch before. The huge house with its winding porch and gabled roof was filled with warmth and laughter, but more importantly, she'd never been around so much love. She tucked the memory of the day away to pull out when the weariness of life attempted to overtake her.

That evening, Brother Whitworth drove them back to town with his family. The twins were tired and really did quite well during church.

After the services, Chloe thanked Brother and Mrs. Whitworth for the wonderful day and walked back to the boardinghouse with Zack and the twins.

"You must be exhausted," Zack said. "I didn't mean to take up your entire day."

"I enjoyed myself."

"I did, too. Is Sunday your only day off?"

"Ah, yes. But I couldn't have spent a finer one."

He chuckled. "I need to get these two into bed, or they'll fall asleep in school tomorrow."

"Would you like for me to help you?"

"I can't impose on you any longer." He sighed. "I realized something today."

"What's that?"

"They call me Zack. My first name doesn't sound right, but what should they call me?"

"Why not ask them?"

He smiled and tugged on each little hand firmly clasped in his. "Curly, Charlie, what do you want to call me?"

"Is something wrong with Zack?" Curly asked.

"As a matter of fact, there is. I'm going to legally be your father when the adoption is completed. So do you want to call me Dad or Papa?"

"I like Papa." Charlie touched her finger to her chin.

"I called my father Papa before he died."

She nodded and appeared to consider the matter. "I like Poppy."

"Poppy?" He glanced at Chloe.

"Very nice," she said.

"Curly, is Poppy all right with you?"

"Sure. If you're our poppy, then is Miss Chloe our mommy?"

Chloe wanted to disappear into the dust that her heavenly Father had used to create her. Now she understood Zack's humiliation this morning in church with the twins' outburst. Heat rose in her face.

"I think it's just the three of us." Zack said.

Curly's little shoulders lifted and fell. "But someday you'll get us a mommy?"

"We'll let God take care of that. Oh, look, here we are at the boardinghouse."

Once inside, Zack led the children up the stairs.

"Would you like for me to make them a sandwich before they go to bed?"

He turned and smiled. "Why is it you think of everything?"

"I think it's part of my job. What about a cup of coffee for you?"

"Only if you'll share one with me—in the hall."

She hoped her smile didn't give away the anticipation of having a few more minutes with Zack. "I think that can be arranged. I'll return shortly with the twins' sandwich."

"What do you say to Miss Chloe?"

Two very tired children mumbled a thank you. They had won her heart for sure. Their poppy had won it many years ago.

Zack picked up the two plates and balanced two glasses on the top. The twins had eaten little but had drunk their milk. Now as they slept, he stole through the shadows to the door. The nutty aroma of coffee filled his senses, yet he preferred the company of Chloe to the finest coffee in the world. Life sure had changed.

She sat in the hallway with her knees drawn to her chest and her blue flowered dress draping about her. *Natural beauty*. Two steaming mugs of coffee and a sandwich rested on the floor.

"Is that a sandwich for me or us?" He eased down beside her.

"You. I'm not hungry."

"Thanks." He chuckled. "You remembered I like my coffee black." He swung his attention toward her. "The little girl has grown into a beautiful woman."

Her cheeks tinted pink. "I hardly know what to say."

"Nothing to say. It's a fact." He picked up the sandwich. "Sure you don't want half?"

She laughed. "Those days are over."

"Praise God that you have grown up so. . .nicely." He took a bite of the sandwich filled with roast beef. "This is really good."

"I'll pass on your compliments to Simeon. What's on your schedule for this week?" Her soft voice gave him a tingling sensation clear to his toes.

"Get a few issues of the paper out to the community. I want to publish a daily paper soon. Talk to the various business owners about advertising. Visit a few of the smaller towns about incorporating their news into the *Frontier Press*. And take care of my twins."

"Your mother is so proud of you."

He lifted the mug of coffee to his lips. "She'd be proud of me if I worked at the livery cleaning out stalls."

They laughed, but that was easy with Chloe. He'd never felt this relaxed with Elizabeth.

"What are you doing this week?" he asked.

She tilted her head. "Working here. Stealing a moment to hug a couple of curly-headed twins when they come for breakfast and dinner."

"Do you have any idea how good it felt tonight when those two said, 'G'night, Poppy'?"

"Must have been special."

"Whenever they say something that is so cute or dear to me, I tell myself to remember it when they misbehave." Then he recalled Charlie's request for a mommy. Should he apologize to Chloe?

"You'll be fine, and they will, too."

"They did make it through a week without getting into trouble at school."

She raised a brow. "Their first week of school was three days."

"Actually, it was two and a half."

They laughed again and finished their coffee. He'd laughed more this week than in a long time. Curly and Charlie weren't the only blessings in his life. Another *C* had suddenly made him a very happy man.

Giggling from inside the room snapped him to attention.

"You hit me."

"You hit me first."

"That's 'cause you kicked me."

"No, I didn't."

"Yes, you did."

Zack groaned. "I'd better go settle my children."

CHAPTER 9

Late Tuesday afternoon, an hour before helping Simeon with dinner, Chloe busied herself by dusting the furniture in the parlor. She loved the richness of the old wood and the elegance of the overstuffed chairs in deep green and gold and the sofa with a mixture of both colors. The small tables were topped with doilies for those times boarders set their coffee cups on the rich wood. Once she couldn't find a speck of dust either on the floor or on the furniture, she rolled up the rugs and took them outside for a good beating. Satisfied that the parlor truly invited everyone to step inside, she turned her attention to bookkeeping and the cash box.

She still basked in memories of the past Sunday with Zack and the twins. And seeing them morning and night rooted her heart in what she thought would never happen—Zack Kahler might one day look at her and not see the pitiful little girl but a full-grown woman who loved him very much. Zack was different. He'd never abuse her. Not like the other men and boys she'd encountered.

"A penny for your thoughts?" Mr. Barton interrupted her musings and sent her thoughts scattering into the corners of her mind like little mice heading for their holes.

In her reverie, she hadn't heard the bell jingle over the door.

"My, Mr. Barton. I didn't hear you come in."

He grinned somewhat boyishly and strolled to her side. "It's good to know your concentration is on the books. I look at them every night while the boarders are sleeping, and they are always in perfect order."

"Thank you. I'm glad you're pleased." She didn't want to think again about what he'd done to her on her first day of work.

"Did you enjoy your day off?"

"Very much."

"I saw you at church on Sunday evening. How commendable of you to help one of our boarders with his children." His tone edged slightly toward condescending.

While her mind searched for the right words, she offered her brightest smile. "They are lovely children."

"The amount of time Zack Kahler has been gone from town and the absence of a wife has a bit of scandal to it. Don't you think?"

"Not really. Mr. Kahler has never married, and the children came from an orphanage in New York. Very dire circumstances."

"I see. That explains it all."

"Yes, sir."

"Mind you don't neglect your duties while he is a guest here."

Chloe stiffened. "My first loyalties are to you, sir."

He offered a faint smile. "Me, Miss Weaver?"

"Precisely, the boardinghouse and my bookkeeping duties."

He glanced down at the registration book. "Perhaps they are one and the same. If you'd permit it." With those words, he gave her a nod and disappeared around the corner. A moment later, the kitchen door creaked open, then shut.

Chloe didn't need a New York university education to understand exactly what Mr. Barton implied. If not for Zack and how she'd loved him for years, she might consider Mr. Barton. He was a good man—simply lonely. And that she understood.

She'd allowed herself to slip into a dream world again. Was she being foolish? Zack needed help, and she'd been there to give it. When she considered his education, status in the community, and ambition to succeed in life, why would he ever give Chloe, a young woman with a Comanche heritage, a second look?

Friday morning, Zack tapped at the typewriter on his desk. He used two fingers and had to be careful not to make a mistake. Someday when he had the money, he'd hire someone to type up his articles. Until then, he'd labor hours over this machine.

He'd spent Tuesday and Wednesday contacting business owners about their advertisements in the *Frontier Press*. Some were a bit skeptical about his new ideas. He wanted to give business owners something fresh and appealing to bring in more revenue, but some folks resented change and preferred the old ads. He'd contacted a few national businesses while still in New York and had secured advertising from Calumet Baking Powder, Maxwell House Blend Coffee, tooth powder, and razor blades. It was a beginning. He needed to plan a day in Houston to study the *Post* and the *Chronicle*.

The first week of December, the weekly paper would officially become a daily. Next week, he planned to call on the folks in neighboring towns. His thoughts were to feature each town and their local news along with what was happening in the county, state, and world. He'd wire Austin for the latest news from Governor Campbell's office, and he had connections in Washington for the current events surrounding the White House and President Taft.

Miss Scott indicated an interest in a women's page, so he'd hired her to write that column. He wanted the folks around Kahlerville to read the society news from their own paper. Everything from communication to cooking interested him, because those topics sold newspapers. He loved this business. It simply excited him, as though his veins were filled with newspaper ink.

And when his day was over and his whole body ached, he had Curly and Charlie to keep him company. Zack lifted his two forefingers from the typewriter and allowed his thoughts to venture toward Chloe. The twins loved her, and she doted on them as though they were the only two children in the whole world. How quickly they had adapted to their new life. And so had he.

Of course, he was partial, and he enjoyed every minute of it. He wanted to ask her about Thanksgiving. Uncle Morgan and Aunt Casey planned to have dinner at their ranch, and Zack really could use Chloe's help with the twins. He shook his head and placed his fingers on the typewriter keys again. Who was he fooling? Chloe had tiptoed into his heart, and he wanted to keep her there. To think he'd allowed Elizabeth in New York to hurt him. She and Chloe were nothing alike.

Before Zack realized what had happened to the day, Lydia Anne and Stuart walked in with the twins. Zack did a double take, then stood.

"Were you two fighting at school today?"

Zack studied Lydia Anne, who was far too blond and pretty for a sixteen-year-old. But she was his parents' problem. Lydia Anne smiled but didn't say a word. His gaze swung to Stuart, the spitting image of Dad.

"Has everyone forgotten how to talk? Unless my eyes have deceived me, Curly has a black eye, and Charlie's dress is dirty." Zack stared at each one, but no one offered an answer. "Somebody had better speak up."

"We were fighting, Poppy." Charlie's best little-girl voice wouldn't melt him this afternoon.

Zack did his best to shove aside the work that still needed his attention and concentrate on the problem at hand. "Did Miss Scott send a note?"

"Yes, sir." Curly handed him a piece of paper.

"Oh my. It's amazing how good your manners are today." He read the note:

Zack,

Although I don't condone fighting for any reason, the children are not entirely at fault for today's incident. I suggest you ask them what happened, and I'll be glad to speak with you about the matter.

Annabelle Scott

"What did she say?" Curly twisted the buckle on the right side of his overalls.

"She said I should ask you two what happened."

The twins exchanged glances, then looked to Lydia Anne and Stuart.

"I'm not tellin'," Stuart said. "And Lydia Anne wasn't around."

Curly's shoulders fell. "We got into a fight because. . .because—"

"Just tell it," Charlie said. "Never mind. I will. One of the big boys called me and Curly a bad name. I kicked him in the knee and told him we were not. . .what he said. That we had a poppy and our real mama and papa died. He said you only took us because you felt sorry for us. I kicked him again."

"Then I punched him in the stomach," Curly said. "And he blacked my eye."

Zack wished he could have been there. He would have escorted that kid to his parents. "Listen, you two." He sat on a chair and pulled them in front of him. "Fighting doesn't solve anything. Now that boy will be picking on you even more. When someone tells lies about you or calls you a bad name, pretend you didn't hear. All right?"

"Yes, sir."

How could two children have such angelic voices? He lifted Curly's chin. "That's quite a shiner. It needs some ice." He glanced about the office. "I have a customer coming by any minute, but I'll let Hank take care of it. Your eye is more important, and I think we have more to talk about."

"I'll take them to the boardinghouse and clean them up," Lydia Anne said. "When Dad or Mama stops by, you can send them there."

Zack reached into his pocket and pulled out his room key. Handing it to his sister, he saw one tear after another roll over Charlie's cheeks. "I'll be along within fifteen minutes."

"Are you mad at us?" the little girl asked.

He bent to her and Curly's level. "No, I'm not mad, just sad that you were fighting." He drew them both into his arms and hugged them. "Who was the boy?"

"Eli Scott," Stuart said. "He's a year older than Lydia Anne."

Seventeen? A year older than Lydia Anne? Anger soared to the top of his head. A boy that old had no business picking on six-year-olds. Why, he was grown. The name didn't sound familiar, but he'd find out who the boy was before the day was over. He wondered if Chloe remembered him from her days at school.

"Thanks, Lydia Anne, for looking after these two. I'm sure Simeon or Miss Chloe will help you with a piece of ice. Believe me, I'll be talking to Miss Scott about Eli Scott."

Thirty minutes later, Zack walked into the boardinghouse with his mother. He'd left work at the newspaper, but he was too furious to do anything but plan his speech to Miss Scott about the bully in her school. He'd already decided to pay a visit to the Scott home. And he would tonight if he could find out where the boy lived.

"Miss Scott can handle him," Mama said. "Getting angry doesn't solve a thing."

Zack didn't respond. Not that he didn't have a mind full of comments about the age difference between the bully and his twins.

"Zack, I can read your mind without your saying a word." Mama straightened to her barely five-foot frame. "Handle this in a proper manner. For right now, think about more pleasant things."

"Yes, ma'am." Now he knew how the twins felt when he corrected them.

"Have you asked Chloe to accompany you for Thanksgiving dinner?"

Maybe she did read his thoughts. "Not yet, but I will."

"She's a beautiful girl and so good with the children."

"Yes, ma'am."

"I'm sure the problem at school can be explained away." Mama nodded to punctuate her words.

Inside the boardinghouse, Zack and his mother found the family in the kitchen. Curly sat on a small worktable, and Chloe held a cloth, obviously containing ice, over his eye.

"How's the patient?" Zack attempted to sound light. "Do we need to take him to the doctor?"

"If you ask me, the bully who did this needs two black eyes." Simeon turned back to dusting slices of beef with flour. "But nobody asked me."

Chloe shook her head, but she didn't turn to acknowledge him or even speak.

"Miss Chloe cried," Charlie said.

Confusion hit him. Had she been so upset over the twins' abuse that she openly wept? He studied Lydia Anne's and Stuart's faces. Nothing. Then Lydia Anne moistened her lips.

"She knows Eli Scott, and that's all I'm saying."

"Chloe, has there been a mistake here, or is he a bully?" Zack asked.

She sniffed. "He's a bully."

"Lydia Anne, has he bothered you and Stuart?"

"No. I think he's afraid of Dad, Uncle Morgan, and Uncle Grant."

"Do you know where he lives?"

Lydia Anne nodded. "He's Miss Scott's nephew."

Zack remembered the note. Miss Scott hadn't blamed the twins.

"I'm going to take care of it tonight."

Chloe slowly turned to face him. Her eyes were red, her face splotchy. "Don't let him get by with this, Zack. If he's not stopped, it'll get worse."

"Believe me, I won't rest until this is settled." Something in her tone told him Chloe had experienced a problem with Eli, too. Later he'd ask. He took the icepack from her and noted her trembling fingers. Her reaction made him even angrier at the Scott kid. She turned away from him. No doubt her tears had embarrassed her.

Zack cringed. Curly's eye was a mass of purple and blue, worse than before.

"I still wish you'd let Miss Scott handle this." Mama peered around Zack to look at Curly's eye. Her face paled.

"He's horrible," Lydia Anne said. "He steals lunch from the other kids and says things that should get him whipped. Miss Scott never hears or sees what he does, or she'd handle the matter."

"All that has been taken care of."

Zack whirled around to see Miss Scott standing in the doorway of the kitchen. She lifted her chin.

Simeon cleared his throat. "Do y'all think you could take your business to the dining room? I don't think my kitchen can hold one more person."

A few moments later, the group sat at a large table. Luckily, no one else was about. Zack had Curly on one knee and Charlie on the another.

"Eli is no longer at the school," Miss Scott said. "I had him removed this afternoon after the incident with Curly and Charlie. I'd have been here sooner, but I needed to tell my brother about my decision."

Zack nodded, observing the determined look on his old teacher's face. A quick step into the past to a time when he used to get into fights flashed across his mind. She didn't put up with it then, either. "I appreciate what you've done, Miss Scott. I understand Eli is your nephew."

She swallowed. "Yes, and I've made excuses for him for far too long. He will not be permitted to return." She paused and turned her attention to Chloe. "I'm sorry, Chloe. I should have removed him long before now."

What had that bully done to her? Zack was furious all over again.

"Thank you, Miss Scott." Chloe rose from her chair. "It's time for me to help Simeon. Please excuse me."

"And I must be getting along." Miss Scott bent down toward the twins. "You have no reason to be afraid at school. Monday will be a new week with all the ugliness of Eli gone." She cupped the chin of each child, then stood to face Zack. "Thank you for your understanding in this unfortunate situation."

Zack had too many thoughts swirling around in his brain, but one thing at a time. His children were safe, and that was most important. He pulled them close to him and wondered when he'd begun to love them—really love them.

CHAPTER 10

Chloe had avoided Zack the rest of the evening. Now that it was nearly breakfast time, she considered how she could steer clear of him. She couldn't let him find out about how Eli used to follow her home. He might think less of her during that time she was homeless.

When Eli had discovered her sleeping by the creek, he'd said horrible things and attempted more, but she'd been successful in fighting him off with Pa's knife. Shortly thereafter, she'd obtained the job at the boardinghouse. The memories of what Eli had tried to do were too fresh. Too frightening. When she'd learned he'd hurt the twins, she had wanted to dig out Pa's knife again.

She bundled up the sheets and pillowcases and placed them in a basket for pickup later. Saturdays always had extra people wanting breakfast, and she wanted to help Simeon as much as possible.

The stairs creaked, and she glanced up to see Zack heading her way with an armful of linens. Despite the darkened stairway, she'd recognize his features anywhere. The mere sight of him took her breath away.

"Good morning." She smiled. Why did he always have to look so perfect?

"Morning. We had a little accident last night."

"But he's doing better."

"Yes, he is." He stopped on a step. "Chloe, are you upset with me?"

"Of course not. Why do you ask?" Her heart thudded against her chest.

"Because ever since the problem at school with Eli yesterday afternoon, you've seemed to ignore me and the twins. I've already surmised that you had problems with Eli, too, and I'm sorry."

She took a deep breath. "Work keeps me busy."

He stared at her. "I thought you and I were friends. Good friends. Maybe the start of more than friends—and not because you help me with the twins."

If he didn't hush, he'd hear her heart pound like a bass drum. Yet what if he was serious? "I was embarrassed by Miss Scott's apology to me."

"Sounds to me like Eli is the one who should be embarrassed."

"Maybe so. I'd like to think I'd grown up and escaped schoolhouse problems."

"I think I understand. If you ever want to talk about it, I'm available. I can be a good listener."

"I remember your listening to a little girl with all of her childish whims."

"Those times were a pleasure. Would you join us for church tomorrow and dinner with my parents?"

You'd like for me to accompany you again? Her pulse raced with the thought. "Are you sure they won't mind?"

"I'd be ordered to turn back around if you refused."

She sensed her lips curving upward. "I'd be delighted."

"Wonderful." He deposited the soiled linens into the basket. "We'll not see you until dinner. I'm taking the twins with me to deliver papers, and we're having lunch with my uncle George and aunt Ellen Kahler—the other side of the family. I haven't seen him since he was elected mayor."

"He's doing a fine job. When word got out about the possibility of moving the county seat to Kahlerville, he worked hard to make it happen."

Zack started up the steps, then swung back around. "Do you have plans for Thanksgiving?"

"I have to work through breakfast, but then Mr. Barton has someone coming in to relieve me."

"Would you accompany us to my uncle Morgan's that day? There's a bunch of us, but we always have a good time."

Chloe wondered if he could ever ask anything she'd refuse. "I'd like that very much. Please let me know what I can bring."

"A smile and a hearty appetite. There will be plenty of food and lots of leftovers. Almost seems a shame at times, but none of it goes to waste with hungry ranch hands."

Chloe heard Simeon whistling "Clementine." Did he hear everything from his post in the kitchen? If she didn't love the dear old man, she'd scold him.

"The last time I came down these stairs he was whistling 'Oh! Susanna.' Does he ever run out of songs?"

"I don't think so." Especially when it came to teasing her about suitors. "Would you like to take a cup of coffee back to your room?"

In the shadows, she could see his smile.

"Can't refuse a cup of Simeon's finest brew."

The two walked into the kitchen, where the older man deftly peeled potatoes. "You two meet at the oddest places and times. Why, when I was in my courtin' days, we went on picnics and took long walks in the moonlight. You two court in the stairway and in my kitchen." He laughed and grabbed another potato. "Guess that makes me a chaperone."

Chloe thought she'd sink right through the floor. A witty remark danced across her mind, but at that moment, Simeon started whistling again. And this time he danced a little jig.

She poured Zack his coffee and met his gaze. He certainly knew how to make her tingle to the tip of her toes. His smile stayed fixed in her mind the rest of the day. She allowed the old dreams to creep back into her heart. *Maybe the start of more than friends.* He wouldn't have said something he didn't mean. Zack Kahler was far too noble for that. Sometimes she wondered if she'd put him on a pedestal too lofty for a mere mortal. But she blamed her kingly opinion of him on love. Surely he had faults. . .somewhere.

Zack enjoyed delivering papers to the rural folks. It gave him time to meet and talk with all of them. Some of them seldom saw anyone else except on Sunday, and they were always eager to talk. A lot of wisdom rested in country people. Today he had the twins to show off. He hoped the two behaved themselves. Once in a while, their language slipped to those words from the streets of New York City, but he was working hard to eliminate those words from their vocabulary.

The air had turned crisp, and the scent of straw filled his nostrils. The rolling fields were bare as though resting until next spring. He glanced to the back of the wagon to see what Curly and Charlie were doing. Knowing them, they were conspiring how to sell more of their poppy's newspapers. They perched atop a stack of the latest edition while taking in the countryside, pointing to this and that. The country air sure smelled a lot sweeter than the sewers of New York. Zack's attitude had improved tremendously, too.

One of the twins laughed about something. Those two. He shook his head. Guess it was about time he set them straight about a matter.

"Hey, you two wild animals."

"Yes, Poppy." Charlie's sweet voice sounded like a tiny bird.

"I love you."

"Both of us?" Curly asked.

"Yes, both of you."

Curly reached from the back of the wagon and touched Zack's suspenders. "We love you, too."

"Mama told us that once," Charlie said. "But most of the time she was too tired 'cept to sleep. Does Miss Chloe love us, too?"

"I bet so." Zack watched the two of them exchange glances, then cover their mouths to conceal a giggle.

"Do you love her like you love us?" Charlie asked.

"Nope. I love you in a whole different way."

They laughed again. What were they up to now?

"Miss Chloe is going with us to celebrate Thanksgiving."

Curly tugged on his suspenders again. "What's Thanksgivin'? Miss Scott talked about it at school, but we don't know what it is."

Had they not shared in a Thanksgiving before? "Well, a long time ago when folks first came to America, they had a hard time growing food and having enough for everyone to eat."

"We've been hungry, Poppy," Charlie said.

He shook off the emotion rising in him and concentrated on his story. "The Indians living around them showed them how to plant corn and other vegetables so they wouldn't starve. One year they had a big harvest, and the people decided to have a feast to thank God for all of their blessings. They invited all of the families and friends, including the Indians. So that is why we celebrate Thanksgiving. It's a time when family and friends get together and thank God for all of their blessings. We have a big turkey dinner with plenty of food for everyone. This year my uncle Morgan and aunt Casey have invited the whole family to their ranch."

"What about the hungry people?" Curly asked.

"Our church has taken care of those people, and we'll do it again at Christmas."

Charlie's eyes widened. "Good. Nobody should be hungry. Does Uncle Morgan and Aunt Casey have kittens, too?"

"*Do* Uncle Morgan, not *does*. Anyway, I'm not sure if they have kittens or not. We'll have to check. They have a lot of horses, but you two stay outside the fence."

"Yes, sir. We promise."

He wondered if heaven heard those two cherub voices.

"I'm glad Miss Chloe is going with us. She'll make a fine mama," Charlie said. "I already told her."

Zack gulped. "You what?"

"Yeah," Curly chimed in. "When she was holding ice on my eye and crying 'bout Eli hitting me, we both told her that."

"What. . .what did she say?"

"Nothing, but she did say she loved us," Charlie said.

"Don't you think if I'm ever to get married and get you two a mama that I should do the choosing?"

Curly shook his head. "We already chose Miss Chloe."

Lord, help me here. I thought You wanted me to run a newspaper—bring the truth to light. In a matter of a month, these two have jumped into my heart, and Chloe is close behind.

"Maybe we should talk about having lunch at Uncle George and Aunt Ellen's." Anything to get those two off the subject of Chloe and needing a mama.

"Do they have a ranch?" Curly asked.

"No. They live in Kahlerville in a big house that Uncle George built. He owns the lumberyard and sawmill. He's also the town's mayor. You will have lots of cousins to play with."

"How many?" the twins chorused.

"Ten. Five boys and five girls. Mind your manners. And don't talk about me and Miss Chloe."

"Why?" Charlie asked. "Are you mad at her?"

"Oh no." *Lord, help me.* "I think all of the cousins will be interested in getting to know you and Curly."

"Do you want us to tell them about New York?" Curly asked.

Zack had to think about that. "I think you could tell them a little but not the bad things."

Curly sighed like an old man trying to get the energy to stand from his rocking chair. "Like pickpocketing?"

"Not much to tell except the bad stuff we did," Charlie said. "But we won't use outhouse words." Her eyes lit up. "I know. We'll talk about Sister Agatha and Sister Catherine. They were nice and loved us even when we did things that Jesus didn't like."

Lord, have mercy.

CHAPTER 11

"Looks to me like an active pair of children need a nap." Mama tilted her head toward Curly and Charlie slouched over on the front porch steps after Sunday dinner.

"We're too big for naps," Curly said and yawned.

"Afternoon naps are a great way to dream about Santa and what you'd like for Christmas."

"We don't want anything, 'cause we have Poppy and a home. And he loves us." Curly turned to Zack and Chloe on the porch swing and offered a big smile. Soon his loose tooth would leave a gap in his smile. Already they were growing too fast.

"Thank you," Zack managed with the tug at his heart. "You two are the best Christmas presents a man could ever want." He glanced toward the fields. How could Curly and Charlie yank at his heartstrings one minute and be naughty the next?

"We got an extra bowl of porridge on Christmas Day at the orphanage." Charlie folded her hands into her lap and smoothed the skirt of her green flowered dress. "We haven't had to eat that horrible stuff since Poppy 'dopted us."

This was fast becoming a tearful occasion. Chloe brushed the dampness from her cheeks.

"How about a story?" Mama bent toward the twins and wrapped an arm around each child's shoulders.

Charlie's droopy eyes gave away her need for sleep. "You read the best, Grandma."

Mama took their hands. "Then I'll read to you on my bed. It's my favorite spot to enjoy a book."

"I need to do some more preparation for tonight's service," Dad said. "I'll read in the parlor."

Once everyone disappeared inside, Zack turned to Chloe. "Why do I suspect we were left alone on purpose?"

The peach in her cheeks deepened. "I thought they all were tired."

He chuckled. "My mother is a matchmaker." He hesitated. "I apologize if her planning bothers you." He waited for several long moments for her answer.

"I—I think it's a nice gesture."

"Good. I do, too. Now I don't know what to talk about."

"Tell me about lunch yesterday with George and Ellen Kahler."

He laughed. "The twins wore themselves out running from one cousin to another, playing inside and outside of the huge house. And they were on their best behavior—except when I caught Curly sliding down the banister. He slid right into my arms."

She giggled.

"It was really funny. You should have seen the surprised look on his face."

"They are cute. What did they like the best?"

"Hmm. I'd say other than all the new playmates, it was a toss-up between Aunt Ellen's sugar cookies and the family dog—a very friendly family dog." He laughed again. "I think they might have been tempted to trade me for the pet."

"Not if I just heard correctly."

"They were trying to avoid a nap."

She smiled, and he smiled. He could get used to this. Were the birds singing, or was his heart playing its own tune?

"I'm glad it went well yesterday." She moistened her lips. "Tell me about your newspaper. Are things progressing as planned?"

He took a breath and silently thanked Chloe for suggesting conversation topics other than Mama's eagerness to see the two of them together. He could be real tempted to steal a kiss. "Well, to begin with, Hank is a mountain of wisdom. I received outstanding experience in New York with reporting and even advertising, but I needed to learn more about the workings of a small-town newspaper—one with high aspirations. Thankfully, Hank plans to stay on until I learn more of those things."

"Miss Scott told me how thrilled she is to be writing a women's column."

Chloe's smile and milky-white teeth were downright distracting.

"Actually, she will help me draw in more women readers from all over the area. And her ideas and writing show a lot of promise. I suppose all of the years of teaching English have something to do with her expertise."

"You are helping this town grow, Zack Kahler."

"That's my dream. I hope to bring the news of the surrounding communities, the country, and the world to the doorstep of ordinary people. They want the farm and stock reports, weather predictions, and help with their crops. I remember following the World Series in October between the Philadelphia Athletes and the New York Giants. . . . Philadelphia won 4–2. At the time, I thought of the folks here who liked baseball. Wouldn't it be grand to give the people in Kahlerville game scores as soon as it happened? Other sports? Economics? U.S. events?"

She turned on the swing to face him directly. "What types of stories affected you the most?"

"Without a doubt, the Triangle Shirtwaist Factory fire that killed the twins' mother."

Chloe shuddered. "You didn't tell me how she died."

Sometimes he still heard the screams of those trapped inside. "It was a tragic fire in a warehouse where many women, mostly immigrants, died. They couldn't get out, and the owners were at fault. I covered the story, which is another reason why I had to help Curly and Charlie."

"You can build your newspaper into something grand. You have the determination, and you're a hard worker. I hear the passion in your voice, Zack Kahler. You and your newspaper will succeed."

Zack feigned surprise. "You can see all those fine things in a matter of a few short weeks?"

She laughed. "I saw those things when you were one of Miss Scott's students."

How did this woman manage to warm his soul and fill him with inspiration at the same time?

〜〜⌒◎⌒〜〜

Monday evening as Zack locked up the newspaper office, he heard a familiar voice speak his name. Miss Scott called to him again and held her hat as a gust of wind whipped around her. The sight of the slightly plump woman struggling to maintain her balance in the midst of school papers flying everywhere caused him almost to laugh aloud. Instead, he helped her retrieve her belongings and ushered her under the overhang of the boardwalk.

"I'm sorry I couldn't get to you fast enough," he said. "How can I help you?"

She paused for a deep breath and regained her composure. "May I have a word with you about Curly and Charlie?"

Chill bumps chased up and down his arms. "Of course." He unlocked the newspaper office and ushered her inside. Trepidation settled on him like a black cloud. After Friday's incident with Eli Scott bullying his children, he was more than a little sensitive to anything about them.

"It's not serious," Miss Scott said as though reading his thoughts.

He forced a chuckle. "I'm constantly reminded of how bad I was in school. Guess I'm nervous—like God may be giving me a dose of my own medicine. And you don't want to know what I've been thinking about the problem last Friday."

Sadness swept over her face. For the first time, he noticed her hair had begun to gray around her face. "Eli has run away from home. But I can understand after the many beatings my brother has given him."

"The many beatings?"

Miss Scott nodded. "My brother's treatment of Eli is no excuse for me to have overlooked my nephew's bad behavior. I think Eli took out his resentment on the other children. None of my talking ever made a difference—to Eli or my brother."

"What a sad situation." And he really believed it.

"Thank you. I pray Eli will find someone who will help him see the right road. As far as my brother goes, he's always been rather brutal in dealing with Eli." She stared off wistfully for a moment, then smiled. "Let's talk about the twins."

"Do we need to have them with us?"

"Calm down. This is nothing we can't work out together."

"Then you'd best tell me soon before this new father becomes ill."

She smiled her teacher smile, which meant there were a few unpleasant matters to deal with. "Curly and Charlie are behind in their schoolwork."

"I figured as much. From what they told me, I doubt if they attended a full week of school at any given time in New York." He attempted to calm himself. "What do you suggest?"

"I'd like to tutor them after school until they can work successfully with their own age group."

He relaxed slightly. "I appreciate your giving them an opportunity to catch up. I was afraid they might need to be held back next year."

"They're bright children, and I think the individual attention will bring them up to where they should be. Lydia Anne and Stuart would then have three free afternoons a week, and I would have a few hours alone with Curly and Charlie. I can work with the twins a little more in the dining room until you return from the newspaper."

"You are taking on a handful."

She laughed. "They are adorable. Shall we start on Wednesday? I think three times a week is a good beginning. Do Monday, Wednesday, and Friday suit you?"

"Perfect for me. You're the one doing all the work. And you will let me know how much I owe you for the tutoring?"

Her eyes pooled. "Oh, Zack, don't you know me by now? The children I teach become my children. I don't want any money for tutoring. Besides, you've given me a column to write."

He started to protest, but then figured he could add to her payment for writing the newspaper column. "I have a difficult time arguing with my former teacher."

"Precisely my point." She nodded to punctuate her words. "Then it's settled."

The clock in the foyer ticked rhythmically, counting down the hours after the boardinghouse had hummed with activity during the dinner hour and the conversation following. The lull in the day's events allowed Chloe to catch up on the chores and Mr. Barton's books. The twins and Miss Scott tended to a spelling lesson. Chloe wanted to help them with arithmetic on Sunday afternoons, but she needed Zack's permission.

"It sure is nice of you to help the twins with their schoolin'." Simeon sidled up to the table where Miss Scott sat with the two.

Chloe bit her lip to keep from laughing. Simeon was sweet-talking Miss Scott for sure.

"I want to see children learn and grow up to be responsible adults. I've taught many fine young people. I think of them as my own."

"And you taught Mr. Zack?"

"Oh yes." She giggled.

I didn't know Miss Scott ever giggled. Is she sweet on Simeon?

"I used to worry about him when he was eleven and twelve years old, but he's such a fine young man now."

"I imagine every successful man and woman in town owes you thanks."

"How kind you are to flatter me so."

"When you're finished, would you like a slice of freshly baked pecan pie and coffee?"

"Mr. Simeon, that sounds perfect."

My, it looks like those two are on the courtin' road. All of this at the end of the first week of tutoring the twins? Chloe fought the notion to hum a few verses of "Clementine."

"I set the pie outside to cool on the windowsill," Simeon said. "Give me a moment to slice it up and pour you a cup of coffee. Cream and sugar, right?"

"How nice of you to remember. You will join me, won't you?"

The sugar in Miss Scott's voice could have sweetened a whole pot of coffee.

"For only a moment. I have dinner to cook for the boarders."

And Simeon poured on the sugar, too.

"Everything you prepare tastes heavenly. I look forward to treating myself to one of your excellent meals."

"Thank ye kindly. I'll be right back."

Chloe peeked around the corner. The twins were writing diligently at a table, no doubt oblivious to the budding romance between Miss Scott and Simeon. Long moments passed. Simeon must really be going to a lot of trouble. Then he hurried into the dining room.

"Something has happened to my pie." His face grew red as he spoke.

Miss Scott's face paled as though he'd given her dire news.

"Yesterday, I had a loaf of bread taken right off my coolin' window.

Today a pecan pie. I believe there's a thief in our town."

"Should I fetch the sheriff?"

Simeon shook his head. "No, I'll be on the lookout for whoever is swipin' my food." He shook his head. "If a hungry person is takin' them, I wish they'd just knock on the back door. I'd be glad to fix 'em a plate. But stealin' makes me mad."

Chloe remembered her hungry years. She'd never considered stealing. Yet when she remembered picking up fallen apples from the livery's apple tree, guilt assaulted her conscience. She took a breath and stepped into the dining room.

"Simeon, I couldn't help but hear about the stolen bread and pie. Do you mind if tomorrow I fix a plate of food after the boarders have eaten and set it on the windowsill?"

The old man frowned. "I guess that's all right. We best check with Mr. Barton to make sure. Hope he doesn't take my plate and fork, too."

"I'll put a note on the top of the food to return them."

A smile spread over Simeon's face. "You know, Miss Chloe, you have a big heart. All I could think about was the missin' food. You're thinkin' about a person goin' hungry."

No matter who it is, I can't condemn them. Going hungry is a horrible feeling.

CHAPTER 12

Chloe counted three days until Thanksgiving knocked at everyone's door and she'd be spending the holiday with Zack and the twins. A calendar lay inside the ledger at the registration desk. Ever since Zack had invited her to spend the holiday with his family, she'd checked off each day in pencil. That way she could erase the markings in case Mr. Barton asked her what they meant. Sometimes she wished she could erase all the ugly reminders of her past. The Bible said God took care of those things, but why was she still plagued with reminders?

Special occasions were a rarity for Chloe, other than her graduation from school. Pa had attended the ceremony and even said he was proud of her. Just when she believed he didn't care, he'd surprised her with a comment that proved otherwise. Poor man. Once her mother died, he found little to live for except the bottle.

Time off from school meant being with Pa, and something about Chloe always made him angry. She guessed it was her resemblance to her mother. But she'd been given a substitute mother in Miss Scott. The dear woman had always given her fruit and nuts at Thanksgiving and more again at Christmas, which Chloe hid from Pa. Maybe that had been wrong, and she should have shared. Women from church always made sure she had food and clothing. One year they gave her a quilt. Two of the girls at school had teased her about wearing their old clothes until Miss Scott scolded them. Eli had amused himself with his own teasing, but Chloe refused to think about those lewd comments. More than once, he'd frightened her with his filthy talk.

She shook her head. No reason to dwell on things she couldn't change or ever tell a soul.

"Miss Chloe, do you have a minute?" Simeon called from the kitchen.

She scurried around the desk to see what he needed. Once inside the kitchen, she saw he had a basin full of carrots and potatoes to peel.

"If ya have a little time, I could use your help cleaning these taters and carrots for dinner."

"Always for you." She snatched up an apron and a paring knife.

"How is Miss Scott doing?"

For certain Simeon fancied the lady. Chloe doubted if he really needed help peeling the vegetables. "Very well, I think. In addition to having her tutor the twins, Zack hired her to write a column for him—recipes, sewing instructions, health tips, fashion, and the like."

"Oh, she'll do a mighty fine job. Isn't her given name Annabelle? What a purdy name for a sweet lady."

Chloe turned her head so he wouldn't see her amusement. "Yes, her name is Annabelle. Did I see you watching her when she came by to check on the twins?"

"Couldn't help myself. Mighty fine woman. Yes, she is." He shook his head as though the memory of her visit had rooted in his head and heart.

"Simeon, are you smitten with Miss Scott?"

The tilt of his head and the twinkle in his eyes confirmed her suspicions. This time she did laugh aloud. Chloe finished peeling a potato and dropped it into a pan filled with salt water. "No need to answer. The look on your face tells it all."

"You are one to accuse me of admirin' someone." Simeon wagged his finger at her and batted his eyes. "Have my ears deceived me? 'Oh, Zack, everything you say and do is just wonderful.'"

Simeon was in for it now. "I don't say those things at all."

"You don't? 'Oh, Zack, yer children are beautiful. Can I get you another piece of pie?'"

She lifted her chin. "How about this? 'Oh, Miss Scott, I love every word that comes from your mouth. You are the best school teacher in the state.'"

Simeon lifted his hands. "All right. I give. I think we're both drownin' in something we don't know what to do about."

She shrugged. "Maybe you are."

He cleared his throat.

"All right. Maybe we both are. If you're finished with the teasing, I have a question, a serious one."

Simeon raised a brow. "Need advice from a wise ol' man? Go right ahead."

"Can you think of something I can do for small Christmas gifts this year?"

He expertly whipped the peeling off a carrot. "I believe I do. I have more apples at my place than I know what to do with. How about makin' a batch of apple jelly? I have some extra jars, too." He grabbed a potato. "We could make it here in the afternoons when work slacks off. Apple butter would be good, too, but it takes too long."

What a perfect idea. "Simeon, that's wonderful. There are a few special people I'd like to give a gift, but money is a problem. With your idea, I could tie the lids with red and green ribbon. What do I need to buy? Sugar?"

He nodded. "Something sweet from somebody sweet."

She laughed. "Are you practicing on me for Miss Scott?"

"I don't need to practice. The words just drip from my tongue like honey." He rubbed his whiskered jaw. "Like I said, she's a mighty fine woman."

Chloe paused again to remember all the fine things Miss Scott had done for her. "After my mother died, she made sure I had food and clothes."

"I heard her say that she thinks of all the young'uns she's taught through the years as hers."

Oh, to put Simeon and Miss Scott together. Perhaps at Christmas when she delivered her gift to the dear lady, Chloe would tell her how much she appreciated the years of teaching and how Simeon had helped her make the jelly. The dear woman may not have had any children of her own, but she certainly had adopted a whole lot more—just as Zack had adopted Curly and Charlie.

Thanksgiving at Morgan and Casey Andrews's ranch? Her stomach fluttered. All those people would make her nervous. What if she said the wrong thing? What if they asked her about Pa's death?

Or where she lived before finding employment at the boardinghouse? But Zack's family had always been kind to her.

Seemed like Chloe's dreams were slowly coming true, like a batch of candy slowly coming to a boil when it was perfect. When Pa died, she had believed her life had taken another turn for the worse. As ugly as he could be at times, she never wanted him dead, and he was her only living family member. Good memories of him when her mother was still alive floated in and out of her head. Perhaps Pa had found peace. He'd been happy before her mother died, and they'd attended church. No matter that they didn't have much money. Love had kept them together.

"Where are your thoughts?" Simeon whispered.

She smiled. "Days gone by."

"Remember the good ones and forget the bad ones. That's the best way to make it through life. I know you love Jesus."

"I do."

"If He can forget the nonsense in our lives when we ask, then we need to do the same."

"You are a wise man."

He smiled. "Naw. Jest lived a lot of years and seen folks make good and bad choices."

She gave him a kiss on the cheek and finished peeling the potatoes and carrots. The grandfather clock in the foyer chimed four o'clock. The time had slipped by this afternoon, and she had many more chores to complete before the evening.

The day wore on until near dinnertime. Chloe lit a lantern on the sideboard in the dining room. As the days shortened, those who dined at the boardinghouse needed light for their evening meal. And today had been cloudy with a steady shower of rain. Sometimes a candle on each table suited her purpose, but she liked to vary things a bit.

She blew out a breath and noted a crooked tablecloth. Once it was straightened, she thought about the days when her stomach had rumbled for food and her life had looked bleak. Then she remembered the incident of Simeon's stolen bread and pie. Mr. Barton had agreed feeding someone made more sense than having food disappear that was needed for the boarders. Beginning on Saturday, she had placed a plateful of food on the windowsill, and the next day the plate and fork were returned. As Chloe considered her own good fortune of late, she questioned if God was no longer upset with her. Her entire life had been plagued with sadness until recently, and she'd assumed God was displeased with her. But life had taken a change for the best. God had blessed her with employment, a place to live, food to eat, and Zack and the twins.

"I'm really pleased with your work."

She swung her attention to the foyer that separated the dining from the living room and smiled at Mr. Barton. She hadn't heard the bell jingle over the boardinghouse door. "Thank you. This is home for me."

"And it shows. There's not a speck of dust in the whole establishment. With the books in excellent condition and Simeon in the kitchen, I don't have a single worry. Is your room adequate?"

"Very much so." She sensed his eyes boring a hole through her, and suddenly she felt uncomfortable. His interest in her was clearly evident, just as Simeon had indicated. "Is there something I can do for you?"

"As a matter of fact there is. I know it's a little early with Thanksgiving not until this Thursday, but I have an idea to help the community for Christmas. And I wanted your opinion and possibly your help."

"I'd be glad to do whatever I can. What is your idea?"

"If I could talk Simeon into baking cookies for the schoolchildren, would you help me distribute them?"

"The children would love your thoughtfulness. It hasn't been that long since I was a student there, and the days before Christmas are spent more in daydreaming than learning. I'd be happy to help Simeon with the baking. He admires Miss Scott."

Mr. Barton chuckled. "I've seen the gleam in his eyes, and more songs seem to have appeared on his repertoire of whistling tunes. I'll be sure to mention her name. I'd also like to open the dining room to needy folks on Christmas Eve. After the incident last Friday, I want to make sure all of the hungry people of this town are fed. Do you think it would be too difficult for you and Simeon with the extra work? I plan on helping, too."

"Not at all. I'd welcome the opportunity to give to others."

"Good. I'll proceed with those plans. I'll ask Brother Whitworth for a list of those who could use a good meal." He shifted from one foot to the other. "Do you have plans for Thanksgiving dinner?"

Her stomach churned. Her suspicions had been more than correct. Although Mr. Barton could be gruff and at times difficult to please, her opinion of him had changed because of his concern for those less fortunate. "Yes, sir, I do."

"Is it anything you could cancel? I'd like to share Thanksgiving dinner with you. Simeon is preparing a huge meal, and I'm sure it will be wonderful." His normal, businesslike facade softened.

"I'm sorry, but I have already made a commitment."

Immediately his features hardened. "I see. If you change your mind, kindly let me know."

"I will. I appreciate your invitation." Chloe walked to the foyer and watched him leave. This could be a sensitive situation with Zack living at the boardinghouse. Mr. Barton probably assumed she'd be spending the holiday with him and the twins. For that matter, Mr. Barton could change his mind about letting her have Thanksgiving Day off after breakfast.

No sooner had Mr. Barton left than he returned. "Miss Weaver, have you had lunch or dinner yet today?"

"No, sir. We've been busy."

"I smell beef stew and corn bread. Would you mind joining me?" He smiled. "It's a good hour before dinner is served for the boarders."

"I'd be delighted."

He gave her a half smile. "As delighted as sharing a meal with Zack Kahler and his children?"

Her face flushed warm. How rude. What should she say?

"I apologize. I've embarrassed and offended you." He picked at a piece of lint on his coat. "My comment was uncalled for. I tend to speak whatever is on my mind without thinking of others."

She swallowed and attempted to control her irritation. "It's all right. Shall I get our food for us?"

"You are a gracious lady indeed. That would be fine, and I'll spend the time contemplating my poor social skills."

Simeon appeared to have dinner in hand, except for arranging the serving dishes. Chloe ladled stew into bowls and placed a few pieces of corn bread on a platter. She placed the food and two cups of coffee onto a tray and headed for the door.

"Who's that for?" Simeon asked.

"Mr. Barton and me."

"You don't look happy about eatin' with the boss."

"Hush. He'll hear you." She blew out a very unladylike sigh. "He has strange mannerisms at times."

"Don't I know it?"

She lifted her chin. "But he has a good heart, and I'm thankful for this job and the way he cares about the community."

Simeon stared at her for a few minutes. "You need to work, don't ya?"

"I'm all I have." She shook her head. "I sound like a whining child."

"I understand. Life ain't always easy. Things will work out."

Forcing a smile, she tilted her head. "I hope so."

Once at the table in the dining room with dinner set before them, she listened to Mr. Barton ask the blessing. "Bless the hands who have prepared this food, and may it nourish our bodies so we can nourish Your kingdom. And I could use a bridle on my mouth. Amen."

Startled, she glanced into his face. His lips curved up and he laughed, urging her to join him.

"We might as well laugh about my lack of manners," he said. "You could have slapped me and quit your job. Then where would I be?"

"Where would I be?"

"You're right." He picked up his spoon and dragged it through the thick stew. "We'd both be in a fine mess. Truce?"

"Truce."

"But your refusal of my invitation to join me for Thanksgiving dinner doesn't mean I won't stop trying to earn your favor."

She picked up her spoon. "Am I supposed to respond?"

"Probably not. I like a good challenge, and I'm afraid Mr. Kahler is in the lead in this race." He leaned in closer. "Do you find my withered hand repulsive?"

"Absolutely not. I look at a man's heart. But sir, you barely know me."

"Sometimes a man knows the blessing in front of him without a word being said."

"I wouldn't want you or Mr. Kahler to be disappointed."

"I assessed you correctly. May the best man win the prize."

The question crossed her mind as to whether she should tell Zack about Mr. Barton's conversation. She hesitated. Not yet, unless Zack chose to deepen their relationship. This could get very complicated.

CHAPTER 13

Out in a chilling rain, Zack pulled up the collar on his coat and dashed across the street to the feed store. He sure hoped this weather changed before tomorrow. Having all of the kids inside the house for Thanksgiving sounded like punishment for the adults.

Jacob Barton's ads for his boardinghouse and feed store had been acquired when Hank owned the paper. They were well drawn up, as Hank had always done, but Zack had a few ideas of his own. Rather than discuss Barton's ads at the boardinghouse, he chose to call on the man at the feed store. There they would stand on neutral ground, whereas at the boardinghouse he'd already felt a heavy dose of animosity between them. Zack had seen Jacob staring at Chloe on more than one occasion.

The smell of dried corn and grain met Zack's nostrils, and a dusting of meal trailed across the wooden floor. Jacob lifted a bag of grain to his shoulder and carried it to the front of the store. Amazing what the man could do with only partial use of his withered arm.

Jacob nodded at Zack. "Be right with you as soon as I take care of this customer."

Zack spoke to the farmer and asked about his wife and family. Once the man left the store, Zack continued the same pleasantries with Barton and shook his hand.

"Two businesses must keep you busy."

"It certainly does. Makes me glad I'm a single man. However, Miss Weaver has made my job a whole lot easier. She is an excellent bookkeeper and makes sure the boardinghouse runs smoothly. I intend to make sure she works for me for a long time."

Zack heard a hint of contention. Was this an open challenge for Chloe's affections?

"So, what brings you to my store today in this cold rain? Newspaper business?"

"I've been working on your ads as we discussed before, and I wanted you to see the sketches for both of your businesses." Zack pulled them from his leather satchel and laid them on the counter. The feed store ad depicted a farmer hoisting a bag of grain on his shoulder. The boardinghouse used a more elegant font and showed a pretty young woman holding a stack of fresh linens.

Barton's attention stayed focused on Zack. "Is there any difference in the cost for advertising if I choose any of these?"

"No, sir. Just an opportunity to have a new look in the paper."

"And my current price includes alternating weeks for my two businesses?"

"That's right. We'll be starting a daily edition beginning Monday, the fourth of December. But as it stands now, your ads will appear in Saturday's edition."

For the first time, Barton picked up the sketches and studied them closely. "These look good. What's the cost to advertise in the Sunday and daily?"

"Eighteen cents a word per week."

"Put that in writing for me, and I'll consider it."

"Will do. Thanks for taking your time to visit with me this morning." Zack reached out and shook his hand again.

"Are you enjoying your stay at the boardinghouse? Everything suitable for you and your children?"

"For certain, but I'm looking for a house. There's only so much confinement my twins can take. They can be a handful with all that energy. I apologize for the noise."

Barton's stoic expression bore into Zack's. "I have received some complaints from a few boarders. You and Miss Weaver share a lot of time together."

"We went to the same school under the tutelage of Miss Scott."

Barton eyed him for a long moment. "Every time I ask her for a stroll or to share a Sunday with me, she's already agreed to do something with you. On Monday she said she had plans for Thanksgiving, and I assume those are with you." He cleared his throat. "Looks to me like those big-city ideas must appeal to her. I should have asked her while we shared dinner what a simple businessman in Kahlerville could do to turn her head."

Zack heard a heavy dose of sarcasm. "Perhaps Miss Weaver should decide whose company she prefers."

"My guess is she doesn't know yet. So I'll continue to be an attentive employer and spend as much time with her as I can."

Fury raced through Zack's veins, but he smiled and tipped his hat. "This will be interesting, I'm sure. Good day, sir." He'd suspected Jacob Barton's interest in Chloe on previous occasions, but now by the man's own admission, Zack knew Barton wanted to court her. Jealousy, an emotion Zack rarely felt, stung him as though he'd angered a swarm of bees. Naturally Chloe should choose whose company she preferred. Had Zack forced his affections on her? After all, he was a guest at the boardinghouse, and she might feel obligated to accept his invitations.

He'd ask her this very evening. Zack stiffened. He'd ask her now.

Chloe had just finished cleaning the room of a boarder who had checked out of the boardinghouse when she heard the bell above the door. She hurried down the stairs to find Zack at the registration desk. He wore a frown, not his usual wide grin that seemed to snatch away her breath. He might be twenty-four years old, but he had not lost his boyish appeal.

"Do you have a minute to discuss something?" he asked.

"I do." She caught her breath and attempted to read the range of emotions on his face. "Is something wrong? Are the twins all right?"

"I just need to make sure I'm not abusing our friendship."

What on earth was he talking about? "Zack, you have never abused our relationship."

"And you're certain of this?" The frown still dug into his brow. "Are you agreeing to accompany me to church and other places because you work here?"

She started. "I assure you that is not what I'm doing."

"Then you enjoy our company?"

Chloe would have laughed if not for the serious look on his face. "Yes. I look forward to our times together."

"And if you were interested in courting another man, you would tell me?"

Was Zack referring to Mr. Barton? "Perhaps you should explain to me what this is all about."

"I had a conversation with Jacob Barton."

Her insides started to quiver. "About me?"

"Yes. He has become attached to you and wanted me to know about it. I thought you and I were establishing a relationship."

She hadn't wanted to reveal the discussion between herself and Mr. Barton, but it looked like her employer was serious about his intentions. "He has expressed interest, but my feelings are not the same as his." She rubbed her perspiring palms together. Anger settled in hard. "I am very uncomfortable being the topic of two grown men's conversation. Do you think I am a pet dog or cat who needs a keeper?"

His eyes widened. "I hadn't thought—"

"Maybe you two should have considered my reaction to this childish bickering as though I am a prize in some contest. My affections are given to whom I choose."

"I understand."

Her anger had risen to another rung on the ladder. "Do you?"

He shifted from one foot to the other. "I'm sorry. Guess I was only thinking about myself."

She took a deep breath. *Calm yourself, Chloe.* "I apologize for my loss of temper. Please be assured that I would never toy with any man's affections."

He nodded and whirled around. At the door he turned. "Am I

forgiven for being a thoughtless, selfish, and jealous man?"

Zack's smile could have charmed the angels, but she dare not let him see how he affected her. She frowned. "I suppose."

"I'll let you have the biggest piece of pumpkin pie tomorrow."

A smile crept to her lips. "How can I resist that?"

"Good." He grinned, reminding her once again of the schoolboy so many years ago. "I'll make sure I have better manners in the future." He tipped his hat. "Good day, Miss Chloe. I'll look forward to your lovely presence at dinner."

Once he closed the door behind him, she laughed. She must find a way to handle the situation with Mr. Barton. Because Zack had her heart tied up in a pretty bow.

Miss Scott read the twins a story about Sam Houston and how he had helped form the state of Texas. When she finished, she asked Curly and Charlie questions pertaining to what they'd heard. The children were bright, and they had been listening.

"Very well done," Miss Scott said. "I have paper and colors here. Would you like to make your poppy a Thanksgiving picture and sign your name?"

"Yes, ma'am," the two chodused.

The dining room grew silent, and Chloe stepped in to greet Miss Scott. The woman rose from her chair and walked into the adjoining parlor where the two women sat down. Miss Scott could look directly into the dining room at her two charges.

"How are they doing?" Chloe asked.

"Progressing nicely, but I knew they would. Those two could not have survived on the streets of New York City unless they were quite intelligent." Her shoulders lifted and fell, and she took Chloe's hand into hers. "If I were but a few years younger, I'd board a train for New York and adopt an orphan or two myself."

"Why not?" Chloe whispered. "You've been a mother to so many of us. Perhaps now is the time for a child to call you 'Mother.'"

The woman pressed her lips together. "I've been thinking about it a great deal. I even discussed it with Simeon last Sunday afternoon."

They are keeping company. "I'm sure he encouraged you."

Miss Scott nodded and blushed. "He is a fine man, and we do get along famously." She smiled. "And what about you and Zack?"

Chloe really needed to talk to a woman. "Our friendship is blossoming."

"That's obvious."

"The problem is Mr. Barton is interested, too. It's becoming a bit discomfiting."

"Some women would be delighted with your problem, but I know you well enough to see this disturbs you."

Chloe nodded and adjusted her posture on the sofa. For a moment, she feared a tear or two might escape.

"Have you told Mr. Barton that you prefer Zack's company?"

"I have in a very nice manner, but he doesn't seem to be the type to take no for an answer. From what Zack has said, Mr. Barton talked to Zack about me."

Miss Scott shuddered. "Oh dear. Did they behave as gentlemen?"

"I think so, but it makes me angry that I'm discussed like I don't have a choice in the matter."

Miss Scott leaned in closer. "One more reason why we women need our rights."

"I'm inclined to agree. Anyway, as you could well imagine, Mr.

Barton could be demanding of my time if he so chose."

Miss Scott swallowed hard, as though the truth hurt her more deeply than she cared to admit. She craned her neck to observe the twins. "Simply conduct yourself as a lady. No matter what those men say and do, you keep your head up and follow your heart. Thank goodness Eli is not bothering you anymore. I still feel badly about his improper advances."

"Zack told me Eli's father abused him."

Miss Scott frowned. "He did—repeatedly. I. . .have decided not to desert my brother in hopes he will someday see the error of his ways. If you remember correctly, his wife passed on about the same time as your mother."

"Neither of our fathers did well after their wives' deaths. Perhaps if I had known about Eli's life at home, I could have been more sympathetic."

"I don't think it would have changed a thing. Wherever Eli is, my prayer is he'll find peace for his soul. I think he plans to join the army. He mentioned it a few times, and it would give him the discipline he needs." She patted Chloe's hand still clasped in hers. "Enough of this gloom. You are a beautiful young woman, Chloe, and I'm sad for the unhappiness in your growing-up years. But God will bring peace and joy to your days, and I think it will happen with Zack and his children."

Chloe smiled. She hoped so, too.

"I have an entirely different topic to discuss with you," Miss Scott said. "We've known each other for a long time, and I don't want you to feel embarrassed about this."

Chloe gave her a curious glance.

"Child, you have one dress to your name. As always at this time of year, I have collected several clothing items. There are a few items that would fit you nicely."

She opened her mouth to object.

"You need them for your job and to look suitable with Zack."

Miss Scott had spoken correctly. Often her dress and under-garments were wet when she crawled into them the next day.

"I see you agree with me," Miss Scott went on. "I'll bring them by discreetly next Monday when I return the twins. Zack and I have decided to skip tutoring this Friday."

"Thank you." Humiliation burned at her cheeks.

"Nonsense." Miss Scott reached over and kissed her cheek. "You give far too much of yourself not to accept something in return." She glanced into the dining room and told the twins, "When you are finished with your paper and crayons, you can go outside if you like."

"Yes, ma'am," they chorused.

Chloe watched them scurry from their chairs, scoot them back under the table, and hurry to the kitchen, which led outside. For the next several minutes, the two women chatted about everything from the upcoming holidays to church news.

In the midst of a discussion about the school's Christmas program, Simeon shouted at Curly and Charlie. Instantly, both women were on their feet and hurrying to the kitchen.

"You two should be ashamed of yourself," Simeon said.

Hissing and screaming met Chloe's ears. She made her way to the back door in time to see two cats with their tails tied together, scratching and clawing at each other.

"Why ever did you do such a thing?" Chloe peered into the faces of first Curly and then Charlie.

"Sorry," Charlie said. "We wanted to see what they'd do."

With a broom in his hand, Simeon burst through the door to the fighting cats. "Chloe, see if you can separate them while I untie the rope on their tails."

Mercy! What would Zack say about this mischief?

CHAPTER 14

Chloe glanced around the long table at Morgan and Casey Andrews's home. Seated around it were people who loved one another. She tingled all over simply to be included with these respected people. Their home reflected elegance yet warmth. Above her head glistened a chandelier that reminded her of a thousand twinkling lights. Zack's hand wrapped firmly around hers as Brother Whitworth began the Thanksgiving prayer.

"Father, here we are together another year. We're another year older, and we pray another year closer to You. I thank You for my fine family and the love so freely given in our midst. Your blessings are many, and we thank You for all of them. It's been a long time since so many of us were gathered together at Thanksgiving. It's a feast of love for sure. Bless this food, we pray, and help us never to forget what Your Son did for us at the cross and His resurrection that gives us life. In Christ Jesus' name, amen."

Zack squeezed her hand lightly before he released it.

Thank You, Lord, for the joy I feel this very minute. There are things about You I don't understand, and I pray I will one day be able to put the pieces of my life's puzzle together. Until then I'll keep asking the questions as to why my mother died and my childhood was so hard. I want to believe there is a reason without concentrating on my own problems and not becoming self-centered. Amen.

"The newest members of the family deserve the first slice of turkey," Brother Whitworth said. "Master Curly and Miss Charlie, what do you want, white meat or dark?"

"We don't know, Grandpa," Curly said. "We ain't, I mean, we've never eaten turkey before." He peered around Zack to where Charlie sat beside Chloe. "What do we pick?"

"Let Poppy decide," the little girl said with her typical seriousness. "He's good at things like that."

Laughter filled the room.

"Hey, Poppy," Doc Grant said. "I hope you're not teaching those children your bad manners. I remember seeing you take a few trips to the woodshed in your younger days."

"Poppy doesn't have bad manners," Charlie said. "He's the best. You should hear how nice he talks to Miss Chloe."

More laughter echoed around the room. Chloe offered a smile even as her face grew warm. What else could she do? *Maybe the hardships in my life were to help Zack with the twins.*

Zack leaned against the corral fence beside his uncle Morgan and uncle Grant and admired Morgan's quarter horses. For the past ten years, Uncle Morgan and Aunt Casey had concentrated on raising thoroughbreds, and the results of their efforts now grazed in the pasture. Zack enjoyed ranching life, but he was destined to be a newspaper man.

"I have the adoption papers completed," Morgan said. "They just need your signature before I post them. Got them with me in the house, so don't forget to sign them today. The judge in New York might require you to finalize it there. We'll have to wait on his decision."

"I hope he approves the paperwork and forgets about that part. The idea of another train ride with the twins makes my stomach churn like butter. The journey here made a believer out of me."

Morgan laughed. "Looks like you're doing a fine job with the two. But it's all up to the judge. I've drafted a good letter in your behalf and attached the four other recommendation letters to it. He might accept those. Then again, he might want visible proof that Curly and Charlie are well taken care of."

"Miss Scott and Hank read me their letters, and I'm assuming the ones from Dad and Uncle Grant state I'm a responsible father." Zack grinned. "As long as none of them recount my boyhood pranks. Sometimes when Curly and Charlie get into mischief, I think God is getting even."

"Ah, I heard about the cats."

Zack blew out an exasperated sigh. "I wanted to string them by their heels, but I maintained my composure."

"What did you do?"

"I confined them to their room for two days after school. I know I was not that bad."

"If that's the case, you don't stand a chance of running a successful newspaper, because you tried the patience of all of us."

"Miss Scott threatened to tell the judge about the time I stole her clothes from her clothesline and strung them up in the school yard tree."

"Best you stay on all of our good sides until the twins are officially yours. Right now you have the recommendations of the town's doctor, lawyer, preacher, and teacher."

"Sounds like free newspapers for a long while."

Morgan nodded. "I like the paper's new look. The ads are more modern. Makes a person look twice, which I guess is what the business owners want. My 'Morgan Andrews, Attorney at Law' needs a little work, too."

"How about a 'painless lawyer'?" Zack grinned. Two could play their teasing game. "A fellow could walk out of a courtroom holding a penny."

"It does sound like one of Morgan's clients," Grant said.

"You two are asking for it. When you least suspect it, I'll get even." Morgan tipped his hat. "I'll get my lovely wife and a pair of six shooters to handle matters outside of court."

"I think the lawyer in town has got us, Zack." Grant punched his brother in the shoulder.

"Some days I feel like I'm on trial with my 'newfangled' ideas," Zack said. "But I appreciate all that everyone is doing for the paper. I've done a bit of bartering for the ads, too. The blacksmith replaced a bad wheel on the wagon for a larger ad, and the town's tailor gave me a good price on a suit."

"I heard the paper's graduating to a daily." Morgan whistled for a mare.

"Very soon. I want the *Frontier Press* to incorporate news from around the community and the world. The fighting in China needs to be reported here on a daily basis, as well as the problems in Italy. I've said this to so many people that I can't back down."

"About time. I like my *Houston Post*, but I have to wait on it. Who knows? I might see one of those ads for an automobile and decide I need to have one." Morgan reached out to the mare and patted her neck.

Grant plopped a hand on his older brother's shoulder. "I heard you already had."

Morgan pushed back his hat. "Almost. I'm still pondering it. The last time an automobile drove through town, I decided to buy one. But the longer time passes, the more I put it off."

"I think you're getting too old to ride a horse." Grant deepened his hold on Morgan's shoulder. "Arthritis. Out of shape. Squeaky voice."

"You're not that far behind me, little brother. And I don't have any of those symptoms."

"When's the last time you broke a horse?" Grant laughed. "Last I heard, the hands were doing all the work."

"I'll match you ride for ride any day." Morgan narrowed his eyes. "Make sure Jenny has all of her nursin' skills down so she can take care of you."

Zack listened to his uncles' banter. They'd teased and sputtered ever since he could remember. Zack's generation had heard the stories about how the two men had taken on outlaws and made sure the ones who survived stayed locked up. The town and the surrounding countryside were safer because his uncles weren't afraid to stand up for what was right. Morgan and Grant Andrews were no men to rile, and Zack was pleased to be a member of the family. The Kahlers were fine, upstanding folks, too. They'd founded the town. Between his mother's and father's families, his twins had good people to look up to. A worthy heritage for Curly and Charlie.

"Did you pick out one of Henry Ford's finest for yourself before leaving New York?" Grant stood on the other side of Zack.

"Not at all. I don't like the noise and all the cranking. Besides, I knew I was coming back here. But after delivering all those papers last Saturday, an automobile is looking better and better."

"As good as that pretty little lady you have hanging on your arm everywhere I look?" Morgan wore a lazy smile.

Here it comes. "Very funny. She's a friend. And she's helping me with the twins."

"How neighborly." Grant leaned in to the fence and patted the mare's neck. "By the time I realized that Jenny was a friend, I'd already fallen in love with her. She had me right in the palm of her hand. The rest is history."

"Casey and I were a little different," Morgan said. "Hard to say no to a lady outlaw who could outshoot me any day of the week."

Zack continued to listen to his aging uncles talk about their sweet wives while gray streaked their hair and a paunch extended over their belts. Mama and her brothers were an odd set. Hard to believe Aunt Casey had really been an outlaw, and she could still hit a target better than anyone in the county. Aunt Jenny was a very proper lady from Ohio, except for an occasional outburst of temper. Mama might be small, but she'd take on the whole town if she believed she was right, and her aim wasn't bad, either. Zack's father had been a sheriff, but after his death, Mama had fallen in love with a preacher from the Ozarks—Brother Whitworth.

His thoughts crept back to Thanksgiving dinner with Chloe. Lovely failed to describe her. He could have feasted on her dark eyes and glowing peach skin. Her wide smile made him hot and cold at the same time. Obviously his uncles detected something more than friendship, but did Chloe share in the same feelings? After he'd made her mad about his talk with Jacob Barton, he decided to be as gentlemanly as possible.

"Zack, where are you?" Grant asked.

He swung his attention back to his uncles, who were having a good time at his expense. "I didn't hear you."

Grant laughed much too long. "We figured as such. We remember how a pretty girl can capture your attention and hold it until you think you'll go insane. Ah, love can squeeze the life out of you."

Were his feelings so transparent? "What did you say? I'm listening now. My mind must have been on the newspaper."

"If you think I believe that, I'd best be prescribing something that brings out the truth in a man." Grant nudged Zack's shoulder. "I asked when you were planning to bring the twins in for a checkup."

Zack cringed. He should have taken care of a health examination the moment he arrived in Kahlerville. Miss Scott had suggested it, too. "I'm sorry. Time gets away from me, and I understand that's no excuse."

"Bring them in before dinner tomorrow evening. They look healthy, but let's be sure. They're a little pale, but the Irish usually are. What is their last name?"

"Sullivan. When the adoption is final, I'll put Sullivan as Curly's middle name. Not sure about Charlie yet. Perhaps after her mother—Maureen. Actually, their given names are Carlin and Caitlain. Got their nicknames on the streets."

Zack caught a glimpse of the twins playing with Stuart near the barn. At least they were in sight and not ready to pull a crazy stunt like they had at his parents' ranch. That escapade nearly got them killed and gave him a heart attack. His gaze lingered on the house. He wondered what the women were talking about. It amazed him the many topics that appealed to women and how they all had something to say. Before he went to New York, women-talk between Mama and Lydia Anne nearly wore him out. Sure glad Chloe was quiet.

∽◌◌◌∼

"So how long have you and Zack been seeing each other?" Zack's pert aunt Jenny Andrews smiled and raised a dainty cup to her lips. "I can see he is quite fond of you."

Strange, Chloe hadn't detected those feelings, just an interest. And she didn't want to read anything into his actions and words that would cause her pain later. "I think you must be mistaken. I work at the boardinghouse where he and the children live. At times I've been privileged to help him with Curly and Charlie." Her voice trembled a little, and she smoothed the skirt of her worn blue dress.

Bonnie Whitworth set her cup on a small round table. "I believe he is as smitten with you as he is with the twins."

A hopeful thought, but Chloe dare not believe a word of it. If she dwelled on her feelings for Zack, he might learn of them. He'd said they were friends working on a possible closer relationship, and he'd admitted to being jealous over Mr. Barton. Still, she needed to be cautious or risk a broken heart.

"Leave the poor girl alone," Casey Andrews said, her auburn hair picking up the light from the parlor window. "If she and Zack want

141

to keep their romance a secret, then we'll all act surprised when we hear the announcement."

What announcement? Mercy, how did she respond to these women? Mrs. Whitworth, Casey, and Jenny did not attempt to conceal their amusement.

"I—I assure you that Zack's time is spent between the newspaper and his children. Anything else is purely coincidental."

Unfortunately, her explanation only increased their mirth.

"Now, now." Mrs. Whitworth raised a small hand to silence the women. "We must stop embarrassing Chloe. My dear, I do apologize for making you feel uncomfortable. This family does love to tease, but only because we like you. Your relationship with Zack is none of our concern." She nodded at Casey and Jenny. "Right, ladies?"

"Of course," Jenny said.

Casey nodded. "I well remember how we teased my poor children when they were courting. Chad never knew what to say, but Lark kept her romance a secret until she and her new husband became engaged."

Mrs. Whitworth frowned. "It's a wonder either of those two married. Where are your daughter-in-law and daughter?"

"Tending to their babies," Casey said. "My beautiful grand-children. Bonnie, you'll feel exactly as I do one day." She smiled at Chloe.

You can talk about something else any time.

"Now that we've laughed at Chloe's expense, let's change our topic of conversation. Am I hosting Christmas this year?" Mrs. Whitworth asked.

"I believe it's your turn," Casey said. "I'm simply excited about all my children and precious grandbabies being home again."

"And Michael Paul will be home from seminary." Mrs. Whitworth turned her attention to Chloe. "You will love our Christmas celebration. Actually, it begins in the afternoon of Christmas Eve."

Whatever did they do for all of that time? "In the afternoon?"

"Before church services, we take meals to those who are less fortunate, ill, or alone, and we invite all of them to come to church. After the Christmas Eve services, we carol through the streets. Once we've sung every Christmas song we know—sometimes twice—we end up at Grant and Jenny's for coffee, hot chocolate, and sweet potato pecan pie. It's very late when we finally arrive home. Some of us have been known to stay up all night, preparing for the next day." Mrs. Whitworth pointed a finger at Casey. "Anyway, with children in our midst, it will be wonderful. And we so want you to join us."

Chloe had mixed emotions about how to respond. She knew they didn't intend to embarrass her, but she sensed the color rising in her cheeks. Were Zack's uncles teasing him about her? She set forth her best manners. "If Zack should ask, I would consider it an honor to be a part of your celebration."

"Perfect." Mrs. Whitworth rested her cup on the table. "I think it's about time we rounded up the men and children to gather pecans."

Chloe instantly rose to her feet. Anything to avoid the topic of her and Zack. Yet when she considered the women's friendship, their faith, and their strength, she was glad to be with them. Perhaps Zack would invite her for Christmas. How very grand. His gesture would be the nicest gift she had ever received.

Lydia Anne entered the parlor. "Mama, I think Chloe should spend some time with me. You and Aunt Casey and Aunt Jenny are asking her awkward questions." The young woman reached for Chloe's hand. "I'll rescue you from these women. I may have to teach you how to handle

CHAPTER 15

Hank stepped into the newspaper office on Saturday morning, blowing on his hands to warm them up. "December 2, and it's already downright cold out there."

"I agree. I'm having Curly and Charlie wear their jackets until the stove warms up the place." Zack glanced at his two sleepy children. For some reason, they'd had a difficult time waking up this morning. "They received a good health report from my uncle Grant yesterday, and I want to keep them that way."

"Poppy, I want to sleep some more." Charlie rubbed her eyes.

"Didn't you two sleep last night?"

Charlie looked at her brother, then at Zack. "I had a bad dream."

She had his complete attention. "Charlie, why didn't you wake me up?"

"I was afraid I'd make you mad. So I woke up Curly."

Zack sighed. "I'm your poppy. When you have a bad dream, wake me up. We'll talk about it. Why did you think I'd be mad?"

"Because you have to work at the newspaper on Saturday, but we don't have school."

"Sweetheart, I'm a poppy who loves you all the time. I want to know when you're frightened."

She nodded. "Can I lie down?"

"My little one, the floor is cold and dirty." Frustrated, Zack wished one more time that he had his own home with blankets and quilts to keep his children warm. Everything belonged to the boardinghouse. Although Chloe never refused him a thing, he still had to request extra blankets or towels. He started to pull off his jacket.

"No need to do that," Hank said. "I have a couple of old blankets in the back of my wagon, but they're clean. We could make a fine bed with them. I left my coffee mug out there, and it's half full." He ruffled Curly's head. "The missus made biscuits stuffed with sausage links this morning. I figure in another couple of hours, these two will be hungry."

"I hope there's a few for me." Gil waved and went back to reading ad copy. His lanky frame looked out of place on the small stool.

"I do, too. Thanks, Hank," Zack said. "I really need to find us a house. At least Lydia Anne could keep them for me at a home rather than all the way back to Mama and Dad's ranch."

"I've been meaning to talk to you about that." The older man winked. "We'll talk later. Right now, let's warm up your young'uns. Have you made coffee?"

"I will right now."

Hank disappeared only to return in a few moments. "Somebody

stole my blankets, the biscuits, and my mug." Irritation rolled off his tongue like bitter medicine. "I'd best not catch him." He swung his attention to Gil.

"Did you try to pull a prank on me?"

"No, sir. I have two babies at home. I wouldn't risk losing my job because you broke both my arms and legs for stealing." He grinned, then sobered. "Stealing from a man's wagon is downright low."

Zack stepped outside to take a look for himself. Hank couldn't have misplaced all of those items. Sure enough. The back of the wagon was bare. Puzzled, he recalled the missing food at the boardinghouse and how Chloe and Simeon had begun placing a plate of food on the windowsill. It disappeared regularly, but no one ever saw the culprit.

Back inside the newspaper office, he made his way to Hank. "We have a thief, and I wonder if it's the same fellow who took food from the boardinghouse."

"You'd think if he was cold and hungry, he'd ask for what he needed." Hank stoked the fire in the stove. He sighed and wiped the soot off his hands. "Sounds like a good news story to me."

Zack snapped his fingers. "We could give it a human-interest angle. Someone homeless and hungry is hiding in our midst. In the spirit of 'Peace on earth, good will toward men,' we want to extend hospitality to whoever is destitute."

"Makes for good reading," Hank said. "I hope whoever stole the food and blankets will confess and stop this nonsense. We have charitable organizations in town that will supply those things."

Gil cleared his throat. "I agree. The fellow who's doing this sure is doing a good job of keeping out of sight. Almost like a ghost."

"A ghost, Poppy?" Charlie asked. "The newsboys used to say a ghost would get me and Curly."

Zack shot a quick look at Gil, who mouthed an apology. "He's teasing. Gil is talking about a man who could steal and not be seen like a ghost."

The twins nodded their heads as if they understood.

"Zack, why don't you take the young'uns to your folks?" Hank said. "Me and Gil will hold down things until you get back."

"Good idea. I'll do that. When I return, I'll start the article about our town's hungry thief. We could run it next Saturday. Oh, and we need an article for the community tree-trimming event next Saturday, too. First thing I'll do when I get back is load up the wagon with today's papers and get them delivered this afternoon."

"I'll load the wagon and do the deliveries," Gil said. "That will get me out of a little hot water over my comment."

Zack laughed. "I'll take that deal." He headed for the door. "Come on, you two. How about a day with Grandma and Grandpa? You can rest there." He hoped his parents didn't mind. Taking advantage of them was the last thing he wanted to do. Once he found a place to live, he could hire a woman to help him. But he knew he didn't want anyone to care for Curly and Charlie but Chloe. *Am I being selfish, or do I love her so much that I want only her to tend to the twins?*

❧⟲◉⟳❧

Mr. Barton bustled through the front door of the boardinghouse with a huge box in his hands. The breakfast dishes had been cleared away, and Chloe busied herself by straightening the dining room. As she scrubbed this morning's pancake syrup from the chairs and tables, she saw from the corner of her eye Mr. Barton set the box on a clean table.

"Miss Weaver."

She whirled around. Lately she dreaded to see the man coming. She never knew if he would be the businessman or the man who wanted to court her. Men could be impossible to deal with.

"It may only be the second of December, but I'm ready to decorate for Christmas. Want to give me a hand?" A smile reached from one ear to the other.

She'd rather deal with the businessman.

"That sounds like fun."

"These ornaments and other decorations were in my attic. I placed them up there a few years ago after my parents died." He started to pull the items from the box. "I haven't gone through these. Thought a woman's touch was in order."

Chloe set her wash bucket and wet cloths by the kitchen door and stepped over to examine the contents of Mr. Barton's box. He carefully unwrapped a couple of delicately etched glass ornaments.

"Mr. Barton, you may not want to use the glass ornaments. They look costly and could easily get broken."

He held up one and allowed the light from the dining room window to reflect on the etchings. "Mother loved these. She had them shipped from England."

"All the more reason to keep them at your home."

"But if folks can't see their beauty, then why have them at all?" He laid the ornament back on the table and smiled into her face.

"How would you feel if one of them were broken?" She pointed at the box. "There are plenty of other things for us to use."

"We do have children staying with us, but I will speak to Zack about making sure they do not enter the parlor without him and that they do not touch any of the decorations."

The comment stung, but the rebuttal threatening to leave her mouth was not appropriate. "I would not want your parents' heirlooms damaged for any reason. I suppose if caution is taken—"

"And we do not light the candles on it."

"Yes, of course. Perhaps Kahlerville will soon have electricity, and in the future the candles could be eliminated."

His gaze lingered a bit too long on her face. "I will make certain my home will be the first to have electricity. Would you like that, Miss Weaver?"

She wasn't going to fall prey to his insinuations. "You mean the boardinghouse?"

"Not at all." His face grew serious. "I mean my home that I would like to share with a deserving young woman. A home that I'd like nothing better than to fill with the sounds of children and the warmth of love."

His words were spoken barely above a whisper, and they touched her not because she had any feelings for him but because his loneliness aroused pity. She swallowed the emotion swirling throughout her. Mr. Barton could be strange at times, even exasperating, but he did have a good heart. Oh how she wished the right woman would walk into his life this very minute.

"Mr. Barton, I—"

He raised his hand. "Please, don't say a word. I fear I may have been so transparent that you've become embarrassed. I apologize for speaking my heart. You've said we barely know each other, but I see in you what I long for—a beautiful woman with a heart of pure gold. Do not discard me, dear Chloe. Give me an opportunity to win you. If you would only let yourself love me, I'd spend the rest of my days showering you with everything you could ever desire."

At that moment, if she could have forced herself to embrace him, she would have. Even so, a relationship based on compassion for a wounded heart was doomed to fail. "You have found these affections for me in such a short time. And—"

"I have no doubts."

Dear Lord, what do I say to him? He sees how Zack and I have started to feel for each other. He also sees how Simeon and Miss Scott are growing closer. Can you bring him the right woman?

"Mr. Barton—"

"Jacob."

She took a deep breath, yet her hands trembled. She couldn't bring herself to pick up an ornament or attempt to change the topic of conversation. Neither could she bring herself to call her employer by his first name. "I am deeply indebted to you for giving me this job. I've told only one other person this—Miss Scott—but I didn't have a place to live after my father died in the fire. She would have taken me in, but pride stopped me. You not only gave me a wonderful job, but you gave me a place to live and food to eat." She took another breath. "If gratitude alone was the foundation for affection, I would welcome your interest in me."

A mixture of pain and tenderness swept over his face. "Your honesty has reached that part of me where few people ever go. I cannot cast away the thought that you might one day care. Now, let's not trouble each other with these hard words. I want to decorate the parlor and the dining room with festive decorations."

"Thank you. Yes, let's make the boardinghouse look positively beautiful."

"And we can discuss the kind of cookies you and I will persuade Simeon to bake for the schoolchildren."

"I'd like that very much. Have you discussed the Christmas Eve dinner for the needy with him?"

Mr. Barton laughed. "Not yet. I already know that I will have to put on an apron and peel potatoes that night."

She joined in his laughter and realized all she could do for Mr. Barton was continue to pray that God put a special woman in his path who would love him with all of her heart.

"I'll enjoy helping."

"And I understand why."

One day soon, she'd tell Zack about those agonizing days before she found work at the boardinghouse. And if he ever asked about Mr. Barton, she'd tell him about this conversation. Chloe had no desire to play each man against the other. Her affections were Zack Kahler's alone.

CHAPTER 16

As soon as Sunday dinner was over at the boardinghouse, the twins twisted in their seats and began to pick at each other. Zack cast a disapproving look their way, but he understood their restlessness. And he wanted them to store up happy childhood memories that lived forever in their little minds, not just remembrances of times they were scolded for being children.

"Are you two in a rush to play?" Chloe asked. They'd shared lunch together, which had become a routine for them on Sundays. "You two are wiggling like a couple of worms after a rain."

"Grandma and Grandpa are coming by to take us to the ranch." The words seemed to spill from Curly's mouth. "First, they were having lunch with Uncle Grant and Aunt Jenny."

"Oh, I see. And you're excited?"

Charlie had a habit of widening her eyes in a way that spoke fathoms. "Yes, ma'am. We're making ginger cookies. They're Poppy's favorite. Grandma says he used to eat them all before Christmas, and there'd be none left for anyone else."

Zack laughed. How did his two little rascals know he always got the last ones? "I admit those are the best cookies around. I love dunking them in coffee."

Curly sat straighter in the chair. "And I'll love dunking them in my milk."

"We both will," Charlie added. "Miss Chloe, what are your favorite cookies?"

She pressed her finger to her chin. "I like the big sugar ones."

"Oh," Charlie said. "Like the ones Mr. Simeon makes?"

Chloe nodded. "But I've never had a ginger one. So before your poppy eats them all, save one for me."

Zack pulled out his pocket watch. "Grandma and Grandpa will be here soon. Why don't you two go on up to the room and change your clothes? But walk. You don't want to disrupt the other guests. I'll be along in a minute to help."

As soon as the children walked from the dining room, Zack heard their little feet scamper up the stairs. He leaned across the table. "Take a walk with me once I'm a free man?"

"You should rest. You could visit old friends. Read. And you want to take a walk?"

"Only with you."

A smile lit up her face. "Where?"

"Anywhere. Everywhere."

Chloe laughed. If given the opportunity, he'd make sure she laughed every day for the rest of her life. "In that case, the answer is yes. I need to get a sweater. It's gotten chilly."

"In New York, this is summer."

She tilted her head. "I've heard your stories about the cold in New York, and I don't like them at all. I think I'd freeze up in September and not thaw out until June."

Not if I were there to keep you warm. "Don't forget snow. You can shovel it, make snowmen with it, and roll it into balls for snowball fights."

"No thanks, Mr. Kahler. I prefer weather best suited to sensible folks." Her eyes sparkled with a hint of teasing.

"Ah, sensible folks? I'll remember that next summer when we're all begging for a little shade."

"I think I'm in trouble."

A smile appeared to surface and remain there whenever he was with her. "You'd best fetch your sweater, Miss Cold-Bones, and I'll check on my children."

Upstairs in their room, he found the twins on their bed exchanging punches.

"That's enough, you two, unless you want to spend the afternoon in bed."

"No, sir," Curly said from his position beneath his sister. "But Charlie told me I was stupid."

"Stupid?" Zack frowned at the little girl. "Your brother is not stupid."

"Yes, he is." She pulled her little dress over her leg and swung it over Curly's back. "He can't do arithmetic as good as me. And he can't remember how many calves are at Grandma and Grandpa's ranch."

"I'm not so sure I remember," Zack said. "Am I stupid?"

Charlie gasped. "No, Poppy."

"Then neither is your brother. Apologize to him this instant, or you will stay here. And then you will hug him and tell him you love him."

The twins' eyes widened.

"Your choice." Zack pressed his lips together to keep from laughing at their horror.

Charlie whirled around and lightly embraced her brother. "I'm sorry, and you aren't stupid."

"And?" Zack raised a brow.

"And I love you."

"Curly, it's your turn."

The little boy looked like he might become ill, but he obeyed. *Will these two ever settle down?*

Shortly thereafter, Curly and Charlie grasped the hand of a grandparent and climbed into a buggy. They'd return at twilight for the evening service. Both the children and the grandparents, along with Lydia Anne and Stuart, would be exhausted.

"How many miles are we walking?" Chloe asked once the buggy disappeared.

"Ten or twenty."

"Are you teasing me, Zack Kahler?"

"Every opportunity I get." He offered her his arm. When she linked hers into his, he realized Chloe needed to be linked with him forever. He'd loved the little girl and now the woman. But it was too soon to express his love and desire for them to have a life together. She might think he'd lost his senses if he gave away his heart before a proper amount of time had passed. Or she might think he simply saw her as a woman to care for Curly and Charlie.

What if she refused him? What if she saw their relationship as friendship and nothing more? If she had any doubts, he intended to chase them away every chance he got. Then there was the problem with Jacob Barton. Zack repeatedly told himself he had nothing to worry about, but Jacob had his sights on Chloe, and the businessman was determined.

Chloe and Zack walked on past the cotton gin. The factory had expanded as well as so much of Kahlerville since the railroad increasingly brought industry to the town. He loved progress, but there were times when he also enjoyed the way things used to be. Perhaps age had crept into his bones.

The peacefulness of nature pulled the stress of his work and problems from his thoughts. A family of crows called to each other. Cows bawled from a neighboring farm. A dog barked. Evergreens provided rich color among the barren trees. A few had leaves of red and gold, not at all like he'd seen in December in New York. Under a blue, cloudless canopy, nature proceeded to tuck late fall into a winter's rest.

Chloe pointed to an area ahead where a lazy creek wound its way through overhanging brush. Zack used to fish in these clear waters when he was younger.

"I lived there for a while." The sadness in Chloe's voice sparked his attention.

Puzzled, Zack glanced about for a shack or at least a shelter. "There's nothing there."

Her features saddened. "I know."

"Do you really want to tell me about this?"

"I believe I need to." She drew in a deep breath. "It will explain my fear and dislike for Eli Scott. Even though he has left town and his situation is sad, I can't seem to forgive or forget what he's done.

I realize God is upset with me for my hard heart, but I can't seem to push away the memory of what Eli has done—both to me and the twins."

He patted her arm, which was still linked with his. How comfortable it felt to have her beside him. He wanted to take away all of her heartache, but only God had the ability to bring peace to her soul.

"When my pa died in the fire, all I had left were the clothes I wore and his old nightshirt."

"His nightshirt?"

She nodded. "I had it hidden in the loft of an old barn near the house. Sometimes when Pa was drunk, he insisted I spend the night in the barn. When I walked home after church the night of the fire and saw the house in flames and folks attempting to put it out, I retrieved the nightshirt. Later the barn burned, too. As bad as things were between Pa and me, the shirt is all I have left of him except for his hunting knife, which I found among the ashes. I used to think he was cruel for making me stay in the barn, but later I realized he may have wanted to protect me from the anger that often accompanied his drunkenness." She paused for a moment. "I had no place to go and was too proud to ask for help. I wandered to the creek and stayed there until I found the job at the boardinghouse."

His insides churned at the thought of his Chloe living in such poverty out in the open wilderness. The memories of the hungry little girl played across his mind. Just as he had in his youth, he wanted to take care of her forever.

"What did you eat?"

She shrugged. "Apples mostly. It doesn't matter, Zack. I have a good job now. What I wanted you to know is during that time,

Eli discovered where I was living and attempted to. . .force himself on me. Before I graduated from school—although he's younger—he had attempted the same behavior. Anyway, I had Pa's hunting knife and knew how to use it. When I pulled it out, he took off. But he threatened to—" She paused, her face flaming.

"No need to say anything else. I understand. Miss Scott did well to dismiss him from school. If he had hurt the twins again, I would have lost my temper. Badly. I have no use for bullies."

"As much as I despise him, I think Eli hurts from what his father has done to him, and that makes him want to do the same to others."

"You are probably correct. I'm not the least bit surprised Miss Scott tried to keep him in school. At least there his father couldn't beat him."

"I wish Eli would let her know where he is. She thinks he may have joined the army." Chloe sighed. "She also thinks the army's discipline might help him."

Zack remembered when he was twelve years old and ready to fight the world. "Discipline, if applied correctly, makes us strong and useful people."

"Pa was both strict and harsh. And then there were times when he surprised me. Tenderness would sound in his voice, or he'd say how much I looked like my mother. I think because I resembled her I was a constant reminder of what he'd lost." She shrugged. "I think I'm talking too much."

"Not at all. I want you to be able to tell me everything." He started to say more, but he didn't want to frighten her away. A thought occurred to him. "Chloe, do you see how God has taken care of you?"

She didn't reply, but her gaze toward the creek with the over-hanging cypress trees revealed her troubled thoughts about God.

Oh Lord, I know my Chloe believes in You, but she's been hurt. Touch her with Your Spirit and show her Your love.

"I see why you and the twins have so much in common: poverty, hard times, hunger. Why didn't you seek out my parents or Miss Scott? They would have taken care of you while you searched for a job."

"I don't believe in charity. I'm a grown woman and can take care of myself."

"My dear Chloe, I wish I'd been here to help."

"I would have been too proud to accept it."

"Now, Chloe."

She lifted her chin. "Pride is a sin, and I'm guilty. But. . .I also see that what I experienced gives me a better understanding of the twins' life before you adopted them. When I stop to ponder the situation, I believe I'd go through my childhood all over again if only to help Curly, Charlie, and you." She sniffed and smiled. "I love those two little ones, and I'm thankful to be a part of their lives."

Do you love me, too? How I long to hear those words, but I can neither tell you my heart nor ask you for yours until my children are secure.

CHAPTER 17

Zack hitched up the wagon feeling as excited as a kid on Christmas Eve. While Curly and Charlie were in school, he planned a surprise that his children would least expect. A bit of a chill had settled in since Thanksgiving, and he loved every minute of it. Not that he missed the snow and cold from New York, but cooler temperatures gave him a lift in his walk. Mama had found jackets for the twins among Stuart's and Lydia Anne's old things, which would do fine until Christmas when Zack produced outer clothing as part of the twins' gifts. Oh, he had to watch himself, or he'd be guilty of spoiling those two by responding to every whim that crossed their minds.

He inhaled the scent of burning wood and noted smoke rising from the chimney tops of the local homes and businesses. The Christmas season had arrived, and he may have found the best gift yet in a dark-haired, dark-eyed woman.

Four miles outside of town, on the way to Morgan and Casey's ranch, a house and fifty acres stood empty and for sale. In truth, Hank's mother had lived there until she passed on a few months ago. He'd offered Zack a good deal—if he liked the house and surrounding acreage.

"Here's the key. Spend all the time you need. Everything is in place as Mother left it. Nothing's changed, but the missus and I cleared out the food and cleaned up a bit. You'll find dishes in the cupboard and fresh sheets on the beds. There are two wells on the place and a creek that flows across the back. Underground springs have always greened up the fields and pasture. A pretty place if I do say so myself. But me and the missus have enough to take care of with our own farm."

"How's the acreage currently used?"

"Pecan trees in one corner and apple trees in another. Also a farmer has been leasing some of the land for the past few years to grow cotton. It's a good little income."

Zack well remembered the white, two-story farmhouse and the trees positioned on both sides of it. He remembered the in-season flowers that made the property look inviting. Already he could envision a rope swing for the twins. With his insides fluttering like a lovesick schoolboy's, he anticipated that the inside of the home would be as welcoming as the outside. If his and Chloe's relationship continued to grow, he'd propose in the proper time, and they'd have a home together with Curly and Charlie.

Here I am making plans without setting foot inside the front door. Slow down, Zack. The last time you rushed into things, you ended up in the middle of an adoption.

But that wasn't such a bad decision, either.

A house for Christmas. Couldn't put it in a stocking, but he and the twins could fill it with love. The boardinghouse had quickly grown old, especially with two high-spirited six-year-olds who needed room to run and play. They were becoming more difficult to manage and control. Many of the guests complained about the noise, and Zack did all he could to keep their voices down. The poor kids had moved from the streets where they had to shout to be heard to a cramped room where everyone expected them to be quiet. His children were as frustrated as he was.

Miss Scott encouraged Curly and Charlie to run around the school-yard after tutoring and before she escorted them to the boarding-house. At least for a little while, their energy had a chance to spread its wings and fly. Simeon always had little chores for them, and he rewarded the two with cookies, corn bread, or biscuits and always with milk.

Zack chuckled. Love was in the air between Miss Scott and Simeon, and all because of Curly and Charlie. Come to think of it, they were in the middle of him and Chloe.

Zack reined in the horse and hitched it to a post in front of the house. Jumping down from the wagon, he took in a panoramic view, wanting to experience every inch of the farmhouse and the picture-perfect land. The trees, two of them statuesque oaks and one a red maple, offered a crisp cool breeze. Ah, to the left of the house was an oak with the perfect branch for a rope swing. Summer heat would be tolerable with these ancient shade trees. He'd need a dog, too. Not a real big one, but one whose care would teach the twins responsibility. A small, red-roofed barn sat behind the house. Hank had said the loft had a few bails of hay in case the twins found themselves with a pony. Not yet, but maybe next spring. To the right of the property lay an apple orchard, and to the left stood a pecan grove. Knowing Hank, the trees were healthy and big producers.

Zack made his way back to the front porch and climbed the steps. The porch reminded him of the old parsonage where his grandparents had lived until their deaths a few years ago. Even a rose trellis climbed up one side of the porch. A twinge of bittersweet memories crept through him as he remembered his white-haired grandfather, who preached the love of God and the justice of His ways. And his grandmother, who was the strongest woman he'd ever met. They had died within weeks of each other, as though one couldn't bear the joy of heaven without the other.

A door slammed, alerting him to the fact he was not alone. Had someone broken into the home? He'd learn soon enough. He hurried down the front steps and around to the side of the house to the back porch in time to see a man race across the barnyard toward the pecan trees.

"Hey, you. Hold up there. What are you doing on private property?"

The man kept right on running. Hopefully Hank's house hadn't been ransacked. The thought angered Zack. Too many people in this world would rather take from others instead of working and earning a decent living. He watched the man disappear into the trees and hoped he didn't return.

Before entering the house, Zack realized it was destined to be his no matter if a vandal's mischief required some repair. The window on the back porch wasn't broken. How had the man gotten inside without a key? The knob to the back door opened with a click. Holding his breath, he stepped inside. *Lord, let this home not be vandalized. And*

Lord, let this be the home for my family.

Zack blinked in the shadows. The curtains had been tightly drawn, keeping out the light of day. He used both hands to pull back the curtains first from one window by a small table and then from another window over a sink and pump. Light streamed in and illuminated a large kitchen. *Plenty big enough for a growing family.* For a moment, he allowed himself to daydream about Curly and Charlie doing homework at the table while Chloe prepared a meal.

Standing in the middle of the room, he glanced in all directions. His nose detected the scent of burning wood. The wooden cookstove felt warm, and when he inserted the lifter to pull out the lid, a log smoldered inside. Someone had been cold for sure. The fellow he'd seen running from the house must not have had anything to cook. Zack replaced the iron lid. Nothing was broken. The man had been staying here with no thought of doing damage. Zack's heart softened a bit. How sad. His thoughts about the fellow began to carry more compassion. Chloe's confession of living by the riverbank after her father's death played across his mind. Sometimes folks didn't have a choice. Maybe he'd learn who that homeless man was and could offer assistance. Once he returned to the paper, he'd discuss his findings with Hank.

To the right of the kitchen was a bedroom where a bed covered with a quilt stitched in the wedding ring pattern seized his attention. He'd recognize that pattern anywhere since his mother presented every newly married family member with one of those. How odd that Hank's mother chose that quilt for her bed. But if Chloe married him, it would be perfect for their room. He laughed aloud at his thoughts. So far, everything was perfect.

He proceeded back into the kitchen and stepped under a wooden arch leading to the dining room, where a round, claw-footed table and sideboard stood ready for folks to share a meal. After drawing back the heavy drapes, he viewed a wall of windows in an L-shape that displayed the pastures of the adjoining farm. Peaceful. No sounds from noisy boarders or goings-on in the streets. But if he closed his eyes, he could hear the sound of bubbly laughter from his children. *His children. Curly and Charlie Kahler. No, Carlin and Caitlain Kahler.* He didn't mind Curly's nickname, but oh how he wanted to call his little daughter Caitlain.

From the dining room doorway, he took in the parlor. Blankets and sheets covered a sofa and two chairs. A piano evened out a corner. Zack sat on the piano bench and stroked the keys to an old childhood tune. The mere sound reminded him of how much he missed his brother Michael Paul. They'd have some fine visiting at Christmas. His brother could out-sing the birds in the trees while playing the piano like a concert pianist. Michael Paul would make a fine preacher. Zack's gaze focused on a brick fireplace where wood was piled high on the hearth. He remembered all the love that centered around the fireplace when he was young. Now he could create that same atmosphere for his children.

From the foyer, Zack climbed a wide, winding staircase upstairs. Two bedrooms on one side and two on the other. Plenty of room for the eight children he wanted one day. One of the beds had a wrinkled quilt. Had the man slept there?

He'd take the house. He had no reservations. It would be a stretch for a man who believed all purchases should be made in cash, but he could do this and have it paid and mortgage-free in five years. What a Christmas surprise for the twins. That meant only a few more weeks at the boardinghouse, but he'd make sure the twins' extra time was spent in doing more constructive things than sliding down the staircase on their behinds and pretending to be birds in the dining room.

Again, he laughed aloud, and the sound reverberated around the house. God had a sense of humor. Nothing about Zack's life of late followed any traditional rules. Watching the events of the next few months would be an adventure for sure. He pulled the key from his pocket and was careful to lock both doors.

I can't wait to show Chloe. I hope she loves the house as much as I do.

CHAPTER 18

Chloe waved at Miss Scott as the older woman entered the boarding-house with the twins in tow. From the looks of the two children, tutoring must have been hard today. Miss Scott carried a bundle wrapped in brown paper. Most likely the clothes she'd promised.

"Good afternoon," Chloe said. "How was school this beautiful Wednesday?"

"Hard." Curly frowned. "But Miss Scott is helping us learn stuff."

Chloe muffled a laugh.

"She's helping us learn a lot so we'll be smart like the other kids." Charlie glared at her brother. "And we're making a Christmas present for Poppy. Two of 'em."

Chloe gasped, then smiled. "Two Christmas presents for Poppy? I can hardly wait to see them."

"We can tell you." Curly glanced at his sister. "Right?"

" 'Course. Miss Chloe won't tell Poppy." Charlie peered all around. "We don't want anyone to give away our secret."

"I agree." Chloe stepped from behind the registration desk and bent down toward the children. "No one will hear down here. We'll whisper. And I promise not to tell anyone."

"I'm making a book about when he found us in New York and what happened." Charlie tilted her head. "We don't want him to ever forget."

"Uh, Charlie, I want him to forget that we took his wallet." Curly pointed a finger at his sister's face, much like she often did to him.

Charlie touched her finger to her lip. "Yeah, but good things happened after that. Remember how Grandma says God takes bad things and makes them good for all the people who love Him?"

"All right. Can I tell my present now?"

Charlie nodded.

"She forgot to say that we're making Christmas ornaments out of paper. They're stars, and we've colored them."

"Oh, that sounds beautiful." Chloe watched the light dance in his eyes and ruffled his red curls.

"And I'm making him a little bird feeder," Curly said. "I put peanut butter on a pinecone and then put seeds on top so the birds won't get hungry."

"Magnificent. He will be so happy with your gifts. Your poppy is a very lucky man."

"We love him very much. Do you love our poppy, too?" Charlie asked.

How did Chloe answer that question?

"I do." Miss Scott said. "Everyone who meets your poppy loves him. I loved him when he was a little boy the same age as you and Curly."

Chloe smiled up at the woman with all the gratitude she could muster.

"Poppy says he's not perfeck—"

"*Perfect*," Charlie said. "The word is *perfect*. You have to work harder on sayin' words right."

Curly narrowed his eyes and clenched his fists. "I was tellin' Miss Scott and Miss Chloe that Poppy says we should always try our best."

"Very good," Miss Scott said. "These two have had a long day." She smiled at Chloe. "I think I will give them a little game to play at the table so you and I can chat—if you have a few moments."

"I am all caught up right now." She hugged the twins, then stood to face the dear woman. "I believe Simeon has corn bread and milk left from lunch. Would you like for me to get the twins a piece with a little butter and honey?"

"Yes, please," they chorused.

"A splendid idea," Miss Scott said. "But I'll take care of getting the corn bread for Curly and Charlie. You finish up what you need to, and then I have exciting news to share."

I think you'd rather see Simeon, and he'd rather see you than me. Chloe went about her duties, knowing Miss Scott's retrieval of corn bread and milk would take a little time. She closed the ledger and placed it in its proper spot. How she longed for Miss Scott and Simeon to find real love together.

Once Miss Scott had the twins nibbling on corn bread and working on a word game, she ventured into the parlor and admired the beginnings of the Christmas decorations.

"Once we have a tree up and decorated, we'll have the parlor finished."

"We, as in you and Mr. Barton?"

Chloe sighed.

"Is the situation any better?"

"Actually, it's worse. The sad part is I feel sorry for him. I can't be what he wants. Neither do I want to be. Yet without a doubt, I'd like for him to find happiness."

Miss Scott frowned. "I'm so sorry. Zack will simply have to propose so Mr. Barton can turn his affections elsewhere."

Chloe nearly choked. "Miss Scott, I hardly think a proposal will happen in the near future. Maybe never."

The woman clicked her tongue. "I am quite observant, and you two are deeper in love than anyone I've seen in a long time." She handed Chloe the bundle. "These are the items I promised you. I think you'll be pleased. I learned from a good source that the clothes came from another town. No need to worry about a contributor seeing you wear her dresses and making you feel uncomfortable."

Chloe's face warmed. "I am grateful. Thank you for thinking of me."

"I'm thinking of you all the time. You are very dear to me, and your happiness gives me much pleasure." Miss Scott folded her hands in front of her, and a smile lit her face. "I have exciting news. My niece from Dallas is coming to spend Christmas with me."

"You mean Rose, the daughter of your oldest brother?"

"Yes, she's a few years older than you and is almost finished with college. She'll graduate in the spring."

"I remember your telling me about her. Doesn't she plan to be a teacher?"

Miss Scott laughed. "Just like me. I'm so proud of her, and to think she plans to spend a few weeks with me at Christmas. It's a shame Eli has taken off. Rose might have been able to help him." She wiggled her shoulders. "My obstinate brother, Eli's father, claims his son is better off dead. Can you imagine? I told him he was wrong and cruel to say such things. Then he asked me to leave his home and not come back."

"I'm really sorry."

"Oh, one day the Lord will grab my brother by the collar and straighten him up."

Her response startled Chloe. Normally the woman chose her words carefully before she spoke. "Everyone deserves a second chance."

"With my brother, it will be his one hundredth. Never mind. I wanted you to know how excited I am about Rose's visit."

"When is she coming?"

"Sunday the seventeenth, and she'll stay until the twenty-ninth. I want all my friends to meet her. She is quite lovely and very intelligent."

"That sounds delightful. I'm looking forward to putting a face and a smile with all the wonderful things you have said about her. And you will have someone to share Christmas with you."

Miss Scott leaned closer. "Simeon and I wanted to spend part of Christmas Day together, but we were concerned about the lack of a chaperone."

Cupid has definitely sent his arrows into Simeon's and Miss Scott's hearts. "Your problem is solved, and I'm glad your relationship is blossoming."

Miss Scott's cheeks flushed. "I've told Rose about Simeon, and she is anxious to meet him."

Chloe blinked back the tears. "Of all the people in this town, you are the one who most deserves the contentment and joy of love."

"I'm not sure what I deserve, but I am happy. Simeon thinks. . ." This time Miss Scott's eyes welled up.

"What? You can tell me."

"Well, he thinks my idea of adopting a street child or two from New York is grand. He says I look as young as a girl. And. . .if our relationship continues to grow, we could raise the children together."

Chloe put her arms around the older woman's shoulder, and in the next moment, both of them were weeping.

"We need to stop this," Miss Scott said. "I feel rather foolish."

"I will if you will."

"All right." Miss Scott pulled away from Chloe's embrace. "I'll count to three, and then we stop this silly schoolgirl nonsense. I never thought a man would make me feel so giddy." She took a breath. "One, two, three."

Chloe reached inside her pocket for a handkerchief and dabbed her nose. "It didn't work."

Then they laughed until they cried again.

In the privacy of her room, Chloe sorted through the bundle of clothes from Miss Scott. One green dress and a black skirt and white blouse seized her attention. They were nearly new. Quickly she shed her worn dress and slipped into the deep green one with its slightly gored skirt and full sleeves. It fit nicely. How wonderful to have something new and different to wear for Christmas. She removed it and folded it on her bed. Next she tried on the shirtwaist blouse and skirt. The two also fit. These could be worn to church beginning this Sunday. Included in the bundle were much-needed undergarments and a pair of shoes. Tears filled her eyes. Zack would never have said a thing about her lack of clothing, but she always wondered what he thought. No matter. With these additional garments, she no longer had to concern herself about embarrassing him. Slipping her feet into the button-up shoes, she noted they were a tiny bit too large. Better that the shoes were too big than too snug, causing her feet to ache. She could wear thick woolen stockings for a better fit.

Holding up the green dress, she thought how grand Christmas would be when she presented herself in something that befit Zack's family. Not that they cared what she wore, but Chloe did. She wanted Zack to be proud of her. And now he would be.

∾◦⟨୨⟩◦∾

"The deed to the Carroll place is clear and ready for you to take over." Morgan handed Zack the document. "I've had my eye on that piece of property for a long time. Glad to see you're able to buy it."

"The twins and I need to leave the boardinghouse before we're thrown out. But it's a surprise. I want to tell the family at Christmas."

"Fine by me. Mind if I tell Casey?"

"I'd expect you to." Zack tapped his finger on the desktop in Morgan's office. "Uh, you and Aunt Casey have been married a lot of years."

"We have, and every one gets better. Good times are a gift from God, and the hard ones move us closer to Him and to each other."

Zack's pulse quickened with the thoughts rolling through his mind. "You two always seem so happy."

"And we are. The worst part of our relationship was before we were married. No secret my sweet wife was an outlaw, and I was a bloodthirsty fool. Once we realized what God had purposed for us, we put Him at the head of our lives." Morgan tilted back in his chair. "All teasing aside with you and Chloe, let your old uncle give you a little advice. Children will gray your hair and cause you to wonder what you were thinking when you had them—I suppose that has already happened with the twins. Difficult times with money and differences of opinion will cause you two to fuss. But remember, if God has put you together, then grab on to her hand and fight for your love."

Zack smiled. "Thanks. I have no idea what the future holds for Chloe and me, but I've loved her since she was eight and I was fourteen."

"Bonnie said she remembered your bringing an extra sandwich every day to school for a little girl and protecting her from school kids who teased her about being part Indian and poor."

"That was Chloe."

Morgan laughed. "I think you swallowed the hook way back then."

"I believe so."

"Zack, I could loan you the money for the mortgage, and—"

"No thanks. I appreciate the offer, but I want to go through the bank. The idea of owing a family member money sounds like the start of bad feelings."

Morgan smiled. "You sound like your father. I'm sure he's looking down from heaven and proud of you. Before I forget it, I expect to hear any day from the judge in New York. I'd think he'd want the matter settled with the twins before Christmas."

"That would set my mind at ease."

"All you'd need then is a weddin' ring for Chloe."

The teasing was heading his way, and he might as well be prepared for it. Zack fished for the right words. "Not yet. I want the twins good and secure first. They lost both parents and had no one to help them through the grieving. They were abandoned, cold, and hungry. As much as I love Chloe, I can't risk frightening them with the prospect of losing my love. I know the Bible says my first priority is to be my wife, and I will honor that. But until I am married, I am devoted to my twins."

Morgan reached out and grasped his hand. "God bless you, Zack." Then he grinned. "I'm glad you're not denying what you feel for Chloe."

Zack laughed and pointed a finger at him. "I need to get back to the newspaper office and see what Hank and Gil are up to."

"I thought after our heart-to-heart talk, you'd volunteer to help me decorate the outside of my office to look like Christmas or at least offer free advertising at the paper."

"Right. Painless Lawyer?" He dipped his hands into his pockets and turned them inside out.

CHAPTER 19

Saturday afternoon, with the temperatures in the low sixties, Zack escorted his children to the town square where everyone gathered to trim the town's tree. Morgan and Casey had planted the nineteen-foot fir twenty years ago for this very purpose.

"Poppy, this feels like summer, not winter." Curly shrugged off his jacket. "I'm gettin' hot."

Charlie proceeded to remove her jacket, too. "I'm glad we live where it's warm."

Zack took Curly's jacket and helped Charlie with hers. "Me, too. I don't know if I could handle slipping on any more ice."

Their little faces shot up at him, and he laughed. "I'm teasing."

Young and old crowded around the tree and talked until Mayor George Kahler quieted them.

"Good afternoon," he said. "And Merry Christmas."

The crowd echoed back their greeting.

"We have some wonderful folks here today who have volunteered to lead groups for decorating the tree. Miss Scott will take the children over to my right. My lovely wife is assisting a group of our older citizens to the left, and I'll help the rest of you. Or should I say, the rest of you need to help me."

Laughter rose from the crowd.

"I promise not to sing. But you folks can sing every Christmas song you know. Some of you already have your storefronts ready for the season, and they look real fine." He pointed to the new pastor of the Lutheran church. "Pastor Schwamp, I sure like the nativity scene in the front yard of your church." He gestured to three tables behind him. "Enjoy the fun, and when we're finished, several of our ladies have cookies and cakes for us. Jacob Barton from the boardinghouse has brought hot apple cider, too. The town here appreciates his hosting a dinner on Christmas Eve for those in the community who have no family to share Christmas with. Anyone who wants to volunteer at the boardinghouse restaurant that evening, please see Jacob."

Had Jacob closed the feed store for today's event? He surely hadn't closed the boardinghouse so Simeon and Chloe could attend the community tree trimming. Zack shook his head. It was wrong to condemn the man because he shared an interest in Chloe and she couldn't be here due to work responsibilities. *Jacob is a good man, despite our love for the same woman. Forgive me, Lord.*

Gathering up Curly's and Charlie's hands, Zack wove his way through the crowd to Miss Scott. He'd already offered to help her with the little ones, and he was beginning to wonder if he'd taken leave of his senses. The twins were hard enough to handle without a dozen more children. He also wanted to take note of what the other folks were doing to trim the tree so he could mention it in an article. Gil was here with his oldest child, while Hank was working hard at the paper with the typesetters.

A glance around the crowd revealed at least fifty Kahler cousins. George and Ellen's children were busy. On the eve of Christmas Day, he and the twins would be at George and Ellen's for a Kahler celebration. Curly and Charlie would be worn out the next day after all the festivities, but Lydia Anne had promised to come early the morning after Christmas so Curly and Charlie could rest while Zack worked.

He missed Chloe. She should be here beside him. He peered around and saw Jacob at the edge of the crowd talking to some folks. The man must have sensed Zack's gaze, for he nodded in his direction. Zack waved and turned back to the task of stringing popcorn. He snatched up a handful of it and a long piece of string that already had a needle attached to it. Bending to the twins' level, he showed them how to carefully insert the needle into the popcorn kernel without sticking themselves. Each child was to contribute to the decorations and be assured they'd played a vital part in trimming the town's community tree. Large baskets of fruit, nuts, paper ornaments, and tinsel set on and around the tables for young and old. The adults were in charge of wiring the candles on the evergreen branches, and all hoped the tree didn't go up in flames. Oh for the day when Kahlerville would have electricity. The Christmas trees in New York looked grand with the lights and trimmings.

"Don't you wish Grandma and Grandpa were here?" Curly asked.

"They are." Zack pointed to a far group.

"Goodie." Charlie jumped up and down. "Grandma. Grandpa."

"We'll head over there as soon as we're finished here."

"Why couldn't Miss Chloe come?" Charlie tilted her little round head.

"She's working."

The little girl frowned. "Next to you, I love her best."

Zack understood. With Chloe, the four of them were complete, as close to a family as they could be right now. He stood and waved at his aunt Ellen. When he turned his attention back to the twins, he saw Jacob had walked his way.

"Afternoon, Zack. Who's mindin' the paper?"

He forced a chuckle. "Hank, of course. I wonder why I'm even there."

Jacob stuffed his hands into his trouser pockets and teetered on his heels. "You're doing a good job." He greeted the twins and helped one with a stubborn popcorn kernel. "Miss Weaver would have enjoyed this celebration. It's a shame I needed her at the boardinghouse. Doesn't give me much of a choice but to hurry back and tell her all about it. In fact, I'll take her one of those sugar cookies."

"Those are her favorite," Charlie said. "She told us."

"Wonderful. Then I'll make her very happy." He nodded at Zack.

You remind me of a schoolboy trying to make me jealous. Unfortunately, it's working. "That's real nice of you. I'm sure she'll appreciate your thoughtfulness."

"I'm doing my best, and in my opinion, my effort is working."

Zack smiled. "But let's see who makes it to the finish line."

"I think you and Chloe should take a stroll." Mama's eyes sparkled, and Zack knew her matchmaking plans were falling into place. Sunday dinner was eaten, the twins were outside playing, and conversation filled the afternoon. "Travis and I will keep Curly and Charlie busy."

Zack didn't want to pass up an opportunity to have Chloe all to himself, even if it meant Mama would claim all the credit if the relationship progressed as he hoped. Yet he refused to take advantage of his parents. "Are you certain? Doesn't Dad need to rest before services tonight?"

"Shoo. We love having those two to ourselves."

"All right, but we won't be gone long." He caught Chloe's attention. "I could show you where a tornado nearly whipped up Dad, Michael Paul, Lydia Anne, and me. I was twelve at the time, and it's where I made some big changes in my life."

A smile lit up her face. "That's a story I want to hear. You were twelve, and I was six—not even in school."

"Good, because I wasn't the nicest kid around."

"It's a good story," Mama said. "I remember the twister and how fear nearly made me crazy. It was also when I realized how much I loved Travis."

"Another reason for me to hear this story."

"Ah, but I was a dashing young man in those days." Dad chuckled and winked at his wife. "Bonnie couldn't resist me."

"That's not exactly how I remember it," Zack said. "The tornado happened before you got a haircut and shaved off your wild beard. None of us knew what you looked like—other than a wild mountain man."

Dad waved away Zack's statement. "Insignificant detail."

Zack caught Chloe's attention. "If we don't leave, we're going to be caught here listening to old stories."

Zack excused himself to find the twins and give them instructions about good behavior. He peered in every direction but didn't see them. When he called, they didn't answer. Dread washed over him. They had headed to the barn in search of the kittens. Zack remembered the cat tail-tying incident, but they knew better than to pull that kind of stunt again.

"Curly, Charlie, where are you?"

"Here, Poppy, behind the barn."

Zack walked behind the barn to discover his twins were covered in cow manure. Curly and Charlie were down on their knees, squashing it between their fingers.

"What on earth are you doing?"

"Making mud pies," Charlie said. "They smell a little, kind of like Simeon's coffee, but they'll get hard in the sun."

"Get out of there this instant."

The two peered up at him and then looked at each other.

"Are we in trouble?" Curly asked.

"Deep trouble," Zack said. "Out of there now, and then we're heading to the watering trough."

Charlie scratched her nose, spreading the mess over her cheeks. And their clothes? Would he ever be able to get them clean? He didn't know where to start.

An hour and a half later, Zack and Chloe finally set off down the road toward his favorite fishing hole and the site of special memories.

"You can start the story about you and the tornado any time. Wait a minute. What did you mean by Brother Whitworth looking like a mountain man?"

When he swung a look her way, her eyes appeared to dance. Did she have any idea how those dark pools affected him?

"Dad came to town to take over Piney Woods Church when my grandfather, Reverend Rainer, decided to retire. He'd come from the Ozarks and looked quite the part."

"I see. Hard for me to picture Brother Whitworth anything but clean shaven."

Zack laughed. "He was a sight, but it was his heart that everyone loved."

"Both of your parents are dear. I sincerely appreciate their inclusion of me in family gatherings."

"And what would I do without you?" Had life ever been without Chloe?

"Have no one to listen to your stories?"

"Oh, Miss Weaver, you are witty today."

"I'm just getting ready for the tornado story."

"I already said I was twelve years old, angry that my father had died, and a bully. In fact, Mama threatened me with military school if I didn't learn to behave. I picked on Michael Paul and Lydia Anne and anyone else who got in my way. I was ready to run off somewhere. In the meantime, I kept getting into one scrape after another. About that time, Brother Travis came to town. He set out to do all he could for the church and the community. So when he learned about all the trouble I was causing, he offered to take me in." Zack laughed. "The town's new preacher had no idea what kind of trouble I could cause, which is why I tend to be a little hard on the twins. I don't want them to ever get into that kind of trouble."

"They need so much love, and you are doing a wonderful job as a father."

"Thanks. I may need you to repeat those words when they have me in a 'twister.'" He caught another of her smiles, and his pulse sped away like a racehorse. "Dad devoted much of his time to me. He schooled me and taught me what it meant to be a godly man. And when false accusations about me sprang up, he defended me. Loved me when I needed a trip to the woodshed. But it took a twister to get my attention."

Chloe's face paled, and he wondered where her thoughts had gone.

"Did I say something wrong?" he asked.

"Oh no. The boy you are describing is not the man before me."

"I'm a miracle of God. Without Him in my life, I'd be behind bars or hung by now."

"I'm glad you allowed Him to work in your life. If not, I'd probably be with—"

"Jacob Barton?"

She frowned, then a slight smile tugged at her lips. "Maybe." She took a deep breath. "What happened in the twister?"

Zack pointed to the river. "Farther down there and beyond those trees, there's a clearing at the bottom of the hill. Dad had taken Michael Paul, Lydia Anne, and me fishing. It was one of my better days. Actually, Dad's way of living was starting to sink in. A storm rushed in, and we headed back to the ranch. But we hadn't gone far before Dad and I saw the twister. We climbed down from the wagon, let the horse loose, and ran for safety. At the foot of the hill, Dad had us lie down, and he covered us with his body. The roar of the twister echoed in our ears. I thought I was going to die, and I wasn't proud of the things I'd done. I asked God to save the others but to take me because I didn't deserve to live. I wanted so badly to live my life for

Jesus, but my day of reckoning had come. I asked Jesus to save me, and I acknowledged Him as Savior and Lord. The twister touched all around us, the sound like a roaring train, but we were safe. When it was over, I told Dad and my brother and sister what happened. I apologized for the things I'd said and done to them. Then we hurried back to Mama, afraid she might not have survived. It was a real tearful reunion. A few months later, Dad asked Mama to marry him."

He heard Chloe sniff.

"Hey, this story has a happy ending."

"I know. That's why I'm crying. It's beautiful and. . ."

He took her hand, and they continued to walk over crackling brush. "Is there something you need to say?"

Silence greeted him, but he chose not to prod her.

"I think my faith needs some help." She stepped over a fallen log. "When I was six and my mother lay dying, she called me to her side and said it was important for me to love Jesus. She was going to live with Him soon and didn't want me to cry. She said her new home in heaven was a beautiful place, and she wanted me to one day live with her there. She prayed with me and assured me that I would one day live with her and Jesus in heaven. I thought I knew what she meant, and I loved my mother dearly, so I told Brother Whitworth what Mama told me to say. He baptized me."

"I remember. The baptismal creek was real warm. August, I think."

She smiled. "When I was a few years older, Miss Scott and I talked about what happened then. I prayed again, because that time I really understood what it meant to love Jesus and have Him rule my life. I've never doubted my faith, but I've been angry with God for a long time. I believed He despised me because of my Indian heritage—caused others to ridicule me, my mother to die, and then my father to burn in such a horrible death. Listening to your story and how God brought you peace has touched me. I—I don't want to feel this way ever again. When we get back to the ranch, I want to talk with Brother Whitworth about getting rid of my bitterness. It's past time I did something about it."

Zack lightly squeezed her hand. "I thought you might be hurt, and I certainly understand why. God loves you, Chloe. He doesn't want you filled with pain."

She nodded and blinked. "Since you've come back to Kahlerville, I've seen the hand of God. You've taken the challenges presented to you and not given up." She shrugged. "You've inspired me to seek the Lord more closely, and for that I thank you. And I also see how God has used my past to help with the twins. I've been homeless without a parent, and so have they."

"You humble me, Chloe. I don't know quite what to say."

She shook her head. "Nothing. I said what was on my heart."

"Living our faith is never easy but always so worth it to please our God."

She pulled a handkerchief from her pocket and dabbed her nose. "Did you find it difficult living your faith in New York?"

"I found it hard at times, but as soon as I made a decision to get involved with a good church, it became easier. My problem was a young woman who caught my attention. She attended the same church, and we saw each other socially for a short while. Later I learned she was searching for a wealthy husband, and I no longer held her interest. I thought I'd never be the same again, but I realized she didn't have a relationship with the Lord." He paused. "I wouldn't have found you if God hadn't stepped in."

"I'm very glad." Her cheeks flushed, and she glanced away. "But I'm also thankful to hear you aren't perfect."

He laughed. "Oh, we are a good pair. Interesting how each one of us has a story. The twins are learning abut Jesus, and I pray for the day when they desire a personal relationship with Him."

"I think it's a legacy that we all have to pass on to the next generation."

Would she be a part of his legacy? He hoped so. He'd have said more about the importance of her life linked with his, but he didn't feel this was the right time. Not with her needing to talk to his dad. His desires sounded selfish, and she needed to have peace with God first before she could contemplate a life with Zack.

CHAPTER 20

The next morning before the boarders were ready for breakfast, Chloe reflected on the previous day with Zack and her conversation with Brother Whitworth. He'd helped her walk through her bitterness in a way that not only brought her peace but also helped her to understand herself a little better.

Before yesterday, trusting Zack was a whole lot easier than trusting God. She loved Him. She served Him, but she couldn't help but think that He'd created the universe, sent Jesus to this miserable world, then sat back and watched. After all, where was God when her mother died? Where was God when her father drank himself to death and burned down the house? Where was God when Eli Scott threatened her? She asked all of those questions of Brother Whitworth, and he responded honestly with scripture.

She stared out into the empty dining room with serenity filling her whole being and her heart lingering on a brighter future. Zack could have turned from her in disgust yesterday when she confessed her problem with God. Instead, he listened and helped. She was so very fortunate to have his attention. She paused in her thinking. She wasn't fortunate but blessed.

Lord, thank You for moving me to give You all of my life, even the parts that hurt. Help me to love You more. I forgive my mother for leaving me and Pa for grieving so that he despised me. I also forgive Eli and all those who have hurt me with their words and actions.

"Are you all right, Miss Chloe?" Simeon asked in the kitchen doorway. "I sure hate to see you crying."

She whisked away the tears. "I'm fine. Simply happy."

"Love will do that to you. Makes you laugh and cry at the same time."

"Yes, it will. I'm grateful to God for all the things He's given me."

"I'm powerfully beholding to Him myself. Me and Miss Annabelle, well, I think we've found something special. Here I am an old man and clearly as in love as a schoolboy."

"I think Miss Scott is partial to schoolboys." She gave him a teasing smile.

He laughed. "I'm glad she finds me fittin'. I want to make her happy every day of her life."

Chloe started to weep again but hastily sent the tears on their way. "I hope everything works out for you. You and Miss Scott are two of the finest people I know." She smiled through watery eyes. "I keep dreaming for myself, but I'm afraid I'll wake up and find out these past weeks with Zack haven't been real—as though I've been living in a fairy tale." For once she didn't care if Simeon knew her heart had toppled for Zack Kahler. "He's been my Prince Charming ever since I was a little girl."

Simeon scratched his whiskered jaw. "I've listened to Miss Annabelle read those fairy tales to Curly and Charlie. Seems to me that every one of them is about someone fightin' to make sure life is good. Yer a fighter, Miss Chloe, and whatever comes your way is nothin' for the blessin's the good Lord is planning to give you."

Maybe Simeon should have been a preacher instead of a cook. No surprise at all that Miss Scott had found her one true love in an apron-covered, weathered old man who had more sense than a dozen other men put together.

One more time Zack proofread the article about the local thief who had captured the hearts of various townspeople. He liked the human-interest angle and the idea that the community could be forgiving of the thefts this time of year as long as the culprit came forward and apologized. Used to be Zack wouldn't have felt so strongly about a situation in which someone was knowingly breaking the law, but the fact the fellow had stolen food and blankets—and Hank's mug of coffee—had *unfortunate* written all over it. In any event, the power of the press was about to push the public and the thief toward reconciliation.

He turned his attention to the article:

> *Jacob Barton reports that a loaf of bread and a pecan pie were stolen from a windowsill at his boardinghouse. However, when he instructed his cook to place a plateful of food on the windowsill daily with a note requesting the plate and utensils*

be returned, the fellow obliged and has continued to comply.

"We do not want to press charges," Sheriff Jackson said. "This is the season of the year when the community wants to reach out and help others. If the man steps forward and identifies himself, all will be forgiven."

Zack continued to the end of the article with a final request for the man in question to make himself known.

"Are you ready with your article?" Hank asked.

"Yes. I'd like to place it on the front page. With all the problems of the world and right here in Kahlerville, a bit of peace on earth and goodwill toward men sounds good. What do you think?"

"I agree. We'll print it and see what happens. I'm sure someone in the community would give the fella a job."

"Would you have written an article like this?"

Hank laughed. "Yes, if the idea had popped into my head. You worry too much, Zack. You're doing a fine job. Brought in new advertisers and changed up the looks of the paper."

"You'll tell me when I'm starting to make a big mistake?"

Hank pushed back his cap and rubbed his bald head, swirling newspaper ink where once hair had grown. "That's my job. I may not have ever worked for a big, fancy newspaper, but I can tell what folks want to read."

"I know you suggested a morning edition of the paper instead of an evening, but I can't do that and still take proper care of the twins."

"They come first. Someday when they're grown, you'll wish you had a dirty face to scrub or two extra mouths to feed."

"I want to make up for all those things they missed in New York.

Every day I wake up and ask God to show me how to love them more. Guess I'm sounding a bit silly."

"Not at all. You sound like a man who loves his children."

"I'm that man." Zack chuckled. "With all of this responsibility, I wonder why folks have kids."

Hank laughed and clasped a hand on Zack's shoulder. " 'Cause we don't know any better."

CHAPTER 21

Chloe righted a crooked candle on the parlor fireplace and adjusted a red ribbon on the Christmas tree. The holiday decorations draped throughout the boardinghouse had seemed to put everyone in a festive mood. And that appeared to enhance the romance unfolding in the kitchen between Simeon and Miss Scott. The twins were with the two lovebirds in the kitchen now. Chloe guessed the children kept Miss Scott and Simeon from speaking their true hearts. How sweet and dear for the older couple to find love in their graying years. She felt a twinge of jealousy when she had to hide her love from Zack. At least she was free to lavish her affections upon Curly and Charlie.

She giggled. The last time Miss Scott had walked the children back to the boardinghouse after their tutoring session, Simeon had arranged for all of them, including Chloe, to have cookies and milk in the kitchen. Curly had wrapped his little arm around Miss Scott's ample waist and leaned his head against her.

"Miss Scott," he said, "you are looking more beautiful than Miss Chloe's Christmas tree."

"You don't say." Miss Scott beamed. "That deserves a hug."

"Watch it, little man." Simeon shook his finger at Curly in feigned annoyance. "You're makin' me jealous."

"You just have to say nice things to court a fine woman," Curly said. "After Miss Scott goes home, I'll give you some pointers."

Miss Scott gasped and her face reddened.

"And how would you know about courtin'?" Simeon appeared to swallow his amusement. Goodness knows, nothing seemed to embarrass him.

"By listening to Poppy talk to Miss Chloe. I think he practices."

Chloe held her breath. Mercy. She sensed the color flooding her cheeks while Simeon enjoyed a good laugh. Soon laughter rang through the entire downstairs. Chloe hastily excused herself and made her way through the kitchen, the dining room, and on to the front desk. She straightened the newspapers from Saturday and brushed away an invisible speck of dust.

Now as she reflected on the moment, Curly's innocence and frankness had been amusing. Did Zack have conversations with the twins about her? She'd sure like to be a fly on the wall if he did. The bell jingled above the door.

"Good afternoon, Miss Weaver."

She recognized Mr. Barton's voice and offered a smile. The tender way he looked at her always made her uncomfortable. "Good afternoon."

"The scent of pine is nearly intoxicating, don't you think?"

"I rather enjoy it."

"Oh, so do I. Fills me with the holiday spirit." He walked through the dining room and stood at the entrance of the parlor. "You've created a breathtaking Christmas."

"Thank you, but I believe you helped."

"Can we have a word?"

"Certainly." She followed him into the parlor.

"Christmas will be here in less than two weeks, and I was wondering if you had plans."

She'd feared this awkward situation. "Yes, sir. I do."

"With our boarder, Zack Kahler?"

Her heart thumped against her chest like the tale of a scared rabbit. "Yes, sir, with him and his family."

Lines plowed across his forehead. "You're spending quite a bit of time with our guest."

She moistened her lips. "I help him with his children when my duties here are completed. I have not shirked my responsibilities."

"I never doubted that you had or would. It's Kahler who has no respect for working hours. He even speaks to you in the dining room, pulling you away from the other guests."

"I—I apologize." Heat assaulted her face and neck. "I'll speak to him about that matter."

"I do not blame you for his indiscretion. But it looks to me like there is something more going on than helping him with those two rambunctious children. Aren't you concerned with what people will say? A lady's reputation can never be righted once it has been tainted."

Chloe's temper quickly rose. Yet she swallowed a retort that would have placed Mr. Barton's words where they belonged—in the outhouse—and gotten her fired. "I don't feel I am behaving inappropriately. Mr. Kahler and I attend church and family functions together."

"I've seen you a time or two together when it wasn't Sunday or with his family."

Was he spying on them? If she had not made plans for Christmas with Zack, the conversation with Mr. Barton would not be happening. He'd be thrilled about making plans with her. Another handful of remarks crossed her mind. Still, she held her tongue.

"Mr. Barton, can you fault my work or say that I am not dedicated to my position here at your boardinghouse?"

"Your work is flawless. You and Simeon keep this place running smoothly." He sighed and moistened his lips as though preparing to give a speech. "I worry about gossip among the boarders and the townspeople. Meddlesome gossips can destroy you."

Chloe took a deep breath. "I assure you that my words and actions are above reproach."

Mr. Barton studied her for several long moments. "For your own good and for the excellent reputation of this establishment, I forbid you to spend any time with Mr. Kahler or his ill-behaved children."

"And does this include the hours I am not in your employ?"

"Yes, it does." His eyes narrowed as though she were an ill-behaved child.

"And if I refuse?"

"I will have no choice but to dismiss you."

Chloe's heart plummeted to her stomach. Was this the same man who had flirted with her? Did he think she'd ever want to spend time with him after his unreasonable demands? "I see you give me no choice since this position is my livelihood."

He smiled. "I'm glad you see things my way. I'll let you know about Christmas plans."

She gasped. How dare he bully her into spending one more minute in his company? Had he been taking lessons from Eli Scott?

By the time she saw Zack in the dining room for dinner, her anger had shifted to despair. She must tell Zack about the ultimatum. But if he lost his temper and argued with Mr. Barton, she might lose her job. Without her current position, she'd be on the streets and at the mercy of those who had preyed upon her before. Every time she considered walking across the room to Zack's table, tears pooled in her eyes, and her love for him crowded out good sense.

She caught Zack's gaze, and he smiled. From across the room, his eyes radiated what his lips had not spoken. Surely, she was not mistaken; he did care. Didn't he? Had he seen the same love in her eyes? Mr. Barton stood in the hallway separating the dining room from the parlor. Without a glance in his direction, she knew he watched her every move.

She skirted around the tables to where Zack and the twins sat and pasted on a smile. "Good evening. How is everyone?"

"Very well, thank you," the twins chorused.

"Your manners are getting better and better," she said.

"Poppy makes us practice." Charlie's red curls bounced.

The little girl's charm broke through Chloe's resolve, and she blinked back the tears.

"What's wrong?" Zack asked. "Don't tell me 'nothing,' because I see it in your face."

She pressed her lips together. If alone, she'd have wept. "Can we talk later, after the twins are asleep?"

"Of course. I see Barton is staring at us. Does he have something to do with this?"

"Yes."

Zack frowned, but she didn't acknowledge it. Maybe he would have a solution when they talked.

She turned her attention to Curly and Charlie. "I'll bring your dinner right out. Simeon has made gingerbread for desert." She breathed in so deeply that her chest hurt. Would love always feel this way?

"Goodie," Curly said. "I'll eat all my veg'ables."

Usually the time spent after dinner sped by until she had a few hours to spend with Zack or read in her room, but tonight she heard every beat of the clock. Its incessant click seemed to rattle through her brain. Not even Simeon or the excitement of Christmas eased the heartache threatening to destroy all she held dear.

Finally, the boardinghouse hushed, and her work was completed for the day.

"I trust you will have a pleasant evening," Mr. Barton said with his hat in hand. "I assume you will need to tell Mr. Kahler tonight of your new terms of employment."

"Yes, sir." She forced herself to sound as cordial as possible when she wanted to tell him what she thought of his "terms of employment." His mandate rose from selfishness. For that matter, her response rose from the same thing. Praying for a man when she wanted to tell him what she thought of his manner of garnering her affections was close to impossible.

"Good evening, Miss Weaver. I will see you tomorrow."

How did his conscience allow him to make such demands? With a rise of fury, she fought asking him how he hoped to sleep tonight.

Once he left the boardinghouse, she swallowed the emotions

tugging at her body. How easy it would be to crumble, but that would solve nothing. Instead, she prayed for guidance and asked for forgiveness for all the ugly thoughts firing across her mind.

Waiting for Zack proved more difficult than rehearsing the right words for telling him that she could no longer enjoy his company. Brother Whitworth had told her trials made one stronger in their faith, and her strength lay in holding on to God's hand.

She heard the stairs creak, and without looking up, she knew it was Zack. She needed a clear mind to talk through this insurmountable problem, and maybe between Zack, herself, and God, they'd have a resolution.

"Tell me what's wrong, Chloe," he whispered.

She glanced up and nearly wept. How handsome and in control. How many years had she loved this man? How many years had he solved the problems in her life, but this time she needed to offer some answers.

"You look miserable." Concern lines etched his brow. "What has Barton done to upset you?"

The sound of his voice settled on her like the warmth of a gently crackling fire on a chilly night. But this night she feared nothing would chase away the cold and emptiness inside.

"He's forbidden me to see you or the twins. Not only here at the boardinghouse, but also during the times I'm not working."

Zack banged his fist on the registration desk. She started and sensed the color draining from her face.

"He has no right to make such demands. Is he still here?"

"He left a few minutes ago." She touched his arm. "Anger won't solve this. Aren't you the one who insists on having God direct our lives?"

He paused and glanced away. Finally, he swung his attention her way. "I'm sorry for that explosion. What's Barton's reason?"

She attempted to settle her nerves. "He said that it looks inappropriate—gossip could result from us being seen together. Since you live here, he fears for my reputation and that of the boardinghouse."

Zack stared at her long and hard. "I don't believe one word of it. He's not giving up on you, is he?"

"I—I don't think so." She shook her head. "I know he's not."

"Jealousy."

She shrugged.

"I'm not the least surprised. When I paid a call on him about advertising in the paper, he made clear his interest in you." Zack sighed. "Guess I didn't want to believe it or that he'd make it nearly impossible to see you."

She swallowed twice to get rid of the lump in her throat. Neither time worked. "I cannot lose my position here."

"I understand." His voice softened. "I will not let him do this to you—to us." He reached for her hand. "Don't you know how much I care for you? I couldn't any more stop seeing you than stop breathing."

Her eyes brimmed with the tears she'd sworn not to show. How she'd longed to hear his words of tenderness, but not like this. Forced. As though he had no other choice. "What can we say or do to change his mind?"

"To begin with, I wanted this to be a surprise, but I found a house. The twins and I can move in sooner than planned."

"I don't think that will make a difference."

"I want to talk to him." He paused. "Unless you prefer his company, then—"

"No." Was she too forward?

He smiled. "All right. I'll find a way to persuade him. In the meantime, I'll move my children this weekend to their new home." He lightly squeezed her hand. "Would you trust me to work out this problem? Will you trust God to guide me in a solution?"

Before she had talked to Brother Whitworth and rededicated her life to God, she wouldn't have been able to respond properly.

"Trust God," Zack whispered.

Chloe took a deep breath. "I am. . .completely." Suddenly, she was conscious of his hand still holding on to hers.

"I can't imagine you not in my life." He opened his mouth, then quickly closed it. "There's so much more I'd like to say, but it's too soon."

She heard all she needed to believe her dreams were coming true.

CHAPTER 22

The next morning while walking to the feed store, Zack did his best to think admirable things about Jacob Barton. But the faster his pace, the more ungodly thoughts tossed about in his head.

Consider his good points.

Jacob planned to feed the poor on Christmas Eve, and he'd provided regular plates of food for whoever was hungry in town. But that had nothing to do with how he'd treated Chloe. Last night, Zack had prayerfully considered how to handle the man, but this morning, he'd wakened as angry as a nest of agitated hornets.

He stopped abruptly on the boardwalk and took a deep breath to calm his soaring temper. Bursting through the door of the feed store like a charging bull said little about his faith or his ability to handle confrontation successfully. He wanted Chloe to trust that he would follow God's leading. And God would not be happy if he broke Jacob's nose.

"Don't ruin all the good things you've accomplished in town," Hank had said earlier. "You asked me to tell you when you were about to make a big mistake. This is it. Jacob Barton is not a man to have on your bad side. A lot of folks like him—he's fair and helps others."

"I agree with all you're saying. He does have a right to state how his employees deal with the boarders, and I don't want Chloe neglecting her job." Zack paused. "But forbidding her to see me at all is unreasonable. Some prayers would help."

"You got 'em. And I think moving into my mother's house before Christmas is a good idea."

Lord, I need some help here. There's a reason this has happened, and I don't have to know why. But if you'd control my fists and put the right words in my mouth, I'd be greatly obliged.

When Zack entered the feed store, Jacob was alone. If the place had been crowded with customers, he might have had a few more minutes to calm down.

"Morning," Jacob called from the rear of the store. His back was turned while he stacked bags of grain. He faced Zack and started.

"Morning, Jacob. I'd like a word with you."

The man strolled toward him, his face tinted red. "I figured you'd be by to see me. If this will be short, I can give you a few minutes."

Do not jump into this. "How is the ad working out for you?"

"Customers have made good comments about it. Not sure if it has brought in any money yet. I'll keep you informed."

Zack nodded, carefully choosing his words. "I wanted to notify you that I'll be moving out on Saturday. I bought a house."

"I'm sure a home will be easier for you and your children."

"Originally I planned to move a few days after Christmas, but circumstances have caused me to consider otherwise."

"As in my business decision regarding Miss Weaver?"

"Precisely. I understand you have a problem with Chloe and me keeping company."

Barton narrowed his eyes. "I don't like gossip. Not good for business—either about my boardinghouse or my employees."

"And what have you heard?"

The knot in the man's throat bobbled. "Nothing yet. I'm trying to prevent any. Prudence is the word here."

"Am I correct in assuming that Chloe accompanying me to church and family functions is against your policy?"

"Correct."

"Then I'll move as soon as possible. My absence should relieve the minds of any folks who are concerned about propriety. I wouldn't want my relationship with Chloe to cause any problems for her or for your establishment. And I apologize for occupying her time during working hours."

Jacob released a sigh that the whole town could have heard. "Are you saying you intend to continue escorting Miss Weaver to various functions and activities?"

"I do."

"She has many duties and responsibilities at the boardinghouse. I must be able to contact her at a moment's notice."

Zack bit his tongue to keep it from getting him into trouble. "I believe she is relieved of duties on Sundays."

"I've invested in teaching her about the boardinghouse and keeping books. With so many boarders, I may need her seven days a week."

"You've just lost three of those boarders."

"Miss Weaver has better things to do than spend time with a man and his children."

"I don't understand." Zack knew exactly what Jacob was inferring, but the man had to state the real reason for his displeasure. "Why do you object to my seeing her?"

Jacob frowned. "You already know the answer to that question. When I want something, I do not give up easily."

"In regards to a young woman's affections, she should make her own choice. Don't you agree?"

Silence stood as a wall between the two, and Zack chose to keep it that way until Jacob decided to end the uncomfortable silence.

"Very well. These are my terms for Miss Weaver to be seen in your company. You cannot visit her at the boardinghouse during working hours."

"Am I and my children barred from the dining room, as well?" Would the man prefer to lose money than allow Chloe to speak to Zack and the twins?

"Not barred, Mr. Kahler, only limited to enjoying a meal at my establishment and promptly leaving. I am assuming you would want your children partaking of their meals in their own home."

Perhaps Zack should propose to Chloe this evening and avoid all of this nonsense. "I would never interfere with the parameters of her position."

"I'm glad we understand each other. Furthermore, Miss Weaver will meet you outside of the boardinghouse on Sunday mornings for church or any other activities."

Now Zack was ready to tear into him. "Trust me, Barton. Your limitations with Miss Weaver regarding our relationship will not stop the inevitable."

The man smiled. "In this instance, you may be wrong. I have plans to win her, so be prepared."

"And you think by disappointing her and making her angry that she will see you as a good man?" Zack stuffed the accusations ready to take flight. "Chloe is a smart woman, and she will see through any deceit."

The door to the feed store opened, and a farmer with two young boys ambled in.

"I'll be right with you. Zack here is just leaving." Jacob smiled and stuck out his hand. "Glad you came by."

"We did have a pleasant conversation. I'll make sure my bill is paid in full on Saturday when I move out."

Zack shook Jacob's hand—rather limp at that—and tipped his hat to the farmer. Jacob Barton had no idea how a man in love could fight for his woman.

That evening after the dining room had thinned out to only a handful of people and while Chloe cleared the tables, Zack turned to Curly and Charlie.

"I have a surprise for you. This was supposed to be saved until Christmas, but I can't wait any longer."

"What is it, Poppy?" Charlie asked. "I thought only children couldn't wait till Christmas."

"Oh, we adults are that way, too."

Curly shook his head. "I'm keeping my Christmas present for you hidden until the right day. Miss Scott has it."

Zack laughed at the little boy's seriousness. "I can't hide this one. It's too big."

"Please, tell us," Charlie said. "It can't be a pony, because we don't have a place for it to eat or sleep."

Zack glanced at Chloe, who balanced a stack of plates. She must have sensed his gaze and smiled at him. Yet her features still held the sadness of the prior evening.

"I found us a wonderful house with some land. The furniture is already there from the previous owner. Even the dishes are in the cupboard. All we need to do is move our clothes and things from the boardinghouse."

Charlie clapped her hands. "A real house? When can we see it?"

"We're going to see it tomorrow after school. And we will move into it on Saturday afternoon once the papers are delivered." He leaned in closer as if telling a secret. "I bet Miss Chloe would like to see our house on Sunday after church."

Chloe stepped closer, her hands full of dirty plates. "I can help you then, too."

"I was thinking more of exploring the pecan grove or the apple orchard."

"Pecans and apples?" Curly said. "I love 'em."

She laughed. "I think you'll have plenty of both. The apples are probably done for the season."

"I have an idea," Charlie said. "Miss Chloe could come live with us."

Chloe whirled around, her face aflame, and hurried off to the kitchen.

Soon, my sweet daughter. Soon, Zack silently promised.

❧❦❧

Chloe had thought about Zack's house ever since he'd made the announcement about leaving the boardinghouse. This afternoon the three people she loved the most would be moving away from her. She attempted to console herself with thoughts of Sunday at their new home, but the days of waiting expectantly for the twins or Zack to enter the boardinghouse door were gone.

"The guests are pleased with the Christmas decorations," Mr. Barton said. Unlike her, he'd been in a jovial mood for the past few days. "One lady said it reminded her of home. Exactly what I wanted to accomplish." He rubbed his palms together. "I have something for you, Miss Weaver."

She forced a smile. "Did I lose something?"

He laughed. "Not exactly." He reached inside his jacket pocket. "I have two tickets for the theater in Houston on New Year's Eve. I also have reservations for dinner. We will travel by train on Sunday morning and return on Monday evening. I've decided to ask Miss Scott to accompany us as our chaperone."

Chloe's stomach rolled. "You should have asked me first. And what about the boardinghouse?"

"How good of you to think about my business. I have all that taken care of. I wanted to surprise you."

"Aren't you concerned about my reputation? An overnight trip to Houston sounds scandalous." If she wasn't careful, she'd lose her temper and get fired.

"Miss Scott is an excellent chaperone."

She moistened her lips and prayed for guidance. "I appreciate your thinking of me and the time you spent planning this trip, but I should have been asked, as well as Miss Scott, before you purchased the tickets and made arrangements."

Shock registered on his face. "Are you refusing me?"

"I am. Even at the expense of my position here."

"That is most unusual, Miss Weaver. I never expected this response."

Courage rooted inside her. "It's not my intent to hurt your feelings or take advantage of your generosity."

His downward glance pulled at her emotions.

"Mr. Barton, we have an employer and employee relationship. I respect you and the good things you do for me and this town. But I do not have feelings for you."

He lifted his gaze. "From my viewpoint, Miss Weaver, you haven't tried."

She wrung her hands. *Honesty.* "Perhaps I haven't."

"We shall see. I'm accustomed to handling matters my own way."

"Does this mean I'm dismissed?"

He crossed his arms over his chest and averted his gaze. "Not at all. I need you here to keep things running smoothly. But, oh, you do this heart much damage." With those words he strode to the kitchen.

CHAPTER 23

Saturday morning sped by much faster than Zack intended, leaving a desk piled high with work in its wake. His parents had picked up the twins early, but even without them, he couldn't get caught up.

"Get on out of here." Hank waved him toward the door. "You need to move and set up housekeeping."

"And leave you with delivering the papers and all of the other chores waiting to be done?"

"Have you forgotten that I did this before you came to town?" Hank shook a finger at him. "Gil and I will tidy up and take care of things."

Zack did need the extra time. He wanted the twins to explore every inch of the house, and then he'd take them for a long walk. Mama and Dad wanted to help, too.

"All right. You convinced me, but I will make it up to you." He grabbed his jacket. "By any chance, has anyone heard from our local hungry fellow since we ran the article?"

"Not a word," Hank said. "Maybe he's thinking about it."

"Or he's a chicken," Gil said. "Not so sure I'd want to come forward after stealin' from folks."

"I could have been wrong about this. I may do a follow-up article as an appeal to him. Maybe invite him to stop by the paper."

Hank nodded. "What I like about the newspaper covering this is we're reaching out to a man who needs to change his ways and appealing to a community to be forgiving. But what do we do if he steals something large or damages property?"

"Then he's at the mercy of the law. We won't have a choice."

"My thoughts, too." Hank grinned wide. "Now get."

Zack headed for the door. "See you in church."

✾❀✾

Once the afternoon settled upon the boardinghouse, Chloe watched Zack and the twins carry their personal belongings down the board-inghouse stairs and out to a wagon. Brother and Mrs. Whitworth came by to offer their assistance, but it didn't take them long. Chloe couldn't help because Mr. Barton stood by the registration desk the entire time. However, her employer did not object when the twins hugged and kissed her good-bye.

That night in the darkness of her room, she wept. Zack had found a way for them to continue seeing each other despite Mr. Barton's demands. And the twins now had a big house and acres to run and play. No more short tempers from being cramped up at the boardinghouse. No more tears on Tuesday nights when Simeon made liver and onions, which neither Curly nor Charlie liked. Chloe should be happy, ecstatic with the outcome of it all. Instead, she felt miserable.

Mr. Barton could decide to dismiss her tomorrow. Then where would she be? She couldn't stay with Miss Scott since her niece would arrive tomorrow from Dallas. Her savings could hold her for a little while, but where? Mr. Barton owned the only reputable boardinghouse.

Staring up at the ceiling, she prayed for strength. Worrying about what might happen meant she didn't trust God to take care of her. Part of her sadness dwelt with not being able to see Zack and the twins as much as before. Since he'd returned to town, she'd seen him at least twice a day. He'd put the color in her cheeks in the mornings, and the prospect of hearing his voice in the evenings made any uncomfortable moments of the day vanish. How she treasured those late-night talks after the twins were asleep. Beginning tonight, those precious times were but memories.

Zack Kahler, I've loved you for so long that I can't remember when I didn't.

Tears dampened her pillow again. Her heart had opened to a pair of red-haired, freckle-faced children, too. She'd get through each lonely day, knowing that on Sunday the four of them would once again be together—beginning tomorrow.

Christmas. Why would Mr. Barton want her to spend the day with him when she had no feelings for him? And whatever had he been thinking to plan a trip to Houston for New Year's Eve? Anger and pity wrestled with her mind.

Sunday morning, she rose and dressed in the dark skirt and blouse that Miss Scott had found for her. At least Zack would see her in something different. And she'd wear a smile, too, a big one that spoke not one word of gloom and sadness.

"You look lovely this morning. That must be a new dress," he said as he helped her into the wagon. "I'd better hold on to you tight or someone might snatch you away."

Like Mr. Barton.

"We're holding her hands, Poppy," Charlie said. "Nobody's going to get our Miss Chloe."

"Thank you." Zack winked. "Well, what do you two want to tell her about our house?"

"It's beautiful," Charlie said. "We have a kitchen and a dining room and a parlor and lots of rooms with beds in them."

"I can hardly wait to see it." Chloe lightly squeezed the little girl's hand and turned to Curly. "And what do you think about your house?"

"Heaben."

"Heaven," Charlie said. "Not a *b* but a *v*."

Curly scowled. "God don't care how I say it."

Zack cleared his throat, and the twins quieted. "We are very pleased. Last evening we took a walk back to the apple and pecan trees and to the creek."

"I'm so happy for you," Chloe said, and she really was.

She glanced up at the row of buggies and the familiar faces. The sky glistened with the brightest blue she'd ever seen, and she knew that very moment that it didn't matter if Mr. Barton dismissed her. One of those smiling faces would take her in until she found another job.

"You are all smiles this morning," Zack said and waved at his mother and dad.

"Strange, isn't it?" She spotted Mr. Barton and waved. "I had a discussion with my employer yesterday morning that nearly devastated me, but right now I'm perfectly happy."

Zack glanced at the twins. "We can talk this afternoon."

Chloe adored sitting by Zack and the twins in church. Curly and Charlie wanted to tell her all about their new home, but she convinced them to wait until after the services.

"I'm cooking lunch," Zack whispered once the music began.

"I'll help," she said.

"Actually, it will be breakfast with scrambled eggs and ham."

She laughed, then turned her attention to what was really important—Brother Whitworth's message.

Afterward, once church members were properly greeted, Zack drove the buggy out of town.

"Why not let me fix lunch for all of us?" she said on the way to see his new home.

He held the reins firmly and shot a smile her way. "But I invited you. I know how to cook. Years ago before my dad and Mama married, I lived with Brother Travis." He hastened the horse to a trot. "He made me learn how to take care of myself. Later when I moved to New York, I had to use all of those skills to survive."

She laughed. Strange how love could make a person forget all the turmoil of life. "I don't doubt your abilities." She nodded to accent her determination. "We could do this together."

Zack frowned; then a smile tugged at his mouth. "All right. Only because you are too pretty to refuse."

"Oh?" She widened her eyes. "I'll make a list of all the things I want in this world and give it to you with my best smile."

He shook his head. "Now I'm trapped."

When the horse and buggy stopped in front of a huge, two-story, white-framed farmhouse, Chloe gasped. "It *is* beautiful."

"Hank's mother lived in the house until she died, and everything is here that we need. I found canned peaches, green beans, and corn in the pantry."

He helped her down from the buggy, and she hoped he didn't sense what his touch did to her. "Curly, Charlie, you are so lucky. I agree with Curly. This is heaven." She tossed a smile Zack's way. "After the boardinghouse, I imagine this seems like a palace. I bet you'd get lonely without two little people constantly surrounding you."

"Actually, they slept with me last night."

"And no accidents," Curly said.

She hadn't been aware of the twins listening to every word. "That's wonderful." Her gaze met Zack's. "You are such a good father."

He shook his head. "Not when I think of all the times I've fished for the right words or questioned something I've done with my children."

"You do your best, and that is what's important. Now show me your wonderful new home."

Zack offered her his arm, and she linked hers to his. Maybe someday this would be *her* home. That would really be a dream come true.

The tour of the inside of the home was like a picture book. Perfect in every way for Zack and the children. He was as excited as Curly and Charlie in showing her every nook and corner. And the kitchen. . .she loved it. A set of beautiful pink-flowered plates with a thin green leaf design caught her attention. Would she one day be able to use these for her husband and children?

"Why don't you two run outside and play while Miss Chloe and

I fix us something to eat?"

The twins didn't need any more encouragement, and they soon disappeared.

"I brought some ice with me yesterday, so the milk, ham, and eggs are in the icebox," he said. "I'll start the ham if you want to break the eggs." He opened the icebox as though it were a banker's vault. But he had every right to be proud.

Chloe reached inside a cabinet and pulled out a bowl. A pair of arms encircled her waist, and Zack nuzzled against her neck. Her pulse raced ahead.

"Aren't you concerned about your children hurrying back inside?"

"No. And since I have you alone, I want to make the most of every moment."

"Shame on you."

"I don't see you pulling away."

"I'm trying to be a good guest."

He chuckled low, and the sound caused her to feel warm—and special. The only other times they'd been alone were drinking coffee in the upstairs hallway of the boardinghouse or in the dining room when the rest of the boarders were asleep. Then there were the mornings when he delivered soiled laundry. This was much more enjoyable. But dangerous. She should have requested that Lydia Anne be with them.

She peered out the kitchen window at the twins running toward the barn, just running as though someone might steal it all from them. She felt the same way. "Goodness, Mr. Kahler, would what Mr. Barton say?"

"He's not here." Zack turned her to face him. "Does it matter?"

Tenderness and another look that she dared hope was love shone into her face. "No. It doesn't. But we should have asked Lydia Anne or your parents to be with us today."

"Probably so. I'll take care of that the next time. Chloe, I want to know what happened between you and Jacob yesterday."

"Why ruin our Sunday?"

"Chloe."

"All right. This is what happened. . . ." And while he held her close, she told him about Mr. Barton's plans for New Year's Eve and her refusal.

"If he no longer needs you at the boardinghouse, I know Mama and Dad would have a place for you to stay until you found another job."

She nodded. For the first time she didn't feel pride invading her senses.

"I know it's only been a short while since I came back to town, but I have to tell you this or I'm going to pop." He smiled, and his fingers ran through her hair while his eyes seemed to look beyond her—beyond time. "You are the most beautiful woman I have ever known, ever seen. It's more than your dark eyes that seem to pierce my soul or your silky hair or even the sound of your voice. It's everything about you. I—"

"Poppy, come see." Charlie burst into the kitchen. "We found kittens behind the barn. They're almost like the ones at Grandma and Grandpa's."

Zack stepped back from Chloe. The moment between them had vanished. But she refused to show her disappointment, even with the longing creeping through her. She wouldn't allow jealousy to rule her emotions when Zack's children needed him.

"Let's go see those kittens." She rubbed her hands together.

"Please hurry, Poppy. They might run away."

"All right. How did you find them?" Zack held the door open for both of them.

"Behind the barn. They are so beautiful, all black with a white stripe down their back."

Zack paled. Chloe gasped.

"Stay here," he said to Chloe and Charlie. "I'll get Curly." He ran toward the barn. "Curly, come here right this instant. Do not touch those animals!"

"What's wrong?" Charlie asked, her round face a mixture of concern and confusion. "Why is Poppy mad?"

Chloe wrapped her arms around the little girl's shoulder. "He's not angry with either of you. Those aren't kittens you found but skunks. Let's step out onto the porch."

"Skunks, Miss Chloe? You mean the ones that smell awful?"

She nodded. "And the smell is very hard to get out of clothes."

She saw a curly red head peek around the back of the barn. "Poppy, we found kittens."

"Run to me now as fast as you can. Those aren't kittens. Those are skunks!"

Chloe couldn't help but laugh. If need be, they'd wash the little boy's clothes in tomato juice and scrub him until he smelled sweet and clean again. Life with Curly and Charlie was never dull.

Zack raced to sweep Curly up into his arms and then carried the little boy to the porch. "We're fine," he said. "No skunks for us."

CHAPTER 24

Late Sunday afternoon, Chloe opened the door into the boarding-house. The familiar jingle offered no comfort, but the events with Zack and the children warmed her to her toes. She laughed aloud at the picture of Zack racing after Curly before the little boy could be sprayed by a skunk.

Inside her home and workplace, the aroma of Simeon's roast beef dinner wafted through the air. Expectancy of Christmas filled her with sincere peace. Friends, good dear friends, always made the ups and downs of life a little easier to bear.

She heard Miss Scott laugh, and Chloe ventured into the dining room. Simeon sat across a table from Miss Scott and another young woman. Could this be Miss Scott's niece Rose?

Chloe stepped into the dining room. "Good evening."

"Oh, Chloe," Miss Scott scooted back from her chair and stood. "Please, come meet my niece."

The young woman in question joined her aunt. Large brown eyes veiled with a thick curtain of lashes peeked from under a mountain of light brown curls. Not at all what Chloe had expected.

Chloe made her way toward the small gathering, not certain if she should interrupt her friends and guest. "I'm delighted to meet you," she said. "Your aunt has told me so much about you."

A sweet smile greeted her. "And the same of you."

"I trust you had a pleasant journey."

Rose laughed lightly. "The train was incredibly crowded. Everyone seemed to be in a hurry to go somewhere in the hustle and bustle of the Christmas season. Won't you join us? It appears that you and I have been frequent topics of conversation between Simeon and Aunt Annabelle."

Chloe liked Rose instantly. "For only a moment. I'm really quite tired."

Miss Scott asked all the proper questions about Zack's home and her little students. All the while, her gaze flitted from Simeon to her niece as if not certain who should have her attention.

Chloe yawned. "Please, excuse me. I think I'll leave you three to visit. Rose, I hope we have time to chat while you are here."

"We'll make time." She shrugged prettily. "It may be a foursome. I've been given the position of chaperone between my aunt and Mr. Simeon."

"We can make sure the two mind their manners." Chloe laughed and turned to leave the room. She nearly ran into Mr. Barton in the hallway.

"Miss Weaver, what a pleasant surprise."

"Mr. Barton." She nodded. "Miss Scott and her niece are visiting in the dining room with Simeon. Perhaps you'd like to greet them."

He stepped into the dining room at the same time as Miss Scott, Rose, and Simeon turned their attention to Chloe and Mr. Barton.

Rose's expressive eyes widened, much like Charlie's did when the little girl was startled. In an instant, the young woman regained her composure. Chloe studied the young woman. Did she know Mr. Barton? She glanced at her employer. For a moment his gaze lingered on the lovely young woman. Was there a spark of romance in the air?

Chloe held her breath. *Jacob Barton, don't you dare be too stubborn not to note what just happened between you two.*

"Mr. Barton, I'm so glad you are here," Miss Scott said. "I'm pleased to present my niece Rose Scott. She's nearly finished with college in Dallas, and she will be teaching school this time next year."

Mr. Barton made his way to the table and took Rose's offered hand. "How good of you to spend the holiday with our Miss Scott."

"Thank you, sir." And the pleasantries passed for a few moments.

"Again, I bid you all good night," Chloe said.

Mr. Barton immediately hastened to her side. "So early, Miss Weaver? Do share a few moments with me in the parlor. You've decorated the room so beautifully, and it seems a waste for us not to enjoy it."

Chloe wanted to shake him. "I'm exhausted—"

"Ten minutes?"

With the other three observing, she gave in to Mr. Barton's invitation. But his attempts at wooing her wouldn't work. He could smile, offer theater tickets, bring flowers, and flatter her until he was exhausted and taken to bed, but her heart belonged to Zack. The afternoon with him and the twins had convinced her that he cared for her as much as she did him.

"I owe you an apology," Mr. Barton said a short while later. He gathered up her hand into his. "I've been thinking all day about what I'd planned for New Year's Eve. How wrong of me to assume you'd welcome the trip to Houston. I will do better in the future."

A hundred responses, or rather retorts, crawled through her mind. Yet responding one more time to torment him was as brutal as mocking his affections. If she trusted God for eternity, then she needed to trust this awkward situation to His safekeeping. This evening, no answers to the dilemma came to her other than to accept Mr. Barton's apology with the sincerity in which it was given. She gently pulled her hand from his.

"I've already forgotten it. No need to concern yourself with the matter."

She also prayed that what she'd seen pass between Mr. Barton and Rose Scott was not wishful thinking but something beautiful— and a way out for her.

❧

Zack stacked the day's papers at the front of the newspaper office so folks could easily pick up a copy and leave their payment in the nearby cup. With his thoughts jumping from the house purchase to the twins to his feelings for Chloe, he didn't hear or see his uncle Morgan walk in.

"Hey, Zack. How's the newspaper business?"

He whirled around and made long strides to shake his uncle's hand. "It's going well. Did you stop by for today's copy?"

"That I did—and to bring you something." He waved a large envelope. "The judge from New York has made a decision."

"And?" Anticipation as big as all Texas settled on him.

"He looked at all we had compiled and signed the adoption papers. Curly and Charlie are now officially Kahlers. Merry Christmas!"

Zack couldn't stop grinning. What a grand Christmas, too. "I'm an official father. For a while, I feared I was playing a child's game of make-believe."

"This document proves differently. I believe this calls for a celebration," Morgan said. "Why don't you and the twins come to dinner tomorrow night? I'll see if Grant and Jenny and Bonnie and Travis can come with Lydia Anne and Stuart. It's not every day that our family increases by two."

"Are you sure? I mean with Christmas coming, does Aunt Casey want to cook for all of us?"

"I'm sure of it. This is a special day, and I'm a selfish enough man to make sure the whole town knows about it." He took in the sights of the newspaper office. "I think the adoption news would make a great newspaper story. Don't you?"

"I know the man to write it."

Morgan handed Zack the envelope. "Congratulations."

"Thanks. We'll be there for dinner. Please, nothing fancy. Bacon and eggs suit my household just fine."

Morgan greeted Hank on the way to the door. "Don't let my nephew forget he's to have dinner tomorrow night at my house." He swung his attention back to Zack. "Will Chloe be with you?"

"She has to work. But I'll be sneaking by the boardinghouse to give her the good news." Even if he had to have someone enter the establishment and coax her to come out.

Zack wanted to tell the twins right then. Glancing at the clock on his desk, he saw it was an hour past noon. He could walk over to the school and give Curly and Charlie the good news. Waiting until evening would drive him insane.

"I'm heading over to the school," he called to Hank. "I won't be gone long."

"I have a ham sandwich for you and Gil from the missus. It'll save for later."

"Don't let Gil eat mine." He laughed and waved at the young man who was thin enough to be a hitching post.

Zack whipped off his apron and wiped his hands on a rag near the typesetter. "Yahoo! I'm a real father." He hurried out the door toward the school. A wisp of cool air gave him the energy of a boy. As he rushed along, he remembered how the way from town to school used to take so long. Since then, the town had grown to encompass the school. Progress had a way of making a man nostalgic. With the tall oak tree in the middle of the schoolyard waving its familiar hello, a dozen boyhood memories danced across his mind. He surely hoped his two children didn't follow in their father's footsteps.

He paused for a moment when he saw Dad's buggy parked in front of the church. The temptation to tell him about the adoption needled at him. Shaking his head, Zack kept his sights on the school—and his children.

Some of the students were playing outside, including his Curly and Charlie. What a good ring Kahler had to his children's names. Suddenly he frowned. Why was Jacob Barton talking to his children? And why was Chloe with him?

"Poppy," Curly and Charlie chorused. They jumped down from a small bench and ran toward him, leaving Chloe and Barton behind.

What were they carrying?

"We have cookies." Curly held up a giant sugar cookie, but the telltale crumbs on his mouth and chin said much more.

Zack bent down and hugged them both—cookie crumbs and all. "Hmm. Where did you get those huge cookies?"

Charlie waved her hand. "We all have them. Mr. Simeon made them for the whole school, and Miss Chloe and Mr. Barton brought them to us."

That made sense, but it didn't make him any happier or any less jealous.

"You wanna bite?" Charlie asked.

"Let's get Poppy his own cookie," Curly said.

"Oh no. I'm fine. I really came to see you two." Zack wondered if his news would be as well received as the sugar cookies. Perhaps he should have waited until this afternoon.

"Are we in trouble?"

"No, Curly." He grinned into his son's amber-colored eyes. Here in the sun, both of his children's eyes looked like bright gold nuggets. "This is good news for all of us."

"Hello, Zack."

Chloe's sweet voice was like a soothing balm and a stick of peppermint candy at the same time. He could listen to her for the rest of his life.

"I see you and Jacob are treating the town's children."

She laughed. "This was Mr. Barton's idea. He wanted to give the school children a special treat. Actually, I should be helping Simeon clean up from lunch. I'm having such a good time while he's washing and drying a huge stack of dishes."

"Poppy has something to tell us," Charlie said. "It's 'posed to be good."

Chloe's gaze flew to his. Did Barton ever receive the same pleasant chill when she smiled?

"I'll leave you to your privacy."

How did she always know the perfect thing to say? "It's all right. Please, stay. I planned to find a way to tell you tonight." He drew the twins into his arms. "The judge in New York signed the adoption papers. You are officially Curly and Charlie Kahler, and I'm your poppy."

The twins scrambled to hug him harder, and in the process, he toppled to the ground. Their laughter mingled with Chloe's and chased away the green demon that had attacked him at the sight of her and Jacob together.

"We won't ever go back to the orphanage?" Curly asked.

"Nope. Your home is my home. We're stuck with each other."

Charlie broke her cookie in half and handed it to him while he still lay on the ground. "Here, Poppy. I want you to have this."

He took a generous bite. "I believe I have the best children in town."

And soon they will have the perfect mother.

"Miss Scott will be so happy," Curly said. "And I'll thank Mr. Barton again for bringing us cookies on our 'doption day."

Jacob made his way to their side. "Sounds like a happy trio here."

Zack stood up, wiped his dirt-covered hand on his trousers, and shook the man's hand. "The adoption papers came through today. We're celebrating."

"Congratulations. The three of you should spend lots of time doing things together. Children need their father's attention with no one else around."

Zack inwardly cringed. *Barton, I understand exactly what you're saying. But this will not always be a trio. Chloe will one day share my name, my house, and our children.*

CHAPTER 25

The morning after the adoption news, Zack woke earlier than usual. Excitement about Christmas, his children, and the love he'd seen in Chloe's eyes the afternoon before filled his head. With the sun rising in spectacular colors of pale orange, yellow, and purple, he noted the temperatures had dropped during the night to near freezing. That was Texas for almost three months of the year. The rest of the time, folks lived in warm to hot weather. He leaned against the porch post and sipped on his black, strong coffee.

For whatever reason, God had blessed him repeatedly this fall. Certainly wasn't anything Zack had done to deserve it, but God's grace covered a lot of valleys and rough spots—and mistakes. Zack praised God for his children, his home, the success of the newspaper, and the wonderful woman He'd placed in his life. Sure was easier praising God for the good things than the bad. But Dad had taught him years ago to praise God no matter what was happening in his life. Three months ago, he thought his life had been carefully laid out: come home to Kahlerville and publish the best newspaper this town had ever seen. And he still labored for that endeavor. But Curly and Charlie had wriggled their way into his heart and caused him to feel things he didn't know existed.

Then there was Chloe. He laughed and took another gulp of coffee. To think he'd almost settled for counterfeit love with. . .all of a sudden he couldn't remember the woman's name who had broken his heart. Or so he thought. Chloe, the mere sound of her name was like the topic of a poem. If he were a poet, he'd compose a piece of literature in her honor. He'd begin by comparing her beauty to a Texas sunrise and end it by comparing her again to a Texas sunset. Wouldn't his uncles get a laugh out of that one?

He breathed in the crisp air, filling his lungs with clean air— and a sense of purpose. He treasured this time of the morning. It offered quiet moments with God along with a reflection on yesterday and how He directed Zack for the day. His gaze moved toward the barn. Something caught his attention. Had a stray dog found its way into the barn for the night? Zack studied a shadowy figure. It was a man. The figure slipped around to the side of the barn. Had he slept there? Was this the subject of the town's talk?

"Hey, there. What are you doing?"

Zack set his cup on the porch step and set out toward the barn. If the man was hungry, then he'd be fed. If the man was up to no good, Zack could handle that, too.

The man took off on a run with Zack close behind. He chased the intruder toward the pecan grove. In the shadows, he looked like the same fellow Zack had chased away the first time he came to view the property.

"Stop there. I just want to talk."

The figure raced ahead, but Zack was faster and quickly caught up. He grabbed the man by the shoulder, then swung him to the ground. Zack straddled him, pinning him with such force that the man groaned. It wasn't a man at all, but a boy nearly grown. Even in the early morning light, Zack recognized the face.

"You're the one I saw when I came to view the house and property. You'd fired up the cookstove, and you were sleeping in one of the beds. Now you're sleeping in my barn. Don't you have a home, boy?"

"I wasn't hurtin' nothin' in the house or in the barn."

"Are you the one swiping food from the boardinghouse?"

"They leave it for me, and I put the plate and fork back."

"And that makes it all right? What about the coffee and blankets you stole from the wagon parked outside the newspaper office?"

The boy swallowed hard. Zack eyed his dirty face and clothes. From the smell attacking his nostrils, he figured it had been a while since the boy had bathed.

"Why don't you come inside the house where it's warm? I'll heat some water so you can take a bath before breakfast." Zack had yet to release the boy beneath him. He wanted to make sure the intruder didn't come at him with flying fists.

"Why would you do that?" The boy eyed him with an air of suspicion and fear.

"Because it looks to me like you're in need of both."

"A real Good Samaritan, huh? Is that why you wrote the newspaper article?"

Zack chuckled. "So you know who I am."

"I might."

"How long were you staying inside my house before I caught you?"

"Why?"

"How'd you get in?"

The young man frowned. "While the old man who owns the place was in the barn. What do you want from me?"

"Nothing. Maybe a name. Maybe a reason why you're using my barn for a bed."

"Can't do either one."

"Why? No guts, boy? You steal around like a thief and hide out, but you haven't the guts to state your name?"

"You might go tell my pa."

"How old are you?"

"Seventeen."

Could this be Eli Scott?

"A boy your age shouldn't be worried about his father unless he's done something that he ought to be ashamed of. All right. Your name and your reason for being here is your business. Let's get you inside before my children get up. I have just enough time to heat the water before they're awake."

"They know me."

"From where? School?"

The boy pressed his lips together hard.

"Are you Eli Scott? Annabelle Scott's nephew?"

The boy shrugged.

"Miss Scott told me about her nephew who ran off, or rather, his father kicked him out after he was expelled from school. So I ask you again. Are you Eli Scott?" Zack held back his anger. He hadn't forgotten what had been done to Curly and Charlie—and Chloe. Yet the boy looked miserable. And where did he get the bruise alongside his left cheek and the scar along his left jaw? Must have been his father. Zack could only imagine how the kid had looked right after he'd been beaten.

The boy glanced away. "And what if I am Eli Scott? You gonna beat me up for what I did to your kids?"

"Is that what you want? Looks like someone already laid a fist into you. Maybe a knife to your face." Zack rose from the ground, offering Eli a chance to run off. "You hurt my children. They're six years old. And you bullied a good friend of mine, Chloe Weaver."

"You gonna take me to jail?" Defiance lined his face—a pale, thin face.

Zack purposefully hesitated. "I'll admit you'd get fed there, and you'd have a better bed than my empty barn."

Eli turned toward the pecan trees. He wasn't wearing a jacket, just a long-sleeved flannel shirt. Too big and probably stolen. He was thin and broad shouldered. Zack considered taking him to jail. Revenge still rooted in him every time he thought about Eli's bullying. But Zack remembered when Dad had taken an interest in him—when most folks in town thought the only place for Zack Kahler was a military school.

"Who bruised your face?"

Eli sighed. "You wouldn't believe me if I told you."

"Miss Scott said your father tended to be hard on you, so I expect I already know."

Eli said nothing but glanced toward the trees again.

"You can run if you want to, or you can come with me to the house." Zack turned and started to walk away, then swung his attention back to the boy. "I'm not hauling you to jail or contacting your father. You're a man, a young one at that. Looks to me like you've paid for what you've done in the way of missing a few meals and losing a little sleep. And I'm not sure I want to know what happened to your face. But for breakfast and a hot bath, I expect an apology to Curly and Charlie."

Eli's jaw clenched, and his lips pressed together so hard that they looked blue. "Yes, sir."

He was either too cold or too hungry to argue. Maybe Zack had made some progress.

Once in the kitchen, the water grew hot in short order. Zack filled the tub in the water closet while Eli drank a hot cup of coffee. As soon as the boy closed the door to the water closet, Zack woke the twins.

"We have a guest for breakfast," he said after morning hugs. "And I want you to use your best manners."

"Is it Miss Chloe?" Curly asked.

Nice thought. "No, but you know him. Do you remember Grandma's story about how Jesus forgave the men who hurt Him?"

"Yes. We're supposed to love everybody." Charlie sat up in bed. "Did you adopt more kids? Some newsboys?"

He smiled. "No, but you might need to remember Grandma's story at breakfast."

"Grandma says we should always forgive bad people," Charlie continued. " 'Cause that makes God happy."

"I'm sure today you two are going to make God very happy."

While the twins dressed, Zack scrambled eggs, fried sausage, baked biscuits, and cooked grits—a little more breakfast than usual. Eli emerged from Zack's bedroom into the dining room wearing jeans and a shirt that hung on him like a feed sack.

Charlie gasped. "Poppy, that's Eli, the bad boy who—"

"What did we talk about this morning?"

"To forgive," Curly said.

"Right. Do you two understand what forgive means?"

The children exchanged looks that spoke of anger and fear. He couldn't blame them. He was itching to tear into Eli himself.

"Not be mad at him anymore?" Charlie asked.

"Making God happy is not always easy." Zack lifted one twin's chin then another. "Remember, He loves us when we do bad things, too."

Zack pulled out a chair from the round oak table in the dining room. "Sit down, Eli, so we can have our breakfast before it gets cold."

Eli awkwardly took a seat. The twins chorused the blessing, and breakfast began. Midway through a heaped plate of food, Eli cleared his throat and aimed his attention at Curly and Charlie.

"I'm sorry for what I did to you," he said.

"You were bad." Curly frowned. "But I forgive you."

"Me, too," Charlie said.

The twins stared at Zack, and he smiled his approval.

Eli had made a good step forward, but what about Chloe? Would he someday ask her for forgiveness, too? For that matter, could she forgive him?

"And I forgive you for what you did to the twins."

"Good, Poppy." Charlie nodded. "I'm proud of you."

After breakfast, the twins helped clean the table and wash the dishes before Zack helped them into the buggy for school.

"You ate a hearty breakfast this morning," Zack said to Eli.

"Yes, sir. It tasted fine. Thank you again."

"Do you have plans for the day?"

"No, sir. With harvest done, farmers have no need for help. The ranchers I've talked to aren't interested, either."

"Why don't you help me out at the newspaper today? That ought to take care of lunch and dinner. This evening we'll talk about some plans for your future."

"Why are you helping me?" Suspicion crept into Eli's voice.

"Because you need it."

"Won't Miss Scott be surprised when we tell her this?" Curly said.

Zack shook his head. "Curly, Charlie, give me your attention."

The two immediately turned to him with their familiar, wide-eyed expressions.

"This is a secret. You cannot tell anyone that Eli is with us. I will do my part and keep him busy at the newspaper in the back where folks won't see him. I need your promise that you two will not breathe a word about Eli."

"Yes, sir," Curly said. "I promise."

"Charlie?"

"Yes, sir. I promise, too."

"This is our special secret for today. If you tell anyone, I'll have to give you lots of chores for a very long time, and I will be very disappointed."

They both nodded.

"I'll tell you when it's the right time to tell Miss Scott or your friends or your cousins." That should cover it. "This morning I'll take Eli to the newspaper office before I take you to school."

Zack studied Eli's face. Sweat streamed from the boy's forehead and dripped onto his cheeks. It had nothing to do with the heat from the cookstove.

All morning long, Zack made sure Eli stayed in the back of the newspaper office. Occasionally folks brought in news articles, and he didn't need anyone finding Eli before Zack figured out what to do with him. The sheriff had agreed to drop all charges if the culprit came forward and confessed, but would he face public humiliation for his actions?

At noon, Zack gave Eli two chicken legs, a roll, and a generous slice of chocolate cake—a lunch made by Gil's wife. "You ready to talk? I know you've read the article."

Eli nearly choked on the chicken. "It made me sound like some poor hick off the river bottom."

Zack shrugged. "What are you then?"

"I can leave right now."

"Go ahead. Make sure you stay off my property. Because the next time I find you there, I'll be taking you to the sheriff."

"I won't go near your place."

"Thank you." Zack swallowed a retort. "How do you plan to take care of yourself or amount to anything?"

Eli's eyes narrowed.

"That's what I thought. You don't have any plans." Zack paused, hoping he hadn't made the young man so angry that he wouldn't listen. "Son, swallow your pride and admit what you've done. Then start all over by living right."

"But my name is gonna be in the newspaper."

"With the way you're headed, your name will be there anyway."

Eli took a deep breath. "After I make a fool out of myself, then what? Oh, I forgot. You'll have more folks reading your paper to see what happens to me. Then you'll make more money."

"Believe what you want. But I'm telling you that I'll help you find a place to live and a job." The kid was too much like Zack used to be. Zack would be eternally grateful for the forgiveness of all those people in Kahlerville whom he'd offended as a troubled boy.

"Yer not lying to me?"

Zack shook his head. "I think the best thing you can do to show others who think you're no good is to make something of yourself. But I don't know if you have what it takes. Could be—"

Eli stiffened. "I'll do it. I'll tell the sheriff. I hate living out in the cold."

"Let's go see Sheriff Jackson."

"Now?"

"Right now." Zack pointed to the door.

Outside the newspaper office, Eli stopped cold. "This is hard."

"But you can do it." Zack directed him down the street. What had happened to Zack in the past few months? First he'd adopted two homeless children, and now he was attempting to turn around a wayward young man.

At the sheriff's office, Eli paled. "What if he wants to take me to my pa? Lock me up?"

"You're seventeen, Eli. If your father wanted you around, he wouldn't have kicked you out. Did he put that scar on your face?"

Eli trembled, his hand touched the door knob, then slid back to his side.

"This is the beginning of a new man." Zack would have touched Eli's shoulder, but he remembered when he didn't want anyone touching him.

Eli opened the door and stepped inside. "Afternoon, Sheriff. I need to talk to you for a few minutes." He swung his attention to Zack. "You comin' with me?"

"I can." Zack tipped his hat. "Sheriff Jackson, this is Eli Scott.

236

He has a few things to tell you."

"Sit down." Sheriff Jackson gestured to a couple of chairs. "What can I do for you?"

The smell coming from the cells behind the sheriff assaulted Zack's nostrils like an outhouse in August. That should cause Eli to think about where his current path was taking him.

Eli paled, and the scar on his face deepened. How could this young man ever trust anyone unless God touched his heart?

"I–I'm the one who took the food from the boardinghouse and the blankets and coffee from the wagon. And I stole this coat from the livery."

The sheriff pressed his lips together. "I suspect you need to apologize to those folks and see what you can do for them."

"Yes, sir."

"Where've you been living?"

"At Mr. Kahler's place mostly. In his barn."

"What are you going to do now?"

Eli shot a look at Zack.

"We haven't gotten that far, Sheriff," Zack said. "But I have some ideas."

The sheriff nodded as though contemplating Eli's situation. "I'd like to know what you decide, because, son, you can't live like this anymore. The people here in Kahlerville are forgivin' now, but that will change after the first of the year when the holidays are over. You need to find a place to live and finish your education. I heard your father kicked you out after some trouble at school."

"Yes, sir. He did."

"Then show him he's wrong and make something of yourself."

"Yes, sir."

"Don't keep yes-sirring me. Get on out of here and do what's right before I'm forced to lock you up."

Eli wasted no time in making his way to the door and grasping the knob with a trembling hand.

A few minutes later, the two made their way back down the street toward the newspaper. "You're a free man," Zack said. "No more hiding. I'll not print your name in tomorrow's article. No point in it. The only folks who'll know your name will be the ones who'll get an apology. Tonight we're going to visit my parents and see if we can find a place for you to live. Even a way to finish your education. Right now—"

"I need to confess to the man at your newspaper office and to the owner of the boardinghouse."

They passed the feed store, and Jacob stepped out. "Afternoon, Zack. Who's your friend?"

Zack glanced at the young man beside him. "Jacob, this is Eli Scott."

"Does he work at the paper?"

The thought had come and gone all morning. Hank wanted to retire, and Gil was capable of replacing him, but that left a hole in Gil's slot, and the paper couldn't afford to lose a typesetter. "If he wants it."

Eli started. "Yes, sir. I'd be proud to work at the newspaper." He stared into Jacob's face. "Sir, I'm the one who took your food. I'm sorry, and it won't happen again."

"What else?" Zack asked.

Eli dragged his tongue over his lips. "If you need for me to work off what I took, I'm willing."

Jacob eyed Eli for several moments. "The newspaper article said the debt was forgiven if you came forth. So we're even, but that means you don't steal any more of my food."

"Yes, sir. Thank you."

Jacob tipped his hat and headed down the street toward the boardinghouse. Zack doubted if Eli had said so many "yes, sirs" in his entire life. Jacob had been generous, and Zack hoped Eli understood that. Things could have been real hard for the young man.

Zack shook away the green demon that attacked him every time he saw or spoke with Jacob. He trusted the look in Chloe's eyes. She cared for him. But a knot twisted in his stomach. How would she feel about Zack befriending Eli after what he'd done to her?

CHAPTER 26

Chloe yawned and massaged her back muscles. If Christmas didn't come soon, she'd be too tired to enjoy it.

Mr. Barton walked through the dining room into the registration area—laughing. "Miss Scott and Simeon are doing some heavy courting."

"Isn't Rose supposed to be chaperoning them?"

"Oh, she is. Mostly she's laughing and encouraging both of them. I believe if I asked Simeon's Miss Scott to wash dishes and mop floors, she'd do it." He smiled, and Chloe shivered. She could only imagine his thoughts.

If only he'd find someone else.

"I saw Zack Kahler today. He had a young man with him that he'd just hired." Mr. Barton paused. "Come to find out he's the one who's been helping himself to my food here. The kid confessed to the sheriff and apologized to me. Seemed scared, and there's a scar on his face and the telltale signs of a bruise. Anyway, while we were speaking, Zack offered him a job."

That's my Zack. He cares for other folks. "Who was the young man?"

"Eli Scott. Any kin to Miss Scott?"

Zack is helping Eli? Why? Look what he did to the twins. . .and me.

"He's her nephew. She thought he had joined the army."

"A shame for such a good woman to have an unruly nephew. Then I heard a while back that his father had a bad temper. Maybe a steady job will keep him from stealing. Good day. I will be by after dinner."

Chloe took a deep breath to steady herself. Zack had a reason for what he was doing, and later she'd ask him why. Yet why would he go to the trouble of helping Eli? She paused in her thinking. Zack had been in trouble as a boy until Brother Whitworth took the time to lead him down a better road.

Rose walked into the hallway between the dining room and parlor and on to the registration desk. She wore a lovely beaded blouse with a dark gored skirt.

"May I have a word with you if you're not busy?" she asked.

Chloe smiled. She welcomed a diversion from her puzzling and confusing thoughts. "Certainly. How can I help you?"

"First of all, I'm so pleased that my aunt has found happiness."

"I am, too. She is such a dear lady, and I want to see her happy. Simeon is one of the kindest and wisest men I've ever met."

Rose nodded. "I'm a little concerned about her idea of adopting a couple of children, but I'm sure God will work that out."

"Indeed He will." Chloe sensed Rose wanted to talk about

something other than her aunt and Simeon. "Is something bothering you? I mean you sound troubled. If it is none of my business, I understand. But I am a good listener."

Rose tilted her head, and a cascade of curls spilled to the side of her face. The young woman was a beauty. "I do have a few things on my mind, and I really would like your opinion. My aunt thinks of you as family, or I wouldn't be troubling you with this."

"I'm honored. And there's not a soul about."

"Well, I graduate next May with my teaching certificate, and I see that my aunt could use another teacher. Has she said anything about needing help? The last thing I'd want to do is insinuate that she can't handle her students. I'd love to move to Kahlerville and begin teaching here."

Chloe leaned over the counter. "I think she'd be thrilled. The school is growing, and if she adopts children, she'll need help."

"Wonderful. I've been praying about it for the past few months, but sometimes it's hard to distinguish what God is directing from what I want to do. I'll ask Aunt Annabelle what she thinks about the idea."

"My guess is she has secretly wished for the same thing."

Rose strolled closer to the desk. "I have another question, a rather personal one. Is Mr. Barton spoken for?"

Chloe's heart quickened. "No. Not at all. His parents passed away a few years ago, and he's been working hard to build his investments."

"He's very handsome and a good conversationalist. I could listen to him talk all day long." She blushed. "Like a girl, I'm quite smitten with him."

And you are an answer to prayer.

"I mentioned this to my aunt," Rose continued, "and she suggested

I speak with you about him. I'm sure that it's because you work for him and see his good points as well as his lesser qualities. However, I have yet to see anything but admirable traits."

Chloe blinked then coughed. "He is a good man, quite successful, a hard worker, and honestly, I think he's lonely. He cares very much for the community. I believe if he found the right woman, he'd be clearly devoted to her."

"Oh, I wouldn't want to take advantage of him. I mean, forwardness is most unbecoming to a lady, don't you think?"

"I agree. Friendship is always a good beginning. For without it, there is no basis for mutual affection. I heard Mr. Barton say that he is stopping by tonight after dinner."

Rose's large eyes fairly glistened. "We were planning on eating dinner here this evening. Perhaps I could engage him in a discussion— a friendly one of course."

"Sounds perfect to me. You are quite lovely, Rose. Mr. Barton must surely see that. Give him a little time."

"I don't have too much of that, but if I come here to teach, we could develop our relationship."

Chloe smiled for more reasons than she cared to verbalize. "If your name is mentioned in any of my dealings with Mr. Barton, I shall surely mention your good qualities."

Rose's blush deepened. "Thank you, Chloe. I never asked about you and Mr. Kahler. My aunt says things between you two are moving along nicely."

"Yes, they are." Then she remembered Zack befriending Eli.

The late afternoon had turned cold by the time Zack and the twins, along with Eli, left the newspaper office. The young man had worked during the day, sweeping up, observing the typesetters, and doing whatever Zack asked of him, but the two had not talked about where Eli would live or much else about his future other than a job at the newspaper. The young man was clearly troubled.

"I'm hungry and cold, Poppy," Curly said once he climbed into the back of the wagon.

Zack wrapped a blanket around the twins. His children were not going to be sick in the cold weather. He remembered their dire circumstances in New York and pulled the blanket tighter around their chins.

"Well, you don't have to eat my cooking tonight. We're going straight to Grandma and Grandpa's for dinner. I saw them both this afternoon."

Eli stiffened. "Is this about me?"

"Possibly." Zack tossed him an extra blanket. "You're going to need this on the ride out there."

"Would you explain what you're thinking?" Eli wasted no time with the blanket. He'd spoken to the livery owner earlier in the afternoon with plans to return the coat tomorrow.

"I want you to ask them if you can live there for a while—probably in the bunkhouse since Lydia Anne and you are close in age."

"You can't mean Brother Whitworth—the preacher."

"He did the same for me before he and my mother were married. And I was younger than you."

"He'll be preachin' to me all the time."

Zack shook his head. "That's not his way. He lives his faith. Of course, it wouldn't hurt for you to listen."

"I don't imagine he'll want to take in the likes of me. Lydia Anne and Stuart know all about what I've done."

"Maybe so. But you're going to ask. They head into town every morning taking the kids to school, so you could come to the newspaper office then. Finishing your school work will have to be worked out."

"Got it all figured out?"

Zack sensed his patience slipping. "On the way out there, you need to decide what you want from your life. If it's not to finish your education, be responsible, and live a decent life, then you'd better jump from the wagon and go on about your business. It's your decision."

Eli stared off down the road. "I should have kept runnin'."

"Running doesn't solve a thing. It just causes you to end up running all your life."

Eli said nothing the rest of the way to Mama and Dad's. Hopefully he was pondering what he'd say to Dad. And Chloe...she didn't know about any of this. With Jacob's ultimatum, the only way Zack would be able to explain things was to take the twins with him to the boardinghouse for breakfast in the morning.

Dad must have heard the wagon pull toward the house, because he was waiting for them.

"Sure glad all of you are here for dinner. What a good way to end the day." Dad stepped toward Eli and reached out his hand. "Pleasure to have you here, son."

Eli mumbled something. Rather than let the kid feel any more awkwardness, Zack introduced him. He could have split the air around Eli with an ax.

Mama's roast beef dinner tasted much better than anything Zack could have done. He could cook, but nothing like his mother. The twins chatted on about school, their new home, and Christmas.

As the food disappeared, Eli became more and more nervous. Dad suggested the men talk in the parlor—and that meant Eli. Mama winked at Zack as though she knew what was about to unfold.

The parlor sparkled with Christmas cheer. A pine bough lay across the fireplace mantel, its fresh scent filling the air. He'd be sneezing before long, but he did enjoy the aroma. Christmas ornaments tied together with red and green ribbon were gathered in a basket beside a chair. He laughed. Mama, despite the protests from her children, had arranged all of the homemade decorations that her children had lovingly crafted throughout the years. She knew which of her children had made each item and when. The pinecone ones had chipped edges, and the paper bells and stars had yellowed, but that didn't stop Mama. Each year they seemed more endearing to her.

The nativity scene was centered on a table in front of the sofa. She'd received it as a gift from Zack's father years ago. It was the only time of the year that Mama brought a little hay into the parlor. Each Christmas Zack remembered again how Papa had loved them all and fought a lung disease courageously until his death.

Zack remembered the reason why they had visited this evening. He observed Eli's twitching eye and decided to break the silence.

"Dad, Eli here needs to talk to you."

Dad turned his attention to the quaking young man. "I thought so. What can I do for you, Eli?"

Eli swung a glance at Zack, then back to Dad. "Well, sir. I have a problem."

"Let's hear it, and I'll see what I can do to help."

Zack cleared his throat. "I'll go check on the twins."

"You're leaving?" Eli nearly gasped.

Zack nodded. "If you're serious about wanting to become a real man, then now is the time to begin."

Out in the kitchen, the smells of Christmas baking caused more memories to swirl about in his head. Family had always meant a lot to him, and this year it meant even more. He'd missed two Christmases while in New York and had spent them volunteering at his church to feed the homeless. But this year, his life was blessed with Curly, Charlie, and Chloe.

The twins were so busy helping Mama with cookies that they didn't realize he'd entered the room. He observed them taking turns heaping spoonfuls of dough onto a flat baking pan. His mother saw him standing in the doorway.

"Should we let Poppy have a cookie?" Mama asked.

"Yes, Grandma. He can have two. These are close to his favorites." Charlie gave Zack her best grin, melting him into a puddle of love for his children.

Mama laughed, a sweet, bell-like tinkle that made her sound like a girl again. No surprise she and Dad acted like newlyweds. Her age increased, but her beauty only deepened. Zack took a cookie from each child. The season's sentiments had him as emotional as a woman. Best he keep that realization to himself.

"Look, Curly, Charlie. The kittens are on the back porch," Mama said.

"Can we see them?" Charlie asked. "Poppy, those aren't skunks."

Mama looked to Zack for permission, her face a picture of mirth.

"Button up your jackets first," he said. "And I'll see if I can convince your grandma to make us all some hot chocolate. This cold weather may not last, and hot chocolate doesn't taste as good on a warm day."

They scurried outside, and Mama urged him to sit down.

"What is the problem with Eli?"

He chuckled. "Did you run the twins outside so you could ask me questions?"

She shrugged. "He looks very sad, and I don't like the scar and bruise on his face. "I'm surprised he's with you since he blackened Curly's eye."

"He's been living out in the open since Miss Scott removed him from school. I'd like to see him make something of himself. If he doesn't come around soon, I'm afraid he'll end up in jail. He's been hardened, but I've seen Dad work miracles. Where would I be without him?"

"He has the touch when it comes to wayward young men."

He took another cookie. "My second-favorite cookie, oatmeal. Any coffee to go with them?"

Mama wagged her finger at him. "Some of these are for Christmas."

"This is my last one. I'll make the hot chocolate for the twins. I shouldn't have assumed you'd do it."

"And take away the joy of seeing chocolate mustaches on my grandchildren's faces?" She scooted into a chair and rested her chin in the palm of her hand. "I'll make the hot chocolate, but first I have an observation to make."

"And what that might be?"

"I think my Zack's in love."

He grinned. "Never could hide much from you."

"That's because I'm your mama. Have you told Chloe how you feel about her?"

"It's too soon, don't you think?" He rubbed the back of his neck. "I've tried a few times, but the words won't come."

"I'm sure she loves you. I can see it in her eyes."

"I want to believe so. Strange, I loved her as a little girl, and now I don't want to think of life without her. She adores the twins."

"Then tell her. What a perfect Christmas present for both of you."

"Mama, I'd ask her to marry me tonight, but I'm afraid of the twins' reaction."

She gave him a sad smile. "Son, they love her."

"I know they do. Yet I'm concerned how they might feel if Chloe and I were married. How would they feel about sharing me? We've been a family for only a short while, and they've gone through some tough changes. When we're at home, they don't let me out of their sight. I know they're afraid I'll leave them like their parents did, and I don't want them to feel abandoned again."

"Trust God to work out those problems. I believe He has a special plan for the four of you. I don't think He's brought you and Chloe together to break your heart."

"They love Chloe, but would that love turn to hurt? Remember how much Lydia Anne loved Dad before you married, and how she later resented you two together? I can't risk hurting them."

"Your dad and I will be praying for His will in all of this."

"Thanks, Mama. I'm stopping by the boardinghouse for breakfast in the morning before taking the twins to school. I need to tell her about Eli."

"Do I need to say a special prayer?"

"Ah, yes. This may be difficult for her." *I want her to trust me, but she can't hear this from anyone else.*

CHAPTER 27

Chloe started when Zack and the twins entered the boardinghouse for breakfast the following morning. Without a doubt, she knew why he was there. Eli Scott. Had Zack given him a place to stay at his home? Anger and hurt twisted inside her—made her stomach churn and her head pound.

"Are you going to get into trouble about us being here for breakfast?" Zack asked.

She smiled in an attempt not to reveal her dismay. "I don't think so."

"We'll have our breakfast and not linger, just as Jacob stated, but I need a moment of your time to tell you something."

Her heart sunk to her toes, but she refused to reveal what plagued her mind. "All right. I'll get you some coffee and some milk for my favorite twins." She pointed to a table along the window wall. "Have a seat there, and I'll be right over."

Chloe took a deep breath and poured their drinks. Plastering on another smile, she weaved around the tables to Zack and the twins. "Scrambled eggs and bacon with some extra-good biscuits this morning."

Zack eyed her strangely. She hadn't fooled him for a minute. "That sounds fine. Have you heard anything about Eli Scott?"

It is true. "Yes. Mr. Barton said he saw you two yesterday."

"Eli was the one taking the food and other things."

Zack appeared as nervous as she, and the twins weren't saying a word. With them listening, he must choose his words carefully. He cleared his throat. "I found him at my place, sleeping in the barn. I'd like to tell you the whole story. Can I stop by midmorning?"

She lifted her chin. "I suppose. Is he staying with you now?"

"No. Dad and Mama are letting him sleep in the bunkhouse. Not sure if it will work out or not. It's up to him."

Mixed feelings swirled through her. Did she want Eli to suffer? God stated otherwise. She hesitated. "I'm glad you were able to help him."

Zack glanced at the twins, then up at her. "Are you upset with me?" he whispered.

She had to consider those words. "I didn't like hearing about it from Mr. Barton, but that's not your fault. I'm working on forgiving Eli, and I know God commands it. But it's hard."

"I understand. It was hard for me, too."

"Us, too," Curly said.

Did those two hear everything?

Suddenly she didn't want him to be concerned about the matter at all. He had responded to Eli as a Christian man. "It's all right. I'm proud you were able to help." She nodded. "I'll get your breakfast."

"Are you sure?"

She laughed lightly. "Absolutely."

Chloe busied herself all morning while keeping one eye on the clock. Zack said he'd stop by midmorning, and he would. Still. . . Eli's improper behavior toward her and the things he'd done to the twins occupied her thoughts. One minute she'd forgiven him, and in the next, she wanted him punished. Zack's dealings with Eli might very well end their fledging relationship. How could she trust a man who ignored her feelings? *Dear God, help me put this to rest.*

Zack arrived promptly at ten. The smile from this morning had faded, and his normally bright eyes were dull.

"Is Jacob around?" he asked and removed his hat.

"No, but I don't want to take advantage of his absence."

"Neither do I." He moistened his lips. "I want to tell you about Eli and what happened. But first, I want to apologize for causing you discomfort." He took a deep breath.

Poor Zack. Maybe she should tell him that the story wasn't important. But it *was*.

"I told you I found him in my barn. From his belligerent attitude, you'd have thought I had trespassed on his property. Anyway, I told him he could have a bath and breakfast in exchange for an apology to Curly and Charlie."

"And he agreed?"

"Yes. Before the twins realized he was there, we talked about

252

forgiveness of those who hurt us."

She stiffened. Had this turned into a lecture? *Calm down.*

"It was hard for them, but they handled his apology wonderfully. On the way to school, they talked about telling the kids at school about Eli. So I told them to keep it a secret for now. I put him to work at the newspaper, but I wouldn't be surprised if he was gone when I get back." He paused and studied her.

"Go on, Zack. I'm listening."

"We took a trip to Sheriff Jackson's office, and Eli owned up to stealing. The sheriff did a good job of letting him know about the future of a lawbreaker. After we left there, we ran into Jacob, and Eli apologized to him, too. When the paper closed, I took him and the twins to my parents. If he can behave himself, he can live there in the bunkhouse, and Dad will see if he can make a man out of him."

"What about Lydia Anne?"

"Dad and I made it clear what was expected of him, and that he would complete his schoolwork."

Chloe nodded. Zack deserved a reply. "I'm—I'm proud of what you're attempting with Eli."

"I haven't forgotten what he's done to the twins or to you."

"I know you haven't."

"Am I forgiven?"

She smiled. "Zack, there's nothing to forgive. Yes, I was very hurt when Mr. Barton told me that you'd given him a job, but that was before I learned the circumstances. I hope for his sake and yours that he abides by the rules and makes some changes in his life."

"Thanks, Chloe. I hope you understand I wouldn't purposely do anything to jeopardize our relationship."

She crossed her arms. "You may be stuck with me. The way I look at it, I'm simply one more homeless waif who needs Zack Kahler to rescue her."

He chuckled. "Wish I shared your confidence, especially when I'm the one who needs you."

What could she say? She blinked back a tear. "You'd better get out of here before Mr. Barton pays an unexpected call."

He grinned and left the boardinghouse. The rest of the morning and into the afternoon she reflected on her Zack, the knight in shining armor. Oh how she appreciated his visit. His caring was evident in every carefully selected word.

Zack really had so many responsibilities with the children and the newspaper. Even his new home added more care and work for him. She didn't regret their move, for they were happy and had a beautiful home. She imagined Zack would soon find a dog for them—possibly a pony, too. Miss Scott claimed Curly and Charlie were doing quite well with their tutoring, but that meant Simeon and Miss Scott did not have the opportunity to see each other as often.

However, Miss Scott and Rose had come by the boardinghouse again this afternoon and stayed on past dinner. She saw Rose speaking with Mr. Barton. He had to be blind not to notice her interest. Simeon and Miss Scott laughed about something. Simeon could afford a wife, and the two of them didn't have many years left to dawdle.

"It's much quieter since Zack Kahler and his children have moved out."

Chloe recognized Mr. Barton's voice and placed a stack of plates on the sideboard. He'd left Rose alone to speak with her. "Oh, I miss the sound of the children's voices and the laughter."

"And Mr. Kahler?"

Chloe slowly turned to face her employer. Must he continue to quiz her about Zack? Did he think her heart might change in a matter of a few hours or a few days? The vulnerable look on his face caused her to pity him despite his attempts to separate her and Zack.

"Yes, sir. I miss seeing him."

"I wish you'd give me an opportunity to win your affections."

The many times others had hurt her filled Chloe with guilt, for she had done the same to Mr. Barton. His ways to win her were wrong, but she couldn't hold a grudge toward him or Eli. "I'm sorry."

"I could give you many fine things."

"But without love, we'd have nothing together. I believe you deserve more than a one-sided relationship."

"I haven't given up completely. Let's see if Simeon has some pie left from dinner. We could share it with Miss Scott and Simeon. Both Miss Scotts."

She wanted to refuse, but Mr. Barton was her employer. "I'll check with him."

A short while later, she sat with Mr. Barton at a table while waiting for the other two women and Simeon to join them. Simeon wanted to show them his birdhouse in back of the boardinghouse. Uneasiness slammed into her and whirled her thoughts like the tornado that Zack had talked about.

"I'm thinking of building a new house," he said. "I could use a woman's touch to assist me in laying out the rooms, especially the kitchen."

"I'm sure it will be lovely. You've done a fine job with the boardinghouse."

"If you will only say yes, Chloe, that house could be yours."

"Mr. Barton—"

"Please, Jacob."

"Mr. Barton, I refuse to take advantage of your kindness. You deserve a woman who would be devoted to you all of her life."

He chuckled. "I don't take no for an answer, and you are just as determined."

"I understand my heart."

"And it's smitten with Zack Kahler."

She nodded.

"I fear he is merely using you to help him with his children. But when you realize that truth, I'll be here."

Mr. Barton was wrong. Zack cared; she was sure of it. Why couldn't he see that Rose was attracted to him? "Zack is not like that at all."

"I see. Unfortunately, you have been duped by a man from the big city. When you are ready, I'll be waiting. Since you don't have any living family members, as your employer, I've taken on the role of guardian. I do know what is best for you." He looked beyond her to the three moving their way.

Chloe watched the expression on Rose's face. The young woman flushed and appeared definitely uneasy. If only Rose and Mr. Barton could talk, get to know each other. Chloe glanced at Mr. Barton and saw he had his gaze fixed on her.

Not me. Rose is the one for you. Perhaps she should look for another job. But when would she find the time to call on other establishments? Her duties kept her busy sunup to sundown, and approaching business owners on Sunday was inappropriate. She inwardly gasped. If Mr. Barton learned about her seeking another employer, he might dismiss her on grounds of disloyalty. He had her in a very vulnerable position, and he knew it.

The days at the boardinghouse grew longer. At first Chloe thought she'd get used to not seeing Zack and the twins every day, but the peace and contentment she longed for hadn't arrived. Maybe it was because she loved the three of them, and being with them was the only thing that eased the longing in her heart. Sunday was just two days away, but it still seemed so far, and Sunday always sped by like a racehorse lunging toward the finish line.

She opened the third jar of green beans for dinner, drained the liquid, and dumped the contents into a huge pot. Her thoughts turned to Christmas. Even if Mr. Barton stood his ground and did not let her spend the day with Zack and his family, she still wanted to give them all something special. And apple jelly was not what she wanted to give to Zack. She planned to purchase candy and new pencils for the twins, but what about Zack? How strange that what she wanted to give him was her heart, and that couldn't be bought at the general store.

"Simeon, I can't think of a proper gift for Zack."

He sighed and appeared to contemplate her dilemma. Without glancing down, he turned a piece of frying chicken. The grease crackled and sputtered.

"Sometimes the most expensive gift in the whole world is not what a man wants."

"What are you suggesting?"

"To pray about it, Miss Chloe."

"I have been. What are you giving Miss Scott?"

"A poetry book."

Chloe swallowed her surprise, or rather her amusement.

"You find that funny?"

"No, sir. I think she'd love a book of poems."

"Thank you. Just because I'm a cook and I don't talk good doesn't mean I don't have good taste."

Good taste? That sounded like something Miss Scott would have said. "I'm sorry, Simeon. Do you think Zack might like a poetry book, too?"

He narrowed his eyes. "No. You come up with your own idea." He laughed. "Got ya going there didn't I? But I did buy that there book."

Without an answer to her problem, Chloe went about her task of helping Simeon with dinner and listening for the bell over the front door. Only four days until Christmas, and she needed an idea soon.

Zack's mind spun with the news of the day and how best to report it. Miss Scott had given him a few recipes and gift ideas for the women's section and a lengthy article about the first Christmas at Piney Woods Church. Morgan had the church history and had passed it on to her. Zack decided to print an article about how New York City celebrated Christmas to contrast with Miss Scott's historical piece. He recalled the ornate churches and cathedrals and the storefronts that glistened with gifts galore, and he tied both articles together with city and country reaching out to help the poor and less fortunate. Kahlerville suited Zack better than any site on earth.

From the neighboring communities, he'd gathered news about the times of their worship services, pageants, and caroling, as well as when they planned to assemble food baskets for the needy. Sure was easy for him to fill up the daily paper during the holiday season. For a moment, he contemplated how his family worshiped during this time, but it was never enough in response to God's giving.

He heard the newspaper office door open. It creaked like an old man with arthritis. His petite mother stepped inside, and he made his way to greet her.

"Mornin', pretty lady." He bent and kissed her cheek.

"How's my favorite son in the newspaper business?"

"Very good. Glad you clarified my position since I'm your only son in the newspaper business."

She laughed. "Michael Paul and Stuart have their special talents, too."

"And Lydia Anne? I've been meaning to talk to you about her. She's entirely too pretty for a sixteen-year-old."

"I see you've noticed. Travis is ready to send her to an all-girls school until she's thirty."

"Grand idea. I'll escort her."

They laughed again. "Are you ready for Christmas?" he asked.

"I think so. I've done more sewing than in the past."

"Have you made another batch of the ginger crinkle cookies?"

"It's on my list for tomorrow. Oh, I saw the little coats that Morgan and Casey purchased for the twins for Christmas. They're royal blue and adorable. And Grant and Jenny bought clothes, too, just like you requested. I'm wondering what you purchased for the twins?"

"A doll for Charlie." Zack grinned. "Did you finish the little dress for it that matches hers?"

"I did, and Travis finished the doll bed."

"She'll be so excited."

"I think Poppy will be, too. So what's for Curly? Travis has a little more painting to finish on the train."

"I bought him overalls and a shirt. This is their first real Christmas. I appreciate Dad building the doll bed and the train." He took a deep breath. "I plan to surprise them with a puppy on Christmas morning."

"Oh good. Children need to learn responsibility. Don't forget the sweets and the fruit for their stockings." Mama swiped at the wetness under her eyes. "Remember their little eyes at Thanksgiving when they saw all the food?"

He nodded. "They'd been hungry so many times in New York that I doubt if they ever had a full stomach until coming here."

Mama took a deep breath, just as she always did when something was on her mind. "Do you need any help in purchasing a gift for Chloe?"

"Are you asking if I need money?" He muffled a laugh.

Mama frowned. "You know exactly what I mean. I wondered if you needed ideas."

"Honestly, I'm lost. Don't know what to get her. What have you done?"

"We purchased a Bible, and I crocheted a bookmark."

"Very nice. I need help—as you well expected."

"Books are good."

He shook his head. "That's what you've done. I considered a necklace." He wished he could give her a ring.

"What about one of your Grandmother Rainer's bracelets, the one with the rubies?"

"I couldn't ask you to part with an heirloom unless—"

"You were married? I understand. A necklace is a lovely idea."

"Then I'll take another look at the cross necklace I saw the other day. I'll purchase it before the day's over. I'm going to pick up some overalls and a shirt for Eli. How's he doing?"

Mama paused. "Nervous. Afraid to trust. Angry. Needy. I understand why Miss Scott kept him at school for so long. He said his father often beat him." She tilted her head. "I'm very proud of Lydia Anne. She's befriended him. Forgiven him for what he'd said and done to her in the past, which I knew nothing about. She's always had a way of encouraging others to talk, and he is doing that very thing."

Zack raised a brow. "Not so sure how I feel about him getting too attached to her."

"Relax, big brother; we're watching things very closely."

"Well, if anyone can get Eli on the right road, you and Dad can."

"I'm very excited about Christmas."

"When will Michael Paul be here?"

"Christmas Eve—maybe in time to sing with Travis at the church service."

"This Christmas will be a memory maker," Zack said. "About as perfect as a Christmas can be."

CHAPTER 28

Zack kissed the foreheads of his sleeping twins beside him. He'd grown to love Saturday mornings. The twins were able to sleep a little later before getting dressed and heading into town for breakfast. That meant seeing Chloe, which set his heart straight for the rest of the day. The twins tried to outdo each other with little tasks around the office until noon when the paper went to press. Mama or Lydia Anne then came by to take them back to the ranch.

"We're not asleep, Poppy," Curly said. "Oh, I love Saturdays."

Charlie rubbed her eyes. "Yes, pancakes and sausage at Miss Chloe's boardinghouse."

Zack laughed. Mr. Barton would appreciate that. "The boarding-house belongs to Mr. Barton. Miss Chloe works there."

Charlie nodded as if she understood. "He doesn't smile much."

"If he had children like you, he'd smile all the time."

"I love you, Poppy," Curly said. "You loved us even when we took your wallet."

"All of us do bad things sometimes. We have to listen to God and do what He says."

"Grandma says we need to have Jesus living in our hearts," Curly said. "How will He get in there?"

Zack wrapped an arm around Curly's shoulder. "You don't see Jesus come into your heart, but you will know He's there by the good way you feel."

"When will He come?"

"Say your prayers and talk to Jesus and ask Him to come into your heart. Then He'll make you one of His children."

"Adopted again?" Charlie asked.

"Oh yes. I've been adopted into God's family, too." He loved hearing his twins talk about the things of God. Zack drew his children closer to him. How he loved these two. Best pickpockets he'd ever had. They'd wanted his wallet, but instead they stole his heart. "Tomorrow night is Christmas Eve. I want you to get lots of rest today."

"We will, Poppy," Curly said and snuggled closer. "We'll rest on Grandma's bed while she reads us a story."

Chloe adjusted the pine greenery on the stairway rail while Simeon spoke with Mr. Barton in the kitchen. Soon dinner would be served—vegetable beef soup and corn bread. She tugged on the greenery. It easily slid out of place with the boarders ascending and descending the stairs. She stepped back and took a peek at the decorated tree in the parlor. The sight nearly took her breath away. The lantern on the mantel flickered lightly, creating a magical backdrop to the holiday.

As a child, she'd longed for a Christmas like this one, lots of people and decorations without the demon alcohol to ruin it. This Christmas her dreams had come true. She had two precious children whom she loved, even if she didn't get to see them as often as before. And she had Zack. He hadn't said *love*, but he'd come very close, and the look in his eyes spilled over with affection. Mr. Barton might be able to tell her where she must spend the holiday, but he held no jurisdiction over her heart.

She returned to the stairway and scrutinized the greenery again. Mr. Barton stepped behind the registration desk and opened the receipt book. He looked up and smiled. She wished he'd meet a young woman who fancied him—like Rose.

"Did you need something, sir? I was adjusting the decorations since they get mussed with all of the boarders."

"I'm quite all right."

"I'll check with Simeon to see if he needs help."

"Could I have a moment with you first?"

She stopped, her heart thudding against her chest. Couldn't he leave her alone?

"Christmas is day after tomorrow. You've done a splendid job here ever since you started, despite the fact you've ignored your employer's best interests."

Had he decided to dismiss her?

"You can relax, Miss Weaver. I have no intentions of making you feel any more uncomfortable than I have in the past. I'd like to give you Christmas Day off to do with as you desire. The whole day. I can help Simeon with the meals."

Chloe thought she'd burst. "Thank you, Mr. Barton. I really appreciate this."

He smiled. "Merry Christmas. I wish you and Zack happiness."

She had to ask. "What changed your mind?"

"Miss Scott. I mean Simeon's Miss Scott. I mean she helped me see my error."

Bless you, sweet lady.

"The truth of the matter is, Miss Scott invited me to join Simeon and her niece for a late Christmas dinner."

"I hope you have an enjoyable celebration."

"I—I think we will."

Thank You, Father. This means so very much to me.

Suddenly, Chloe had an idea of a gift for Zack—other than being off from work for Christmas. The owner of the largest of the general stores often lunched on Sunday at the boardinghouse, and she hoped he'd fetch something from his store for her. Tomorrow at church, she'd not tell Zack about her good news.

∽◦⟅◦∾

Saturday afternoon, Zack straightened the slips of paper and notes on his desk. Hank and Gil were delivering papers while Eli swept up the back. When Zack returned on Tuesday after Christmas, he didn't want a pile of work. He could at least put it all in one stack. One thing he had to do was get organized. Hank had a system of keeping track of customers, the cost of their ads, and when they paid, but Zack could neither follow his method nor take the time to develop one of his own. But he had to do something soon. He was a people man and loved to talk and dig up news, but the idea of attending to financial details was like taking a dose of castor oil.

He rubbed his temples and continued through the disorganized notes and papers. When he finally had them sorted by size, not content, he studied the office to see what other chores needed to be done before he fetched the twins at his parents' ranch.

The door of the newspaper office opened, and Jacob stepped inside. Zack's mood soured the moment the man's face appeared.

"Zack, can I speak with you a moment?"

Do I have a choice? "I'm a little busy."

"This won't take long."

Jacob's voice sounded more congenial than usual. "Have a seat. Are you ready for Christmas?"

"Ready as I'll ever be." The man made his way to Zack's desk and sat opposite him. "I owe you an apology."

Zack peered into the man's face. "For what?"

"The mess I've made of things where Miss Weaver is concerned."

"I'm listening."

"I made a terrible mistake in trying to win her. Instead of making her a friend, well, more than a friend, I succeeded in making a fool of myself. I'm sorry. She cares for you, and there's not a thing I can do about it." He offered a tight-lipped smile. "I apologized to her earlier today and thought you deserved the same."

Zack reached over to shake Jacob's hand. "I appreciate that. You're a good man—always have been. Takes a big man to admit he's wrong."

"But a fool in love with the wrong woman can do some stupid things. I hope you and I can remain friends."

"Of course."

Jacob stood. "I need to get back to the feed store. Have a Merry Christmas."

"Thanks. Will you be at church tomorrow night?"

"I doubt it. With the number of people we're feeding at the boardinghouse, I'll be helping Chloe and Simeon."

"Merry Christmas to you and a blessed New Year." And Zack sincerely meant every word.

He laughed aloud after Jacob left. What a perfect Christmas for those he loved. Couldn't ask for a thing this year other than what he already had. It would have been perfect to have Chloe with him for the day, but at least they didn't have to worry about Jacob trying to break them apart. With a better attitude, he worked for the next hour on editing articles. He would have continued longer, but someone had arrived. Probably needing a newspaper.

"I'll be right there," he called.

"No need. I'll find ya."

Zack frowned. He didn't recognize the voice. Pushing himself back from his desk, he walked toward the front of the office. The man before him didn't look familiar. Neither did he look happy. He needed a bath, and his overalls were splattered with mud.

"What can I do for you? Need a newspaper?"

"Nah. Understand my boy's working here." The stench of alcohol seemed to seep from the pores of his skin.

Zack suspected the man was Eli's father. "Depends on who your son is."

"Eli Scott. I ran him off. No good. Told him not to set foot near this town, and here he is working for you." He turned his head and spit tobacco on the floor. "I came to make sure he never shows up again."

Zack looked at the spot on the floor and then up at the man. "Why do you care where he lives?"

"He's givin' me a bad name."

"Looks to me like you've already done a good job of that yourself. Your boy has a scar on his face. You did that?"

"He needed to learn a lesson. Maybe you do, too."

"Why don't you leave him alone?"

The man stepped closer. "He's my son, and I'll do as I want."

"He's seventeen years old. Not a boy anymore."

Zack saw Eli step from the shadows but kept his eyes on the elder Scott. "Leave now, and I won't report this to the sheriff."

"I'll go see him myself and straighten this matter out."

"Go right ahead. Make sure you bring him back with you."

The man staggered around and stomped out of the office.

"What will the sheriff do?" Eli asked.

"Probably throw him in jail until he sobers up, then tell him to leave you alone."

"I sure hope so." Eli made his way to Zack's side. "I don't want to end up like him."

"You've got a good man showing you the right road."

"He says some hard things. I can't believe them."

"Listen to him, Eli. He knows the right way."

CHAPTER 29

On Christmas Eve, after delivering food to needy families, Zack escorted his children to church, wishing Chloe was there with them. This was supposed to be her day off, but Jacob needed her to help with the dinner preparations. The boardinghouse expected about ten families. Tomorrow they'd all be together after breakfast at the boardinghouse, and he'd have her all to himself. Zack helped the twins down from the buggy and noted the darkness had brought a chill.

"Brr," he said. "Almost as cold as New York."

The twins stared at each other. "No, Poppy, New York is very cold," Curly said.

They'd been strangely quiet all day. Perhaps the excitement had exhausted them.

"Let's hurry inside and hear what your grandpa has to say about Christmas."

Candles lit the church, much different from the lanterns on a regular evening service. The tree was lit, too, the candlelight flickering like the star-studded sky on the first Christmas. A bucket of water sat on each side of the tree with a youth watching just in case the tree burst into flames.

Sheriff Jackson eased up beside him. "I told Brother Whitworth, and now I'll tell you. Eli's father won't be bothering him or you. If he attempts anything, let me know. Now it's up to Eli to change things around."

"Thanks. He's got himself a good man to help him along the way."

After Dad welcomed the congregation, the choir sang several Christmas carols, and the older children presented the nativity story. Zack stole a look at Curly and Charlie. They seemed dazed by what they saw.

"Next year, you can be a part of the Christmas program if you like," he whispered to each of his children.

Charlie nodded and smiled, but Curly didn't seem to be so sure. Good. Zack wanted them to have different interests. Dad made his way to the pulpit with his Bible in hand.

"Tonight we celebrate our Lord's birth." Dad opened his Bible. "I'm going to read from Luke, chapter 2. . . ."

The familiar story settled into Zack's mind. Although he had heard the words many times, they'd never lost their freshness or their ability to inspire awe and wonder.

" 'Fear not: for, behold, I bring you good tidings of great joy.' " Dad paused and looked out on the people. "Everyone who came in contact with the angel was instructed to fear not. God's message was not to be feared. He had a special gift for them. What about you? What are you afraid of? Is it a special gift from God to you?"

Zack listened. He understood fear. It seized him every time he contemplated raising Curly and Charlie. And it gripped him when he thought of Chloe. Fear. All the uncertainty over taking a wife—providing for her, hoping Curly and Charlie still felt loved, running the newspaper while still having time to be a good husband and father. Fear. He had a heavy dose of it.

"Has God called you to do something for Him, and you're afraid?"

Zack scooted the twins closer to him. Perhaps God had a message for him in this tonight. Maybe he was supposed to propose to Chloe.

"I love you," he whispered to each child.

"I love you," they whispered back.

⌘

Christmas morning, Zack woke to the sound of someone or something moving downstairs, like the clanging of a skillet on top of the stove. He blinked. Must be dreaming. But when he smelled wood burning, he rose to investigate. What were Curly and Charlie up to this morning?

A stab of fear shot through him. What if the twins were cooking him breakfast? Yet darkness veiled even a hint of sunrise. This could be a prowler, but prowlers didn't break into people's homes to cook. He'd find the source of the noise and hope his children didn't get burned before he got there. Slipping into his trousers and a shirt, he snatched up a boot to use as a weapon—just in case.

He crept to the door and realized that if a person had broken into the house, he was doing a poor job of keeping quiet. Across the hallway came a lantern light from the kitchen table. His Chloe had milk and eggs on the table along with flour and sugar.

She must have sensed his presence, for she peered up and smiled.

"Merry Christmas. I'm sorry I woke you."

Speechless, he simply stared into her face, her lovely features enhanced by the lantern light.

"Aren't you going to say anything?" Her sweet whisper shook his senses.

"Uh...merry Christmas. I thought you had to work this morning."

"Mr. Barton gave me the entire day off and an apology."

He laughed. "I knew he had a good man hidden inside. He stopped to see me yesterday afternoon and apologized, too. You didn't walk?"

She giggled. "Simeon let me borrow his horse and wagon."

With her straight black hair swept back from her face and trailing down her back, and her face tinged with peachy shades of health and beauty, Chloe appeared more radiant than the star in the east.

"I wanted to make you and the twins Christmas breakfast. This is my gift to you." She folded her hands before her. "And I have a little something else, too."

Why is she nervous? "Having you here is the perfect gift."

She picked up a brown paper package tied with a red ribbon lying on the table beside the milk and eggs. "I will be able to relax once you open this."

He took the package, shook it, then grinned. "Can I guess?"

"No." Her smile enchanted him.

Carefully, he untied the ribbon and slipped his fingers around the taped edges and lifted a book. "A ledger."

"I heard your complaining about not being able to keep track of customers and payments, so with the ledger comes my assistance as your personal bookkeeper."

He stepped closer, and with a smile that he hoped spoke fathoms of his love, he drew her into his arms. "Thank you. I love the way you are sensitive to my needs. My gift for you is in the parlor." He paused. "I told myself I would not speak of my feelings today, but I can't keep this inside any longer."

She lifted her gaze to meet his, her dark eyes brimming with trust and more.

"I love you, Chloe. It took me a lot of years to realize that the little girl who shared my lunch would one day share my heart. But here you are before me, all grown up and in my arms." He wanted to kiss her, seal his words of love. Hesitantly, so as not to frighten her, he bent to taste her lips. "Do I dare ask how you feel?"

"I love you." Her face glistened with tears through her smile. "I've loved you for as long as I can remember."

Zack brushed away the dampness on her cheek with his finger. "This is supposed to be a happy occasion."

"It is. I've dreamed of this day. And now that it's happening, I can't believe it's true."

As he drew her closer, she laid her head against his chest. Holding and protecting Chloe—that's how he wanted to spend the rest of his life.

"I hear your heart," she said.

"Good. Does it tell you merry Christmas?"

"Truthfully, your heart is attempting to keep pace with mine."

They laughed, and the lightness of the moment helped ease the weakness in his knees.

"I came here to make your breakfast, and instead, I've found the feast of a lifetime."

"What a grand feast, too." He kissed her forehead, the tip of her nose, and her lips again. "You taste sweeter than peppermint candy." He held her a moment longer. "I could do this all day."

"Me, too. I'm surprised the twins haven't come bounding out of bed with the excitement of Christmas."

He nodded. "They were exhausted last night and didn't fall asleep until after eleven. They need to get up soon so they can enjoy this fine breakfast."

"I have to finish it first."

"And what are you planning?"

"All of their favorites and yours, too."

"Wonderful. Good thing Christmas dinner isn't until two o'clock." He caressed her face, just to make sure what had happened between them was real. *She loved him.* "We have much to discuss later."

"I know, but the day will be filled. I'm content with your words of love. We can talk tomorrow or the next day or the next."

"I can hardly wait. I'm worse than my own children anticipating Christmas."

"Can we postpone telling them about us?" she asked. "This is their first Christmas with their poppy, and I don't want to take away any of the celebration from them."

"I understand, and I agree." He stepped back and took her hands into his. "Once Christmas is over, we can talk to them about us. Probably ought to prepare them slowly." Then he laughed. "They've been real matchmakers. Oh, how they love you."

"And I feel the same about them. They are irresistible."

He would have proposed right then, but it was too soon. One giant step at a time. He needed to change the topic of discussion about them before he dropped to one knee and begged her to marry him.

"I want to give you my gift," he said.

"You already have."

He shook his head and grinned. "Close your eyes, and don't move while I get it." He kissed the tip of her nose and hurried into the parlor, where he snatched up the small box containing her necklace. "Keep your eyes closed."

"I am."

He laughed and quickly lifted the lid of the box and pulled out the delicate gold chain. "Don't move or peek." He placed the chain and cross around her neck and clumsily fastened the clasp.

"Oh, Zack."

"Hush and don't open those pretty brown eyes until I tell you." He stepped around to face her. "All right. You can look now."

Her trembling fingers flew to touch the cross and lifted it so she could see. "I want to see it better."

He'd already thought of that and held up a small mirror. She peered at her image, and tears pooled her eyes. "It's beautiful. Thank you so much."

"It's nothing compared to the woman who is wearing it. I hope to always be able to make you smile and give you beautiful things."

"Your heart is all I ever want."

"It's yours."

She moistened her lips. "I have a request."

"Whatever you wish, my lady."

"Can I help you dress the twins later? I'd love to fix Charlie's hair."

"Be my guest. I am all thumbs." He smiled. "Do you suppose she will ever let me call her Caitlain? The sound of it has such a lovely ring."

Chloe laughed. "We'll have to coax her."

"*We.* I like the sound of it."

"Hmm. I do, too. But if you don't leave me alone, I'll never get breakfast finished."

His eyes lingered on her flushed face, his mind dwelling on one more kiss.

"Go." She laughed and shooed him away as though chasing away chickens. "Do whatever you do before waking Curly and Charlie."

Chloe trembled with excitement dancing through her body. *Zack loved her!* He hadn't said *marriage*, but he wanted to talk about the future. Imagine a life with Zack. It sounded too good to be true.

In the past, she'd envied those who celebrated Christmas with decorated trees and lavish parties. Now she realized that those regrets took away from the worship of Jesus' entrance into the world. She'd had very little as a child, but when her mother was alive, she'd read the Christmas story, and the three of them had attended church. Chloe's mother was gone, but she'd left a legacy, and Chloe intended to do the same with the twins. These things and much more would be passed on to Curly and Charlie, and maybe one day to more children for her and Zack.

She laughed aloud. What a perfect Christmas. With the pancakes ready to fry and the eggs whipped up nicely, she pulled out the plates to set the table. The thud of Zack hurrying down the steps seized her attention.

"Chloe."

She whirled around. Zack's pale face told her something was wrong.

"Chloe, the twins are gone."

"Are you sure? Maybe they slipped out of the house for a moment."

He shook his head and headed for the door. "I've got to find them."

She pulled the frying pan from the stove and grabbed her jacket. Where had the twins gone?

"Maybe they're doing something special for you—a gift for Christmas." Yet she remembered their gifts of paper star ornaments, a pinecone bird feeder, and a book about how Zack had met the twins.

"It's barely daylight. Neither of them likes the dark. I—I found gifts for me on the bed." He jammed his arms through his coat sleeves.

He yanked open the door, and the two stepped into the brisk morning.

"Did either of them indicate a problem last night?" she asked.

"Not at all. Simply all the anticipation for today. But they were quieter than usual. I thought they were simply preoccupied with Christmas." He stiffened. "Charlie did make an odd comment. She asked if it hurt to have my heart broke. And when I asked her what she meant, she asked if it hurt to love them."

"Strange question for a little girl."

"I thought so, too. So I told her that it didn't hurt at all to love them. I ignored the question about a broken heart." He sighed and gazed toward the barn and the surrounding area. "Where could they be?"

"Perhaps they found the puppy."

"Let's check in the barn."

Inside the shadowy barn, Zack took long strides to the corner where he'd made a warm bed inside a stall for the puppy. The little furry collie was still there. Zack stared up at the hayloft. "Do you suppose they're up there?"

She peered up into the rafters where slivers of starlight peeped through the corners of the barn. "They could have fallen asleep."

He climbed the ladder to the hayloft, but it was empty. "Where could they be? Curly!" he yelled. "Charlie!"

Nothing.

He called for them again before descending the ladder. "I don't know where to look. They haven't indicated a special play spot." His gaze focused on the pecan trees. "I'll go see if they decided to gather pecans."

The desperation in his voice alarmed her. Zack was a man of control and answers. *Dear Lord, where are the twins?* "I'm not sure whether I should join you, look somewhere else, or stay right here."

"Why don't you stay close by the house? They could get hungry or cold." When she agreed, he took off at a run toward the pecan trees.

Dear Lord, help us find Curly and Charlie. Watch over them and keep them safe and unhurt.

By now, they might feel they were in trouble. "Curly, Charlie. No one's angry with you. We're simply worried, and this is Christmas. We are going to have a wonderful celebration."

Silence greeted her, almost echoing in her ears. She had no choice but to wait in the house. Once inside, she slipped into a kitchen chair and prayed Zack would find the children soon. After several minutes, she decided to finish setting the table and complete breakfast. *Trust God.* He loved them more than she and Zack could ever comprehend. If she failed to believe God did not have them safe in the palm of His hand, then she had no faith at all.

About thirty minutes later, a knock at the front door seized her attention. She set the butter dish on the table and hurried to answer it. Startled, she faced Eli.

He stepped back. Obviously, he had not expected to see her, either. "Mornin', Chloe. I mean, merry Christmas." He didn't smile.

Be civil. Remember how his father treated him. "Merry Christmas. If you're looking for Zack, he's not here."

"Mrs. Whitworth wanted him and the twins to come as soon as you arrived. But I see you're already here."

Chloe sensed her face warming. How terrible it looked for her to be at Zack's home before the sun had risen, as though she had. . . Her face grew hot.

"Mr. Barton gave me the day off, so I thought I'd surprise Zack and the twins by preparing Christmas breakfast."

"That's nice of you." He shifted from one foot to the other.

Should she invite him into a house not her own?

"Where are the twins? I need to tell them somethin'."

"Well, they aren't here, either." In the next breath, she explained the missing children.

"Do you think they run off?"

"I don't know. Zack said nothing unpleasant happened last night. He's very worried."

"Sometimes people's minds get confused."

Chloe realized Eli spoke from his own pain. Although she'd forgiven him, for the first time, she felt pity toward him.

His hands hung awkwardly at his side. "I'm sorry for the way I acted—the things I said and done."

"I forgave you some time back. I didn't know our mothers died within a few weeks apart. We could have comforted each other."

His gaze darted about. "Two kids hurtin' over their ma's deaths would have been better than what happened."

"I do understand how you feel. I thought God was mad at me for many years. Instead of allowing the problems in my life to make me a better person and help others, I felt sorry for myself. It wasn't until I met the twins that I realized I could help Zack with them because I'd been abandoned, too."

"Sounds like you have religion like the rest of the family."

"I'm a believer, if that's what you mean."

"It's not for me." He hesitated. "I reckon I know every spot to hide around here. I think I'll go look for the twins."

"I really appreciate that, Eli." And she meant every word. "Zack started his search in the grove of pecan trees. I have no idea where he'd go from there."

CHAPTER 30

Zack didn't know where else to look for his children. They must have run off, but where and why? How had he failed them? Being a father had proved harder than anything he'd ever attempted.

Have you asked Me how to be a good father?

Shaking, Zack understood the origin of that voice. *I neglected to ask You for directions. Is it too late to ask for help?*

He'd believed adopting Curly and Charlie was a plan ordained by God, but he had assumed he'd receive guidance and instructions instead of asking for them. How insolent. How wrong he'd been.

Lord, forgive me for my foolishness. I'm asking You to help me find my children and to be a good father. Please keep them safe. And while I'm at it, I'm going to need Your help in being a good husband.

Standing in the pecan grove with no sign of his redheaded twins in sight, he did spot a man walking his way. Closer scrutiny revealed Eli.

"I stopped at the house to give you a message from your parents, and Chloe told me the twins were gone, maybe run off."

"That they are, and I don't know where to look."

"I can help. There are a few secret places that I found while I was hiding out."

"Then let's go. I'm real worried."

Eli led the way east, away from Zack's acreage toward a thick, treed area and the creek.

"I apologized to Chloe," Eli said.

Zack had realized a long time ago that the bit of unfinished business between the two needed to take place. But he'd sensed urging the two to talk wasn't the answer. "I'm real glad for both of you."

Eli nodded. The boy, nearly a man, struggled with a wagonload of guilt and shame.

"God will guide you," Zack said. "Sometimes we simply have to ask Him to lead the way."

"Brother Travis says the same. He's making me read the Bible."

Zack remembered his own days of rebellion. "Do you have something else to say?"

"It's hard to think of a heavenly Father who cares about me when my own father. . ."

"I think we can both say that your father was not a good example of your heavenly Father."

Eli stopped and pointed to a hill. "At the foot of that hill and beyond the winding creek is an overhang of brush. I slept there a few nights."

The two walked in silence. Zack's heart ached to hold his children.

Suddenly he saw a little red head. *Thank You.* Then he saw a second red head. Curly and Charlie stood at the edge of the creek.

"Curly. Charlie." He garnered speed and ran toward the twins. He snatched up both of them, one in each arm and drew them close. For a moment, he thought he'd cry.

"How did you find us?" Curly asked.

"Eli and God helped me."

Eli bent down beside them. "I want to tell you again how sorry I am for what I did. I want you to forgive me."

"Oh, we did that," Charlie said. "Grandma helped us in Sunday school."

Zack turned them both to face him. "Why did you leave?"

Charlie peered into his face. "So your heart wouldn't get broken. You have too many people to love."

"Yeah," Curly said. "Grandma said Miss Chloe might break your heart, but you said you had us. We didn't want your heart to break and have you die like our other papa and mama, so we thought we should run away."

This time Zack blinked back the tears. He remembered bits and pieces of the conversation with Mama when he thought the twins were playing with kittens on the porch. He swallowed hard to keep back his emotions. "Grandma meant I'd be sad, not die."

"We love Miss Chloe, too," Charlie said. "It makes us sad when we can't see her every day."

"Our hearts are big enough to love all the people of the world. Promise me you'll never run away again. I love you too much to ever have you gone from my life."

"But what about Miss Chloe. Can't you adopt her, too?" Curly asked.

"Grown-ups don't adopt each other." Charlie shook her finger at her brother. "They should get married so Miss Chloe can be our mama."

Zack wasn't prepared to get into that discussion. "She's at our house fixing breakfast and waiting for you. I know I saw pancakes and sausages."

The twins' eyes widened. "Will she stay with us forever?"

A plan began to form in his mind. "She might if you ask her. Right now, she's very worried about you."

"Is Eli gonna have breakfast with us, too?" Curly asked.

"Would you like him to join us?" Zack asked.

"No." Eli's curt reply startled the little boy. "I need to be getting back." Without another word, Eli raced toward the house where he had left his horse.

Zack grabbed up his children's hands. "Let's hurry back for our Christmas breakfast."

Chloe's body stiffened as she waited for signs of Zack and the twins. Perhaps Eli had been a messenger from God to help find Curly and Charlie. She hoped so. She prayed so. She'd prayed for help, and then Eli had announced he wanted to do that very thing.

She scanned the fields beyond the barn. Eli ran by and on to his horse. She waved, but he ignored her.

In the distance, she saw the outline of Zack and two little ones hurrying toward her.

She held her breath and waved. No longer able to contain her joy, she lifted her skirts and raced toward them. They were the ones she loved—Zack, Curly, and Charlie. The twins called out for her, broke free from Zack's hands, and rushed into her arms. She nearly toppled over.

"Oh, you scared me so. Where have you been?" She glanced up at a smiling Zack.

"I'll tell you later," he said. "Right now the twins have something to ask you."

"What's that?" She kissed each twin's cheek.

"We want you to live with us forever," Curly said.

"And be our mama so Poppy won't have a broken heart," Charlie said.

Chloe sensed her heart flutter like a butterfly's wings.

"Not a very romantic proposal, but I can do better later," Zack said.

"Yes," she cried. "It's a perfect proposal."

"Yea!" the twins shouted.

Charlie looked up at Zack. "God gave us a poppy for Thanksgiving and a mama for Christmas. Right, Curly?"

"Right. The best Christmas ever."

"I have the best gift of all." Zack bent and wrapped his arms around all of them.

"God gave me a family."

Zack grasped Chloe's hand and brushed a kiss across her cheek. "When I think of how my uncles teased me about you on Thanksgiving, I can only imagine how bad the teasing will be today."

She giggled as he lifted her down from the buggy. "You should have been in the house with your mother and aunts. Lydia Anne finally came to my rescue."

"Poppy, we don't understand what you're talking about," Curly said and jumped from the wagon.

Zack grabbed Charlie before she did the same. His precious daughter had her arms wrapped around the furry puppy and would not let go. The two had shared the puppy all the way here.

Oh, his ladies looked fine this morning in their Christmas dresses, and Curly was dashing. Chloe wore a lovely green dress that he'd never seen before, and his twins looked like they had just walked out of a department store in New York City. Curly's green-and-blue-plaid shirt matched Charlie's plaid dress.

"Poppy, tell us." Charlie placed a kiss on Zack's cheek before he set her gently onto the ground.

"Well, today your poppy and Miss Chloe will tell everyone that we are getting married. But you have to keep it a secret until we tell them at dinner." He glanced at each child. When they nodded, he breathed a quick sigh. "And the same goes tonight when we go to Uncle George and Aunt Ellen's house. Our families believed we would get married before we did."

The confused look on the children's faces caused him to laugh.

"Never mind. This is Christmas Day, our Lord's birthday, and we will be among all those people we love." Zack caught a smile from Chloe. "They will want to know when," he said.

A pretty blush spread over her face. "New Year's Day, and not one day later."

ZACK'S GINGER CRINKLE COOKIES

⅔ cup butter
1 cup sugar
1 egg
4 tablespoons molasses
2 cups sifted flour
2 teaspoons soda
½ teaspoon salt
1 teaspoon cinnamon
1 teaspoon ginger
¼ cup sugar for dipping

Heat oven to 350 degrees. Mix butter and sugar thoroughly. Add egg and beat well. Stir in molasses. Sift together dry ingredients and add to butter and sugar mixture. Form into balls and roll in sugar until well coated. Place on ungreased cookie sheet three inches apart. Bake for fifteen minutes. Cookies will flatten and crinkle. Makes five dozen cookies. Great coffee and milk dunkers!

Award-winning author DiAnn Mills launched her career in 1998 with the publication of her first book. Currently she has nineteen novels, fifteen novellas, a nonfiction book, and several articles and short stories in print.

DiAnn believes her readers should "expect an adventure." Her desire is to show characters solving real problems of today from a Christian perspective through a compelling story.

Five of her anthologies have appeared on the CBA best-seller list. Three of her books have won the distinction of Best Historical of the Year by Heartsong Presents, and she remains a favorite author of Heartsong Presents' readers. Two of her books have won Short Historical of the Year by American Christian Romance Writers for 2003 and 2004. She is the recipient of the Inspirational Reader's Choice award for 2005 in the long contemporary and novella category.

DiAnn is a founding board member of American Christian Fiction Writers and a member of Inspirational Writers Alive, Chi Libris, and Advanced Writers and Speakers Association. She speaks to various groups and teaches writing workshops. She is also a mentor for the Christian Writers Guild.

She lives in sunny Houston, Texas, the home of heat, humidity, and Harleys. In fact, she'd own one, but her legs are too short. DiAnn and her husband have four adult sons and are active members of Metropolitan Baptist Church.